THE CRUSADE OF
THE EXCELSIOR

BRET HARTE

1st WORLD
LIBRARY
Literary Society

The Crusade of the Excelsior

Bret Harte

© 1st World Library, 2007
PO Box 2211
Fairfield, IA 52556
www.1stworldlibrary.com
First Edition

LCCN: 2007927829

Softcover ISBN: 978-1-4218-4508-1
Hardcover ISBN: 978-1-4218-4424-4
eBook ISBN: 978-1-4218-4592-0

Purchase *"The Crusade of the Excelsior"*
as a traditional bound book at:
www.1stWorldLibrary.com/purchase.asp?ISBN=978-1-4218-4508-1

1st World Library is a literary, educational organization
dedicated to:

- Creating a free internet library of downloadable ebooks

- Hosting writing competitions and offering book publishing
  scholarships.

Interested in more 1st World Library books? contact:
literacy@1stworldlibrary.com
Check us out at: www.1stworldlibrary.com

1ˢᵗ World Library Literary Society

Giving Back to the World

"If you want to work on the core problem, it's early school literacy."

- James Barksdale, former CEO of Netscape

"No skill is more crucial to the future of a child, or to a democratic and prosperous society, than literacy."

- Los Angeles Times

"Literacy... means far more than learning how to read and write... The aim is to transmit... knowledge and promote social participation."

- UNESCO

"Literacy is not a luxury, it is a right and a responsibility. If our world is to meet the challenges of the twenty-first century we must harness the energy and creativity of all our citizens."

- President Bill Clinton

"Parents should be encouraged to read to their children, and teachers should be equipped with all available techniques for teaching literacy, so the varying needs and capacities of individual kids can be taken into account."

- Hugh Mackay

CONTENTS

PART I—IN BONDS

PART II—FREED

PART I

IN BONDS

CHAPTER I

A CRUSADER AND A SIGN

It was the 4th of August, 1854, off Cape Corrientes. Morning was breaking over a heavy sea, and the closely-reefed topsails of a barque that ran before it bearing down upon the faint outline of the Mexican coast. Already the white peak of Colima showed, ghost-like, in the east; already the long sweep of the Pacific was gathering strength and volume as it swept uninterruptedly into the opening Gulf of California.

As the cold light increased, it could be seen that the vessel showed evidence of a long voyage and stress of weather. She had lost one of her spars, and her starboard davits rolled emptily. Nevertheless, her rigging was taut and ship-shape, and her decks scrupulously clean. Indeed, in that uncertain light, the only moving figure besides the two motionless shadows at the wheel was engaged in scrubbing the quarter-deck—which, with its grated settees and stacked camp-chairs, seemed to indicate the presence of cabin passengers. For the barque Excelsior, from New York to San Francisco, had discharged the bulk of her cargo at Callao, and had extended her liberal cabin accommodation to swell the feverish Californian immigration, still in its height.

Suddenly there was a slight commotion on deck. An order,

issued from some invisible depth of the cabin, was so unexpected that it had to be repeated sternly and peremptorily. A bustle forward ensued, two or three other shadows sprang up by the bulwarks, then the two men bent over the wheel, the Excelsior slowly swung round on her heel, and, with a parting salutation to the coast, bore away to the northwest and the open sea again.

"What's up now?" growled one of the men at the wheel to his companion, as they slowly eased up on the helm.

"'Tain't the skipper's, for he's drunk as a biled owl, and ain't stirred out of his bunk since eight bells," said the other. "It's the first mate's orders; but, I reckon, it's the Senor's idea."

"Then we ain't goin' on to Mazatlan?"

"Not this trip, I reckon," said the third mate, joining them.

"Why?"

The third mate turned and pointed to leeward. The line of coast had already sunk enough to permit the faint silhouette of a trail of smoke to define the horizon line of sky.

"Steamer goin' in, eh?"

"Yes. D'ye see—it might be too hot, in there!"

"Then the jig's up?"

"No. Suthin's to be done—north of St. Lucas. Hush!"

He made a gesture of silence, although the conversation, since he had joined them, had been carried on in a continuous whisper. A figure, evidently a passenger, had appeared on deck. One or two of the foreign-looking crew who had drawn near the group, with a certain undue and irregular familiarity, now slunk away again.

The passenger was a shrewd, exact, rectangular-looking man, who had evidently never entirely succumbed to the freedom of the sea either in his appearance or habits. He had not even his sea legs yet; and as the barque, with the full swell of the Pacific now on her weather bow, was plunging uncomfortably, he was fain to cling to the stanchions. This did not, however, prevent him from noticing the change in her position, and captiously resenting it.

"Look here—you; I say! What have we turned round for? We're going away from the land! Ain't we going on to Mazatlan?"

The two men at the wheel looked silently forward, with that exasperating unconcern of any landsman's interest peculiar to marine officials. The passenger turned impatiently to the third mate.

"But this ain't right, you know. It was understood that we were going into Mazatlan. I've got business there."

"My orders, sir," said the mate curtly, turning away.

The practical passenger had been observant enough of sea-going rules to recognize that this reason was final, and that it was equally futile to demand an interview with the captain when that gentleman was not visibly on duty. He turned angrily to the cabin again.

"You look disturbed, my dear Banks. I trust you haven't slept badly," said a very gentle voice from the quarter-rail near him; "or, perhaps, the ship's going about has upset you. It's a little rougher on this tack."

"That's just it," returned Banks sharply. "We HAVE gone about, and we're not going into Mazatlan at all. It's scandalous! I'll speak to the captain—I'll complain to the consignees—I've got business at Mazatlan—I expect letters —I"—

"Business, my dear fellow?" continued the voice, in gentle protest. "You'll have time for business when you get to San Francisco. And as for letters—they'll follow you there soon enough. Come over here, my boy, and say hail and farewell to the Mexican coast—to the land of Montezuma and Pizarro. Come here and see the mountain range from which Balboa feasted his eyes on the broad Pacific. Come!"

The speaker, though apparently more at his ease at sea, was in dress and appearance fully as unnautical as Banks. As he leaned over the railing, his white, close-fitting trousers and small patent-leather boots gave him a jaunty, half-military air, which continued up to the second button of his black frock-coat, and then so utterly changed its character that it was doubtful if a greater contrast could be conceived than that offered by the widely spread lapels of his coat, his low turned-down collar, loosely knotted silk handkerchief, and the round, smooth-shaven, gentle, pacific face above them. His straight long black hair, shining as if from recent immersion, was tucked carefully behind his ears, and hung in a heavy, even, semicircular fringe around the back of his neck where his tall hat usually rested, as if to leave his forehead meekly exposed to celestial criticism. When he had joined the ship at Callao, his fellow-passengers, rashly trusting to the momentary suggestion of his legs on the gangplank, had pronounced him military; meeting him later at dinner, they had regarded the mild Methodistic contour of his breast and shoulders above the table, and entertained the wild idea of asking him to evoke a blessing. To complete the confusion of his appearance, he was called "Senor" Perkins, for no other reason, apparently, than his occasional, but masterful, use of the Spanish vernacular.

Steadying himself by one of the quarter stanchions, he waved his right hand oratorically towards the sinking coast.

"Look at it, sir. One of the finest countries that ever came from the hand of the Creator; a land overflowing with milk and honey; containing, sir, in that one mountain range, the products of the three zones—and yet the abode of the oppressed and down-trodden; the land of faction, superstition, tyranny, and political revolution."

"That's all very well," said Banks irritably, "but Mazatlan is a well-known commercial port, and has English and American correspondents. There's a branch of that Boston firm— Potter, Potts & Potter—there. The new line of steamers is going to stop there regularly."

Senor Perkins' soft black eyes fell for an instant, as if accidentally, on the third mate, but the next moment he laughed, and, throwing back his head, inhaled, with evident relish, a long breath of the sharp, salt air.

"Ah!" he said enthusiastically, "THAT'S better than all the business you can pick up along a malarious coast. Open your mouth and try to take in the free breath of the glorious North Pacific. Ah! isn't it glorious?"

"Where's the captain?" said Banks, with despairing irritation. "I want to see him."

"The captain," said Senor Perkins, with a bland, forgiving smile and a slight lowering of his voice, "is, I fear, suffering from an accident of hospitality, and keeps his state-room.

The captain is a good fellow," continued Perkins, with gentle enthusiasm; "a good sailor and careful navigator, and exceedingly attentive to his passengers. I shall certainly propose getting up some testimonial for him."

"But if he's shut up in his state-room, who's giving the orders?" began Banks angrily.

Senor Perkins put up a small, well-kept hand deprecatingly.

"Really, my dear boy, I suppose the captain cannot be omnipresent. Some discretion must be left to the other officers. They probably know his ideas and what is to be done better than we do. You business men trouble yourselves too much about these things. You should take them more philosophically. For my part I always confide myself trustingly to these people. I enter a ship or railroad car with perfect faith. I say to myself, 'This captain, or this conductor, is a responsible man, selected with a view to my safety and comfort; he understands how to procure that safety and that comfort better than I do. He worries himself; he spends hours and nights of vigil to look after me and carry me to my destination. Why should I worry myself, who can only assist him by passive obedience? Why'—" But here he was interrupted by a headlong plunge of the Excelsior, a feminine shriek that was half a laugh, the rapid patter of small feet and sweep of flying skirts down the slanting deck, and the sudden and violent contact of a pretty figure.

The next moment he had forgotten his philosophy, and his companion his business. Both flew to the assistance of the fair intruder, who, albeit the least injured of the trio, clung breathlessly to the bulwarks.

"Miss Keene!" ejaculated both gentlemen.

"Oh dear! I beg your pardon," said the young lady, reddening, with a naive mingling of hilarity and embarrassment. "But it seemed so stuffy in the cabin, and it seemed so easy to get out on deck and pull myself up by the railings; and just as I got up here, I suddenly seemed to be sliding down the roof of a house."

"And now that you're here, your courage should be rewarded," said the Senor, gallantly assisting her to a settee, which he lashed securely. "You are perfectly safe now," he added, holding the end of the rope in his hand to allow a slight sliding movement of the seat as the vessel rolled. "And here is a glorious spectacle for you. Look! the sun is just rising."

The young girl glanced over the vast expanse before her with sparkling eyes and a suddenly awakened fancy that checked her embarrassed smile, and fixed her pretty, parted lips with wonder. The level rays of the rising sun striking the white crests of the lifted waves had suffused the whole ocean with a pinkish opal color: the darker parts of each wave seemed broken into facets instead of curves, and glittered sharply. The sea seemed to have lost its fluidity, and become vitreous; so much so, that it was difficult to believe that the waves which splintered across the Excelsior's bow did not fall upon her deck with the ring of shattered glass.

"Sindbad's Valley of Diamonds!" said the young girl, in an awed whisper.

"It's a cross sea in the Gulf of California, so the mate says," said Banks practically; "but I don't see why we" . . .

"The Gulf of California?" repeated the young girl, while a slight shade of disappointment passed over her bright face; "are we then so near"—

"Not the California you mean, my dear young lady," broke in Senor Perkins, "but the old peninsula of California, which is still a part of Mexico. It terminates in Cape St. Lucas, a hundred miles from here, but it's still a far cry to San Francisco, which is in Upper California. But I fancy you don't seem as anxious as our friend Mr. Banks to get to your journey's end," he added, with paternal blandness.

The look of relief which had passed over Miss Keene's truthful face gave way to one of slight embarrassment.

"It hasn't seemed long," she said hastily; and then added, as if to turn the conversation, "What is this peninsula? I remember it on our map at school."

"It's not of much account," interrupted Banks positively. "There ain't a place on it you ever heard of. It's a kind of wilderness."

"I differ from you," said Senor Perkins gravely. "There are, I have been told, some old Mexican settlements along the coast, and there is no reason why the country shouldn't be fruitful. But you may have a chance to judge for yourself," he continued beamingly. "Since we are not going into Mazatlan, we may drop in at some of those places for water. It's all on our way, and we shall save the three days we would have lost had we touched Mazatlan. That," he added, answering an impatient interrogation in Banks' eye, "at least, is the captain's idea, I reckon." He laughed, and went on still gayly,—"But what's the use of anticipating? Why should we spoil any little surprise that our gallant captain may have in store for us? I've been trying to convert this business man to my easy philosophy, Miss Keene, but he is incorrigible; he is actually lamenting his lost chance of hearing the latest news at Mazatlan, and getting the latest market quotations, instead of offering a thanksgiving for another uninterrupted day of freedom in this glorious air."

With a half humorous extravagance he unloosed his already loose necktie, turned his Byron collar still lower, and squared his shoulders ostentatiously to the sea breeze. Accustomed as his two companions were to his habitually extravagant speech, it did not at that moment seem inconsistent with the intoxicating morning air and the exhilaration of sky and wave. A breath of awakening and resurrection moved over the face of the waters; recreation and new-born life sparkled everywhere; the past night seemed forever buried in the vast and exundating sea. The reefs had been shaken out, and every sail set to catch the steadier breeze of the day; and as the quickening sun shone upon the dazzling canvas that seemed to envelop them, they felt as if wrapped in the purity of a baptismal robe.

Nevertheless, Miss Keene's eyes occasionally wandered from the charming prospect towards the companion-ladder. Presently she became ominously and ostentatiously interested in the view again, and at the same moment a young man's head and shoulders appeared above the companionway. With a bound he was on the slanting deck, moving with the agility and adaptability of youth, and approached the group. He was quite surprised to find Miss Keene there so early, and Miss Keene was equally surprised at his appearance, notwithstanding the phenomenon had occurred with singular regularity for the last three weeks. The two spectators of this gentle comedy received it as they had often received it before, with a mixture of apparent astonishment and patronizing unconsciousness, and, after a decent interval, moved away together, leaving the young people alone.

The hesitancy and awkwardness which usually followed the first moments of their charming isolation were this morning more than usually prolonged.

"It seems we are not going into Mazatlan, after all," said Miss Keene at last, without lifting her conscious eyes from the sea.

"No," returned the young fellow quickly. "I heard all about it down below, and we had quite an indignation meeting over it. I believe Mrs. Markham wanted to head a deputation to wait upon the captain in his berth. It seems that the first officer, or whosoever is running the ship, has concluded we've lost too much time already, and we're going to strike a bee-line for Cape St. Lucas, and give Mazatlan the go-by. We'll save four days by it. I suppose it don't make any difference to you, Miss Keene, does it?"

"I? Oh, no!" said the girl hastily.

"I'M rather sorry," he said hesitatingly.

"Indeed. Are you tired of the ship?" she asked saucily.

"No," he replied bluntly; "but it would have given us four more days together—four more days before we separated."

He stopped, with a heightened color. There was a moment of silence, and the voices of Senor Perkins and Mr. Banks in political discussion on the other side of the deck came faintly. Miss Keene laughed.

"We are a long way from San Francisco yet, and you may think differently."

"Never!" he said, impulsively.

He had drawn closer to her, as if to emphasize his speech. She cast a quick glance across the deck towards the two disputants, and drew herself gently away.

"Do you know," she said suddenly, with a charming smile which robbed the act of its sting, "I sometimes wonder if I am REALLY going to San Francisco. I don't know how it is; but, somehow, I never can SEE myself there."

"I wish you did, for I'M going there," he replied boldly.

Without appearing to notice the significance of his speech, she continued gravely:

"I have been so strongly impressed with this feeling at times that it makes me quite superstitious. When we had that terrible storm after we left Callao, I thought it meant that—that we were all going down, and we should never be heard of again."

"As long as we all went together," he said, "I don't know that it would be the worst thing that could happen. I remember that storm, Miss Keene. And I remember"—He stopped timidly.

"What?" she replied, raising her smiling eyes for the first time to his earnest face.

"I remember sitting up all night near your state-room, with a cork jacket and lots of things I'd fixed up for you, and thinking I'd die before I trusted you alone in the boat to those rascally Lascars of the crew."

"But how would you have prevented it?" asked Miss Keene, with a compassionate and half-maternal amusement.

"I don't know exactly," he said, coloring; "but I'd have lashed you to some spar, or made a raft, and got you ashore on some island."

"And poor Mrs. Markham and Mrs. Brimmer—you'd have left them to the boats and the Lascars, I suppose?" smiled Miss Keene.

"Oh, somebody would have looked after Mrs. Markham; and Mrs. Brimmer wouldn't have gone with anybody that wasn't well connected. But what's the use of talking?" he added ruefully. "Nothing has happened, and nothing is going to happen. You will see yourself in San Francisco, even if you don't see ME there. You're going to a rich brother, Miss Keene, who has friends of his own, and who won't care to know a poor fellow whom you tolerated on the passage, but who don't move in Mrs. Brimmer's set, and whom Mr. Banks wouldn't indorse commercially."

"Ah, you don't know my brother, Mr. Brace."

"Nor do you, very well, Miss Keene. You were saying, only last night, you hardly remembered him."

The young girl sighed.

"I was very young when he went West," she said explanatorily; "but I dare say I shall recall him. What I meant is, that he will be very glad to know that I have been so happy here, and he will like all those who have made me so."

"Then you have been happy?"

"Yes; very." She had withdrawn her eyes, and was looking vaguely towards the companion-way. "Everybody has been so kind to me."

"And you are grateful to all?"

"Yes."

"Equally?"

The ship gave a sudden forward plunge. Miss Keene involuntarily clutched the air with her little hand, that had been resting on the settee between them, and the young man caught it in his own.

"Equally?" he repeated, with an assumed playfulness that half veiled his anxiety. "Equally—from the beaming Senor Perkins, who smiles on all, to the gloomy Mr. Hurlstone, who smiles on no one?"

She quickly withdrew her hand, and rose. "I smell the breakfast," she said laughingly. "Don't be horrified, Mr. Brace, but I'm very hungry." She laid the hand she had withdrawn lightly on his arm. "Now help me down to the cabin."

CHAPTER II

ANOTHER PORTENT

The saloon of the Excelsior was spacious for the size of the vessel, and was furnished in a style superior to most passenger-ships of that epoch. The sun was shining through the sliding windows upon the fresh and neatly arranged breakfast-table, but the presence of the ominous "storm-racks," and partitions for glass and china, and the absence of the more delicate passengers, still testified to the potency of the Gulf of California. Even those present wore an air of fatigued discontent, and the conversation had that jerky interjectional quality which belonged to people with a common grievance, but a different individual experience. Mr. Winslow had been unable to shave. Mrs. Markham, incautiously and surreptitiously opening a port-hole in her state-room for a whiff of fresh air while dressing, had been shocked by the intrusion of the Pacific Ocean, and was obliged to summon assistance and change her dress. Jack Crosby, who had attired himself for tropical shore-going in white ducks and patent leathers, shivered in the keen northwest Trades, and bewailed the cheap cigars he had expected to buy at Mazatlan. The entrance of Miss Keene, who seemed to bring with her the freshness and purity of the dazzling outer air, stirred the younger men into some gallant attention, embarrassed, however, by a sense of self-reproach.

Senor Perkins alone retained his normal serenity. Already seated at the table between the two fair-headed children of Mrs. Brimmer, he was benevolently performing parental duties in her absence, and gently supervising and preparing their victuals even while he carried on an ethnological and political discussion with Mrs. Markham.

"Ah, my dear lady," continued the Senor, as he spread a hot biscuit with butter and currant jelly for the youngest Miss Brimmer, "I am afraid that, with the fastidiousness of your sex, you allow your refined instincts against a race who only mix with ours in a menial capacity to prejudice your views of their ability for enlightened self-government. That may be true of the aborigines of the Old World—like our friends the Lascars among the crew"—

"They're so snaky, dark, and deceitful-looking," interrupted Mrs. Markham.

"I might differ from you there, and say that the higher blonde types like the Anglo-Saxon—to say nothing of the wily Greeks—were the deceitful races: it might be difficult for any of us to say what a sly and deceitful man should be like"—

"Oor not detheitful—oor a dood man," interpolated the youngest Miss Brimmer, fondly regarding the biscuit.

"Thank you, Missie," beamed the Senor; "but to return: our Lascar friends, Mrs. Markham, belong to an earlier Asiatic type of civilization already decayed or relapsed to barbarism, while the aborigines of the New World now existing have never known it—or, like the Aztecs, have perished with it. The modern North American aborigine has not yet got beyond the tribal condition; mingled with Caucasian blood as he is in Mexico and Central America, he is perfectly capable of self-government."

"Then why has he never obtained it?" asked Mrs. Markham.

"He has always been oppressed and kept down by colonists of the Latin races; he has been little better than a slave to his oppressor for the last two centuries," said Senor Perkins, with a slight darkening of his soft eyes.

"Injins is pizen," whispered Mr. Winslow to Miss Keene.

"Who would be free, you know, the poet says, ought themselves to light out from the shoulder, and all that sort of thing," suggested Crosby, with cheerful vagueness.

"True; but a little assistance and encouragement from mankind generally would help them," continued the Senor. "Ah! my dear Mrs. Markham, if they could even count on the intelligent sympathy of women like yourself, their independence would be assured. And think what a proud privilege to have contributed to such a result, to have assisted at the birth of the ideal American Republic, for such it would be—a Republic of one blood, one faith, one history."

"What on earth, or sea, ever set the old man off again?" inquired Crosby, in an aggrieved whisper. "It's two weeks since he's given us any Central American independent flapdoodle—long enough for those nigger injins to have had half a dozen revolutions. You know that the vessels that put into San Juan have saluted one flag in the morning, and have been fired at under another in the afternoon."

"Hush!" said Miss Keene. "He's so kind! Look at him now, taking off the pinafores of those children and tidying them. He is kinder to them than their nurse, and more judicious than their mother. And half his talk with Mrs. Markham now is only to please her, because she thinks she knows politics. He's always trying to do good to somebody."

"That's so," exclaimed Brace, eager to share Miss Keene's sentiments; "and he's so good to those outlandish niggers in the crew. I don't see how the captain could get on with the crew without him; he's the only one who can talk their gibberish and keep them quiet. I've seen him myself quietly drop down among them when they were wrangling. In my opinion," continued the young fellow, lowering his voice somewhat ostentatiously, "you'll find out when we get to port that he's stopped the beginning of many a mutiny among them."

"I reckon they'd make short work of a man like him," said Winslow, whose superciliousness was by no means lessened by the community of sentiment between Miss Keene and Brace. "I reckon, his political reforms, and his poetical high-falutin' wouldn't go as far in the forecastle among live men as it does in the cabin with a lot of women. You'll more likely find that he's been some sort of steward on a steamer, and he's working his passage with us. That's where he gets that smooth, equally-attentive-to-anybody sort of style. The way he skirmished around Mrs. Brimmer and Mrs. Markham with a basin the other day when it was so rough convinced ME. It was a little too professional to suit my style."

"I suppose that was the reason why you went below so suddenly," rejoined Brace, whose too sensitive blood was beginning to burn in his cheeks and eyes.

"It's a shame to stay below this morning," said Miss Keene, instinctively recognizing the cause of the discord and its remedy. "I'm going on deck again—if I can manage to get there."

The three gentlemen sprang to accompany her; and, in their efforts to keep their physical balance and hers equally, the social equilibrium was restored.

By noon, however, the heavy cross-sea had abated, and the Excelsior bore west. When she once more rose and fell regularly on the long rhythmical swell of the Pacific, most of the passengers regained the deck. Even Mrs. Brimmer and Miss Chubb ventured from their staterooms, and were conveyed to and installed in some state on a temporary divan of cushions and shawls on the lee side. For even in this small republic of equal cabin passengers the undemo-cratic and distinction-loving sex had managed to create a sham exclusiveness. Mrs. Brimmer, as the daughter of a rich Bostonian, the sister of a prominent lawyer, and the wife of a successful San Francisco merchant, who was popularly supposed to be part-owner of the Excelsior, was recognized, and alternately caressed and hated as their superior. A majority of the male passengers, owning no actual or prospective matrimonial subjection to those charming toad-eaters, I am afraid continued to enjoy a mild and debasing equality among themselves, mitigated only by the concessions of occasional gallantry. To them, Mrs. Brimmer was a rather pretty, refined, well-dressed woman, whose languid pallor, aristocratic spareness, and utter fastidiousness did not, however, preclude a certain nervous intensity which occasionally lit up her weary eyes with a dangerous phosphorescence, under their brown fringes. Equally acceptable was Miss Chubb, her friend and traveling companion; a tall, well-bred girl, with faint salmon-pink hair and complexion, that darkened to a fiery brown in her shortsighted eyes.

Between these ladies and Mrs. Markham and Miss Keene existed an enthusiastic tolerance, which, however, could never be mistaken for a generous rivalry. Of the greater popularity of Miss Keene as the recognized belle of the

Excelsior there could be no question; nor was there any from Mrs. Brimmer and her friend. The intellectual preeminence of Mrs. Markham was equally, and no less ostentatiously, granted. "Mrs. Markham is so clever; I delight to hear you converse together," Mrs. Brimmer would say to Senor Perkins, "though I'm sure I hardly dare talk to her myself. She might easily go into the lecture-field—perhaps she expects to do so in California. My dear Clarissa"—to Miss Chubb—"don't she remind you a little of Aunt Jane Winthrop's governess, whom we came so near taking to Paris with us, but couldn't on account of her defective French?"

When "The Excelsior Banner and South Sea Bubble" was published in lat. 15 N. and long. 105 W., to which Mrs. Markham contributed the editorials and essays, and Senor Perkins three columns of sentimental poetry, Mrs. Brimmer did not withhold her praise of the fair editor. When the Excelsior "Recrossed the Line," with a suitable tableau vivant and pageant, and Miss Keene as California, in white and blue, welcomed from the hands of Neptune (Senor Perkins) and Amphitrite (Mrs. Markham) her fair sister, Massachusetts (Mrs. Brimmer), and New York (Miss Chubb), Mrs. Brimmer was most enthusiastic of the beauty of Miss Keene.

On the present morning Mr. Banks found his disappointment at not going into Mazatlan languidly shared by Mrs. Brimmer. That lady even made a place for him on the cushions beside her, as she pensively expressed her belief that her husband would be still more disappointed.

"Mr. Brimmer, you know, has correspondents at Mazatlan, and no doubt he has made particular arrangements for our reception and entertainment while there. I should not wonder if he was very indignant. And if, as I fear, the officials of the place, knowing Mr. Brimmer's position—and my own connections—have prepared to show us social courtesies, it may be a graver affair. I shouldn't be surprised if our Government were obliged to take notice of it. There is a Captain-General of port—isn't there? I think my husband spoke of him."

"Oh, he's probably been shot long ago," broke in Mr. Crosby cheerfully. "They put in a new man every revo-lution. If the wrong party's got in, they've likely shipped your husband's correspondent too, and might be waiting to get a reception for you with nigger soldiers and ball cartridges. Shouldn't wonder if the skipper got wind of something of the kind, and that's why he didn't put in. If your husband hadn't been so well known, you see, we might have slipped in all right."

Mrs. Brimmer received this speech with the languid oblivi-ousness of perception she usually meted out to this chartered jester.

"Do you really think so, Mr. Crosby? And would you have been afraid to leave your cabin—or are you joking? You know I never know when you are. It is very dreadful, either way."

But here Miss Chubb, with ready tact, interrupted any possible retort from Mr. Crosby.

"Look," she said, pointing to some of the other passengers, who, at a little distance, had grouped about the first mate in animated discussion. "I wonder what those gentlemen are so interested about. Do go and see."

Before he could reply, Mr. Winslow, detaching himself from the group, hurried towards them.

"Here's a row: Hurlstone is missing! Can't be found

Bret Harte

anywhere! They think he's fallen overboard!"

The two frightened exclamations from Miss Chubb and Mrs. Brimmer diverted attention from the sudden paleness of Miss Keene, who had impulsively approached them.

"Impossible!" she said hurriedly.

"I fear it is so," said Brace, who had followed Winslow; "although," he added in a lower tone, with an angry glance at the latter, "that brute need not have blustered it out to frighten everybody. They're searching the ship again, but there seems no hope. He hasn't been seen since last night. He was supposed to be in his state-room—but as nobody missed him—you know how odd and reserved he was—it was only when the steward couldn't find him, and began to inquire, that everybody remembered they hadn't seen him all day. You are frightened, Miss Keene; pray sit down. That fellow Winslow ought to have had more sense."

"It seems so horrible that nobody knew it," said the young girl, shuddering; "that we sat here laughing and talking, while perhaps he was—Good heavens! what's that?"

A gruff order had been given: in the bustle that ensued the ship began to fall off to leeward; a number of the crew had sprung to the davits of the quarter boat.

"We're going about, and they're lowering a boat, that's all; but it's as good as hopeless," said Brace. "The accident must have happened before daylight, or it would have been seen by the watch. It was probably long before we came on deck," he added gently; "so comfort yourself, Miss Keene, you could have seen nothing."

"It seems so dreadful," murmured the young girl, "that he

wasn't even missed. Why," she said, suddenly raising her soft eyes to Brace, "YOU must have noticed his absence; why, even I"—She stopped with a slight confusion, that was, however, luckily diverted by the irrepressible Winslow.

"The skipper's been routed out at last, and is giving orders. He don't look as if his hat fitted him any too comfortably this morning, does he?" he laughed, as a stout, grizzled man, with congested face and eyes, and a peremptory voice husky with alcoholic irritation, suddenly appeared among the group by the wheel. "I reckon he's cursing his luck at having to heave-to and lose this wind."

"But for a human creature's life!" exclaimed Mrs. Markham in horror.

"That's just it. Laying-to now ain't going to save anybody's life, and he knows it. He's doin' it for show, just for a clean record in the log, and to satisfy you people here, who'd kick up a row if he didn't."

"Then you believe he's lost?" said Miss Keene, with glistening eyes.

"There ain't a doubt of it," returned Winslow shortly.

"I don't agree with you," said a gentle voice.

They turned quickly towards the benevolent face of Senor Perkins, who had just joined them.

"I differ from my young friend," continued the Senor courteously, "because the accident must have happened at about daybreak, when we were close inshore. It would not be impossible for a good swimmer to reach the land, or even," continued Senor Perkins, in answer to the ray of hope that gleamed in Miss Keene's soft eyes, "for him to have been picked up by some passing vessel. The smoke of a large steamer was sighted between us and the land at about that time."

"A steamer!" ejaculated Banks eagerly; "that was one of the new line with the mails. How provoking!"

He was thinking of his lost letters. Miss Keene turned, heart-sick, away. Worse than the ghastly interruption to their easy idyllic life was this grim revelation of selfish-ness. She began to doubt if even the hysterical excitement of her sister passengers was not merely a pleasant titillation of their bored and inactive nerves.

"I believe the Senor is right, Miss Keene," said Brace, taking her aside, "and I'll tell you why." He stopped, looked around him, and went on in a lower voice, "There are some circumstances about the affair which look more like deliberation than an accident. He has left nothing behind him of any value or that gives any clue. If it was a suicide he would have left some letter behind for somebody—people always do, you know, at such times—and he would have chosen the open sea. It seems more probable that he threw himself overboard with the intention of reaching the shore."

"But why should he want to leave the ship?" echoed the young girl simply.

"Perhaps he found out that we were NOT going to Mazatlan, and this was his only chance; it must have happened just as the ship went about and stood off from shore again."

"But I don't understand," continued Miss Keene, with a pretty knitting of her brows, "why he should be so dread-fully anxious to get ashore now."

The young fellow looked at her with the superior smile of youthful sagacity.

"Suppose he had particular reasons for not going to San Francisco, where our laws could reach him! Suppose he had committed some offense! Suppose he was afraid of being questioned or recognized!"

The young girl rose indignantly.

"This is really too shameful! Who dare talk like that?"

Brace colored quickly.

"Who? Why, everybody," he stammered, for a moment abandoning his attitude of individual acumen; "it's the talk of the ship."

"Is it? And before they know whether he's alive or dead— perhaps even while he is still struggling with death—all they can do is to take his character away!" she repeated, with flashing eyes.

"And I'm even worse than they are," he returned, his temper rising with his color. "I ought to have known I was talking to one of HIS friends, instead of one whom I thought was MINE. I beg your pardon."

He turned away as Miss Keene, apparently not heeding his pique, crossed the deck, and entered into conversation with Mrs. Markham.

It is to be feared that she found little consolation among the other passengers, or even those of her own sex, whom this profound event had united in a certain freemasonry of sympathy and interest—to the exclusion of their former cliques. She soon learned, as the return of the boats to the ship and the ship to her course might have clearly told her, that there was no chance of recovering the missing passenger. She learned that the theory advanced by Brace was the one generally held by them; but with an added romance of detail, that excited at once their commiseration and admiration. Mrs. Brimmer remembered to have heard him, the second or third night out from Callao, groaning in his state-room; but having mistakenly referred the emotion to ordinary seasickness, she had no doubt lost an oppor-tunity for confidential disclosure. "I am sure," she added, "that had somebody as resolute and practical as you, dear Mrs. Markham, approached him the next day, he would have revealed his sorrow." Miss Chubb was quite certain that she had seen him one night, in tears, by the quarter railing. "I saw his eyes glistening under his slouched hat as I passed. I remember thinking, at the time, that he oughtn't to have been left alone with such a dreadful temptation before him to slip overboard and end his sorrow or his crime." Mrs. Markham also remembered that it was about five o'clock—or was it six?—that morning when she distinctly thought she had heard a splash, and she was almost impelled to get up and look out of the bull's-eye. She should never forgive herself for resisting that impulse, for she was positive now that she would have seen his ghastly face in the water. Some indignation was felt that the captain, after a cursory survey of his stateroom, had ordered it to be locked until his fate was more positively known, and the usual seals placed on his effects for their delivery to the authorities at San Francisco. It was believed that some clue to his secret would be found among his personal chattels, if only in the form of a keepsake, a locket, or a bit of jewelry. Miss Chubb had noticed that he wore a seal ring, but not on the engagement-finger. In some vague feminine way it was admitted without discussion that one of their own sex was mixed up in the affair, and, with the exception of Miss Keene, general credence was given to the theory that Mazatlan contained his loadstar—the fatal partner and accomplice of his crime, the siren that allured him to his watery grave. I regret to say that the facts gathered by the gentlemen were equally ineffective. The steward who had attended the missing man was obliged to confess that their most protracted and confidential conversation had been on the comparative efficiency of ship biscuits and soda crackers. Mr. Banks, who was known to have spoken to him, could only remember that one warm evening, in reply to a casual remark about the weather, the missing man, burying his ears further in the turned-up collar of his pea-jacket, had stated, "'It was cold enough to freeze the ears off a brass monkey,'—a remark, no doubt, sir, intended to convey a reason for his hiding his own." Only Senor Perkins retained his serene optimism unimpaired.

"Take my word for it, we shall yet hear good news of our missing friend. Let us at least believe it until we know otherwise. Ah! my dear Mrs. Markham, why should the Unknown always fill us with apprehension? Its surprises are equally often agreeable."

"But we have all been so happy before this; and this seems such an unnecessary and cruel awakening," said Miss Keene, lifting her sad eyes to the speaker, "that I can't help thinking it's the beginning of the end. Good heavens! what's that?"

She had started at the dark figure of one of the foreign-looking sailors, who seemed to have suddenly risen out of the deck beside them.

"The Senor Perkins," he said, with an apologetic gesture of his hand to his hatless head.

"You want ME, my good man?" asked Senor Perkins paternally.

"Si, Senor; the mate wishes to see the Patrono," he said in Spanish.

"I will come presently."

The sailor hesitated. Senor Perkins took a step nearer to him benignantly. The man raised his eyes to Senor Perkins, and said,—

"Vigilancia."

"Bueno!" returned the Senor gently. "Excuse me, ladies, for a moment."

"Perhaps it is some news of poor Mr. Hurlstone?" said Miss Keene, with an instinctive girlish movement of hope.

"Who knows?" returned Senor Perkins, waving his hand as he gayly tripped after his guide. "Let us believe in the best, dear young lady, the best!"

CHAPTER III

"VIGILANCIA"

Without exchanging another word with his escort, Senor Perkins followed him to the main hatch, where they descended and groped their way through the half obscurity of the lower deck. Here they passed one or two shadows, that, recognizing the Senor, seemed to draw aside in a half awed, half suppressed shyness, as of caged animals in the presence of their trainer. At the fore-hatch they again descended, passing a figure that appeared to be keeping watch at the foot of the ladder, and almost instantly came upon a group lit up by the glare of a bull's-eye lantern. It was composed of the first and second mate, a vicious-looking Peruvian sailor with a bandaged head, and, to the Senor's astonishment, the missing passenger Hurlstone, seated on the deck, heavily ironed.

"Tell him what you know, Pedro," said the first mate to the Peruvian sailor curtly.

"It was just daybreak, Patrono, before we put about," began the man in Spanish, "that I thought I saw some one gliding along towards the fore-hatch; but I lost sight of him. After we had tumbled up to go on the other tack, I heard a noise in the fore-hold. I went down and found HIM," pointing to

Hurlstone, "hiding there. He had some provisions stowed away beside him, and that package. I grabbed him, Patrono. He broke away and struck me here"—he pointed to his still wet bandage—"and would have got out overboard through the port, but the second mate heard the row and came down just in time to stop him."

"When was this?" asked Senor Perkins.

"Guardia di Diana."

"You were chattering, you fellows."

"Quien sabe?" said the Peruvian, lifting his shoulders.

"How does he explain himself?"

"He refuses to speak."

"Take off his irons," said Senor Perkins, in English.

"But"—expostulated the first mate, with a warning gesture.

"I said—take off his irons," repeated Senor Perkins in a dry and unfamiliar voice.

The two mates released the shackles. The prisoner raised his eyes to Senor Perkins. He was a slightly built man of about thirty, fair-haired and hollow-cheeked. His short upper lip was lifted over his teeth, as if from hurried or labored breathing; but his features were regular and determined, and his large blue eyes shone with a strange abstraction of courage and fatuity.

"That will do," continued the Senor, in the same tone. "Now leave him with me."

The two mates looked at each other, and hesitated; but at a glance from Perkins, turned, and ascended the ladder again. The Peruvian alone remained.

"Go!" said the Senor sharply.

The man cast a vindictive look at the prisoner and retreated sullenly.

"Did HE tell you," said the prisoner, looking after the sailor grimly, "that I tried to bribe him to let me go, but that I couldn't reach his figure? He wanted too much. He thought I had some stolen money or valuables here," he added, with a bitter laugh, pointing to the package that lay beside him.

"And you hadn't?" said Perkins shortly.

"No."

"I believe you. And now, my young friend," said Perkins, with a singular return of his beaming gentleness, "since those two efficient and competent officers and this energetic but discourteous seaman are gone, would you mind telling me WHAT you were hiding for?"

The prisoner raised his eyes on his questioner. For the last three weeks he had lived in the small community of which the Senor was a prominent member, but he scarcely recognized him now.

"What if I refuse?" he said.

The Senor shrugged his shoulders.

"Those two excellent men would feel it their duty to bring the Peruvian to the captain, and I should be called to interpret to him."

"And I should throw myself overboard the first chance I got. I would have done so ten minutes ago, but the mate stopped me."

His eye glistened with the same fatuous determination he had shown at first. There was no doubt he would do as he said.

"I believe you would," said the Senor benevolently; "but I see no present necessity for that, nor for any trouble whatever, if you will kindly tell me WHAT I am to say."

The young man's eyes fell.

"I DID try to conceal myself in the hold," he said bluntly. "I intended to remain there hidden while the ship was at Mazatlan. I did not know until now that the vessel had changed her course."

"And how did you believe your absence would be accounted for?" asked the Senor blandly.

"I thought it would be supposed that I had fallen overboard before we entered Mazatlan."

"So that anybody seeking you there would not find you, and you would be believed to be dead?"

"Yes." He raised his eyes quickly to Senor Perkins again. "I am neither a thief nor a murderer," he said almost savagely, "but I do not choose to be recognized by any one who knows me on this side of the grave."

Senor Perkins' eyes sought his, and for an instant seemed to burn through the singular, fatuous mist that veiled them.

"My friend," he said cheerfully, after a moment's pause, "you have just had a providential escape. I repeat it—a most providential escape. Indeed, if I were inclined to prophesy, I would say you were a man reserved for some special good fortune."

The prisoner stared at him with angry amazement.

"You are a confirmed somnambulist. Excuse me," continued the Senor, with a soft, deprecating gesture; "you are, of course, unaware of it—most victims of that singular complaint are, or at least fail to recognize the extent of their aberration. In your case it has only been indicated by a profound melancholy and natural shunning of society. In a paroxysm of your disorder, you rise in the night, fully dress yourself, and glide as unconsciously along the deck in pursuance of some vague fancy. You pass the honest but energetic sailor who has just left us, who thinks you are a phantom, and fails to give the alarm; you are precipitated by a lurch of the ship through an open hatchway: the shock renders you insensible until you are discovered and restored."

"And who will believe this pretty story?" said the young man scornfully.

"The honest sailor who picked you up, who has related it in his own picturesque tongue to ME, who will in turn interpret it to the captain and the other passengers," replied Senor Perkins blandly.

"And what of the two mates who were here?" said the prisoner hesitatingly.

"They are two competent officers, who are quite content to carry out the orders of their superiors, and who understand their duty too well to interfere with the reports of their subordinates, on which these orders are based. Mr. Brooks, the first officer, though fairly intelligent and a good reader of history, is only imperfectly acquainted with the languages, and Mr. M'Carthy's knowledge of Spanish is confined to a few objurgations which generally preclude extended conversation."

"And who are you," said Hurlstone, more calmly, "who are willing to do this for a stranger?"

"A friend—equally of yours, the captain's, and the other passengers'," replied Senor Perkins pleasantly. "A man who believes you, my dear sir, and, even if he did not, sees no reason to interrupt the harmony that has obtained in our little community during our delightful passage. Were any scandal to occur, were you to carry out your idea of throwing yourself overboard, it would, to say nothing of my personal regret, produce a discord for which there is no necessity, and from which no personal good can be derived. Here at least your secret is secure, for even I do not ask what it is; we meet here on an equality, based on our own conduct and courtesy to each other, limited by no antecedent prejudice, and restrained by no thought of the future. In a little while we shall be separated—why should it not be as friends? Why should we not look back upon our little world of this ship as a happy one?"

Hurlstone gazed at the speaker with a troubled air. It was once more the quaint benevolent figure whom he had vaguely noted among the other passengers, and as vaguely despised. He hesitated a moment, and then, half timidly, half reservedly, extended his hand.

"I thank you," he said, "at least for not asking my secret. Perhaps, if it was only"—

"Your own—you might tell it," interrupted the Senor, gayly. "I understand. I see you recognize my principle. There is no necessity of your putting yourself to that pain, or another to that risk. And now, my young friend, time presses. I must say a word to our friends above, who are waiting, and I shall see that you are taken privately to your state-room while most of the other passengers are still on deck. If you would permit yourself the weakness of allowing the steward to carry or assist you it would be better. Let me advise you that the excitement of the last three hours has not left you in your full strength. You must really give ME the pleasure of spreading the glad tidings of your safety among the passengers, who have been so terribly alarmed."

"They will undoubtedly be relieved," said Hurlstone, with ironical bitterness.

"You wrong them," returned the Senor, with gentle reproach; "especially the ladies."

The voice of the first mate from above here checked his further speech, and, perhaps, prevented him, as he quickly reascended the upper deck, from noticing the slight embarrassment of his prisoner.

The Senor's explanations to the mate were evidently explicit and brief. In a few moments he reappeared with the steward and his assistant.

"Lean on these men," he said to Hurlstone significantly, "and do not overestimate your strength. Thank Heaven, no bones are broken, and you are only bruised by the fall. With a little rest, I think we can get along without laying the captain's medicine-chest under contribution. Our kind friend Mr. Brooks has had the lower deck cleared, so that you may gain your state-room without alarming the passengers or fatiguing yourself."

He pressed Hurlstone's hand as the latter resigned himself to the steward, and was half led, half supported, through the gloom of the lower deck. Senor Perkins remained for an instant gazing after him with even more than his usual benevolence. Suddenly his arm was touched almost rudely. He turned, and encountered the lowering eyes of the Peruvian sailor.

"And what is to be done for me?" said the man roughly, in Spanish.

"You?"

"Yes. Who's to pay for this?" he pointed to his bandaged head.

Without changing his bland expression, Senor Perkins apparently allowed his soft black eyes to rest, as if fondly, on the angry pupils of the Peruvian. The eyes of the latter presently sought the ground.

"My dear Yoto," said Senor Perkins softly, "I scarcely think that this question of personal damage can be referred to the State. I will, however, look into it. Meantime, let me advise you to control your enthusiasm. Too much zeal in a subordinate is even more fatal than laxity. For the rest, son, be vigilant—and peaceful. Thou hast meant well, much shall be—forgiven thee. For the present, vamos!"

He turned on his heel, and ascended to the upper deck.

Here he found the passengers thrilling with a vague excitement. A few brief orders, a few briefer explanations, dropped by the officers, had already whetted curiosity to the keenest point. The Senor was instantly beset with interrogations. Gentle, compassionate, with well-rounded periods, he related the singular accident that had befallen Mr. Hurlstone, and his providential escape from almost certain death. "At the most, he has now only the exhaustion of the shock, from which a day of perfect rest will recover him; but," he added deprecatingly, "at present he ought not to be disturbed or excited."

The story was received by those fellow-passengers who had been strongest in their suspicions of Hurlstone's suicide or flight, with a keen sense of discomfiture, only mitigated by a humorous perception of the cause of the accident. It was agreed that a man whose ludicrous infirmity had been the cause of putting the ship out of her course, and the passengers out of their comfortable security, could not be wronged by attributing to him manlier and more criminal motives. A somnambulist on shipboard was clearly a humorous object, who might, however, become a bore. "It all accounts for his being so deuced quiet and reserved in the daytime," said Crosby facetiously; "he couldn't keep it up the whole twenty-four hours. If he'd only given us a little more of his company when he was awake, he wouldn't have gallivanted round at night, and we'd have been thirty miles nearer port." Equal amusement was created by the humorous suggestion that the unfortunate man had never been entirely awake during the voyage, and that he would now, probably for the first time, really make the acquaintance of his fellow-voyagers. Listening to this badinage with bland tolerance, Senor Perkins no doubt felt that, for the maintenance of that perfect amity he so ardently apostrophized, it was just as well that Hurlstone was in his state-room, and out of hearing. He would have been more satisfied, however, had he been permitted to hear the feminine comments on this incident. In the eyes of the lady passengers Mr. Hurlstone was more a hero than ever; his mysterious malady invested him with a vague and spiritual interest; his escape from the awful fate reserved to him, in their excited fancy, gave him the eclat of having ACTUALLY survived it; while the supposed real incident of his fall through the hatchway lent him the additional lustre of a wounded and crippled man. That prostrate condition of active humanity, which so irresistibly appeals to the feminine imagination as segre-gating their victim from the distractions of his own sex, and, as it were, delivering him helpless into their hands, was at once their opportunity, and his. All the ladies volunteered to nurse him; it was with difficulty that Mrs. Brimmer and Mrs. Markham, reinforced with bandages, flannels, and liniments, and supported by different theories, could be kept from the door of his state-room. Jellies, potted meats, and delicacies from their private stores appeared on trays at his bedside, to be courteously declined by the Senor Perkins, in his new functions of a benevolent type of Sancho Panza physician. To say that this pleased the gentle optimism of the Senor is unnecessary. Even while his companion writhed under the sting of this enforced compassion, the good man beamed philosophi-cally upon him.

"Take care, or I shall end this cursed farce in my own way," said Hurlstone ominously, his eyes again filming with a vague desperation.

"My dear boy," returned the Senor gently, "reflect upon the situation. Your suffering, real or implied, produces in the hearts of these gentle creatures a sympathy which not only exalts and sustains their higher natures, but, I conscientiously believe, gratifies and pleases their lower ones. Why should you deny them this opportunity of indulging their twofold organisms, and beguiling the tedium of the voyage, merely because of some erroneous exhibition of fact?"

Later, Senor Perkins might have added to this exposition the singularly stimulating effect which Hurlstone's supposed peculiarity had upon the feminine imagination. But there were some secrets which were not imparted even to him, and it was only to each other that the ladies confided certain details and reminiscences. For it now appeared that they had all heard strange noises and stealthy steps at night; and Mrs. Brimmer was quite sure that on one occasion the handle of her state-room door was softly turned. Mrs. Markham also remembered distinctly that only a week before, being unable to sleep, she had ventured out into the saloon in a dressing-gown to get her diary, which she had left with a portfolio on a chair; that she had a sudden consciousness of another presence in the saloon, although she could distinguish nothing by the dim light of the swinging lantern; and that, after quickly returning to her room, she was quite positive she heard a door close. But the most surprising reminiscence developed by the late incident was from Mrs. Brimmer's nurse, Susan. As it, apparently, demonstrated the fact that Mr. Hurlstone not only walked but TALKED in his sleep, it possessed a more mysterious significance. It seemed that Susan was awakened one night by the sound of voices, and, opening her door softly, saw a figure which she at first supposed to be the Senor Perkins, but which she now was satisfied was poor Mr. Hurlstone. As there was no one else to be seen, the voices must have proceeded from that single figure; and being in a strange and unknown tongue, were inexpressibly weird and awful. When pressed to remember what was said, she could only distinguish one word—a woman's name—Virgil—Vigil—no: Virginescia!

"It must have been one of those creatures at Callao, whose pictures you can buy for ten cents," said Mrs. Brimmer.

"If it is one of them, Susan must have made a mistake in the first two syllables of the name," said Mrs. Markham grimly.

"But surely, Miss Keene," said Miss Chubb, turning to that

Bret Harte

young lady, who had taken only the part of a passive listener to this colloquy, and was gazing over the railing at the sinking sun, "surely YOU can tell us something about this poor young man. If I don't mistake, you are the only person he ever honored with his conversation."

"And only once, I think," said the young girl, slightly coloring. "He happened to be sitting next to me on deck, and I believe he spoke only out of politeness. At least, he seemed very quiet and reserved, and talked on general topics, and I thought very intelligently. I—should have thought—I mean," she continued hesitatingly—"I thought he was an educated gentleman."

"That isn't at all inconsistent with photographs or sleep-walking," said Mrs. Brimmer, with one of her vague simplicities. "Uncle Quincey brought home a whole sheaf of those women whom he said he'd met; and one of my cousins, who was educated at Heidelberg, used to walk in his sleep, as it were, all over Europe."

"Did you notice anything queer in his eyes, Miss Keene?" asked Miss Chubb vivaciously.

Miss Keene had noticed that his eyes were his best feature, albeit somewhat abstracted and melancholy; but, for some vague reason she could not explain herself, she answered hurriedly that she had seen nothing very particular in them.

"Well," said Mrs. Markham positively, "when he's able to be out again, I shall consider it my duty to look him up, and try to keep him sufficiently awake in the daytime to ensure his resting better at night."

"No one can do it, dear Mrs. Markham, better than you; and no one would think of misunderstanding your motives," said

Mrs. Brimmer sweetly. "But it's getting late, and the air seems to be ever so much colder. Captain Bunker says it's because we are really nearing the Californian coast. It seems so odd! Mr. Brimmer wrote to me that it was so hot in Sacramento that you could do something with eggs in the sun—I forget what."

"Hatch them?" suggested Miss Chubb.

"I think so," returned Mrs. Brimmer, rising. "Let us go below."

The three ladies rustled away, but Miss Keene, throwing a wrap around her shoulders, lingered by the railing. With one little hand supporting her round chin, she leaned over the darkly heaving water. She was thinking of her brief and only interview with that lonely man whose name was now in everybody's mouth, but who, until to-day, had been passed over by them with an unconcern equal to his own. And yet to her refined and delicately feminine taste there appeared no reason why he should not have mingled with his fellows, and have accepted the homage from them that SHE was instinctively ready to give. He seemed to her like a gentleman—and something more. In her limited but joyous knowledge of the world—a knowledge gathered in the happy school-life of an orphan who but faintly remembered and never missed a parent's care—she knew nothing of the mysterious dominance of passion, suffering, or experience in fashioning the outward expression of men, and saw only that Mr. Hurlstone was unlike any other. That unlikeness was fascinating. He had said very little to her in that very brief period. He had not talked to her with the general gallantry which she already knew her prettiness elicited. Without knowing why, she felt there was a subtle flattery in his tacit recognition of that other self of which she, as yet, knew so little. She could not remember what they had talked about—

nor why. Nor was she offended that he had never spoken to her since, nor gone beyond a grave lifting of his hat to her when he passed.

CHAPTER IV

IN THE FOG

By noon of the following day the coast of the Peninsula of California had been sighted to leeward. The lower temperature of the northwest Trades had driven Mrs. Brimmer and Miss Chubb into their state-rooms to consult their wardrobes in view of an impending change from the light muslins and easy languid toilets of the Tropics. That momentous question for the moment held all other topics in abeyance; and even Mrs. Markham and Miss Keene, though they still kept the deck, in shawls and wraps, sighed over this feminine evidence of the gentle passing of their summer holiday. The gentlemen had already mounted their pea-jackets and overcoats, with the single exception of Senor Perkins, who, in chivalrous compliment to the elements, still bared his unfettered throat and forehead to the breeze. The aspect of the coast, as seen from the Excelsior's deck, seemed to bear out Mr. Banks' sweeping indictment of the day before. A few low, dome-like hills, yellow and treeless as sand dunes, scarcely raised themselves above the horizon. The air, too, appeared to have taken upon itself a dry asperity; the sun shone with a hard, practical brilliancy. Miss Keene raised her eyes to Senor Perkins with a pretty impatience that she sometimes indulged in, as one of the privileges of accepted beauty and petted youth.

"I don't think much of your peninsula," she said poutingly. "It looks dreadfully flat and uninteresting. It was a great deal nicer on the other coast, or even at sea."

"Perhaps you are judging hastily, my dear young friend," said Senor Perkins, with habitual tolerance. "I have heard that behind those hills, and hidden from sight in some of the canyons, are perfect little Edens of beauty and fruitfulness. They are like some ardent natures that cover their approaches with the ashes of their burnt-up fires, but only do it the better to keep intact their glowing, vivifying, central heat."

"How very poetical, Mr. Perkins!" said Mrs. Markham, with blunt admiration. "You ought to put that into verse."

"I have," returned Senor Perkins modestly. "They are some reflections on—I hardly dare call them an apostrophe to—the crater of Colima. If you will permit me to read them to you this evening, I shall be charmed. I hope also to take that opportunity of showing you the verses of a gifted woman, not yet known to fame, Mrs. Euphemia M'Corkle, of Peoria, Illinois."

Mrs. Markham coughed slightly. The gifted M'Corkle was already known to her through certain lines quoted by the Senor; and the entire cabin had one evening fled before a larger and more ambitious manuscript of the fair Illinoisian. Miss Keene, who dreaded the reappearance of this poetical phantom that seemed to haunt the Senor's fancy, could not, however, forget that she had been touched on that occasion by a kindly moisture of eye and tremulousness of voice in the reader; and, in spite of the hopeless bathos of the composition, she had forgiven him. Though she did not always understand Senor Perkins, she liked him too well to allow him to become ridiculous to others; and at the present moment she promptly interposed with a charming assumption of coquetry.

"You forget that you promised to let ME read the manuscript first, and in private, and that you engaged to give me my revenge at chess this evening. But do as you like. You are all fast becoming faithless. I suppose it is because our holiday is drawing to a close, and we shall soon forget we ever had any, or be ashamed we ever played so long. Everybody seems to be getting nervous and fidgety and preparing for civilization again. Mr. Banks, for the last few days, has dressed himself regularly as if he were going down town to his office, and writes letters in the corner of the saloon as if it were a counting-house. Mr. Crosby and Mr. Winslow do nothing but talk of their prospects, and I believe they are drawing up articles of partnership together. Here is Mr. Brace frightening me by telling me that my brother will lock me up, to keep the rich miners from laying their bags of gold dust at my feet; and Mrs. Brimmer and Miss Chubb assure me that I haven't a decent gown to go ashore in."

"You forget Mr. Hurlstone," said Brace, with ill-concealed bitterness; "he seems to have time enough on his hands, and I dare say would sympathize with you. You women like idle men."

"If we do, it's because only the idle men have the time to amuse us," retorted Miss Keene. "But," she added, with a laugh, "I suppose I'm getting nervous and fidgety myself; for I find myself every now and then watching the officers and men, and listening to the orders as if something were going to happen again. I never felt so before; I never used to have the least concern in what you call 'the working of the ship,' and now"—her voice, which had been half playful, half pettish, suddenly became grave,—"and now—look at the mate and those men forward. There certainly is something going on, or is going to happen. What ARE they looking at?"

The mate had clambered halfway up the main ratlines, and was looking earnestly to windward. Two or three of the crew on the forecastle were gazing in the same direction. The group of cabin-passengers on the quarterdeck, following their eyes, saw what appeared to be another low shore on the opposite bow.

"Why, there's another coast there!" said Mrs. Markham.

"It's a fog-bank," said Senor Perkins gravely. He quickly crossed the deck, exchanged a few words with the officer, and returned. Miss Keene, who had felt a sense of relief, nevertheless questioned his face as he again stood beside her. But he had recovered his beaming cheerfulness. "It's nothing to alarm you," he said, answering her glance, "but it may mean delay if we can't get out of it. You don't mind that, I know."

"No," replied the young girl, smiling. "Besides, it would be a new experience. We've had winds and calms—we only want fog now to complete our adventures. Unless it's going to make everybody cross," she continued, with a mischievous glance at Brace.

"You'll find it won't improve the temper of the officers," said Crosby, who had joined the group. "There's nothing sailors hate more than a fog. They can go to sleep in a hurricane between the rolls of a ship, but a fog keeps them awake. It's the one thing they can't shirk. There's the skipper tumbled up, too! The old man looks wrathy, don't he? But it's no use now; we're going slap into it, and the wind's failing!"

It was true. In the last few moments all that vast glistening surface of metallic blue which stretched so far to windward appeared to be slowly eaten away as if by some dull, corroding acid; the distant horizon line of sea and sky was still distinct and sharply cut, but the whole water between them had grown gray, as if some invisible shadow had passed in mid-air across it. The actual fog bank had suddenly lost its resemblance to the shore, had lifted as a curtain, and now seemed suspended over the ship. Gradually it descended; the top-gallant and top-sails were lost in this mysterious vapor, yet the horizon line still glimmered faintly. Then another mist seemed to rise from the sea and meet it; in another instant the deck whereon they stood shrank to the appearance of a raft adrift in a faint gray sea. With the complete obliteration of all circum-ambient space, the wind fell. Their isolation was complete.

It was notable that the first and most peculiar effect of this misty environment was the absolute silence. The empty, invisible sails above did not flap; the sheets and halyards hung limp; even the faint creaking of an unseen block overhead was so startling as to draw every eye upwards. Muffled orders from viewless figures forward were obeyed by phantoms that moved noiselessly through the gray sea that seemed to have invaded the deck. Even the passengers spoke in whispers, or held their breath, in passive groups, as if fearing to break a silence so replete with awe and anticipation. It was next noticed that the vessel was subjected to some vague motion; the resistance of the water had ceased, the waves no longer hissed under her bows, or nestled and lapped under her counter; a dreamy, irregular, and listless rocking had taken the place of the regular undulations; at times, a faint and half delicious vertigo seemed to overcome their senses; the ship was drifting.

Captain Bunker stood near the bitts, where his brief orders were transmitted to the man at the almost useless wheel. At his side Senor Perkins beamed with unshaken serenity, and hopefully replied to the captain's half surly, half anxious queries.

"By the chart we should be well east of Los Lobos island, d'ye see?" he said impatiently. "You don't happen to remember the direction of the current off shore when you were running up here?"

"It's five years ago," said the Senor modestly; "but I remember we kept well to the west to weather Cape St. Eugenio. My impression is that there was a strong northwesterly current setting north of Ballenos Bay."

"And we're in it now," said Captain Bunker shortly. "How near St. Roque does it set?"

"Within a mile or two. I should keep away more to the west," said Senor Perkins, "and clear"—

"I ain't asking you to run the ship," interrupted Captain Bunker sharply. "How's her head now, Mr. Brooks?"

The seamen standing near cast a rapid glance at Senor Perkins, but not a muscle of his bland face moved or betrayed a consciousness of the insult. Whatever might have been the feeling towards him, at that moment the sailors— after their fashion—admired their captain; strong, masterful, and imperious. The danger that had cleared his eye, throat, and brain, and left him once more the daring and skillful navigator they knew, wiped out of their shallow minds the vicious habit that had sunk him below their level.

It had now become perceptible to even the inexperienced eyes of the passengers that the Excelsior was obeying some new and profound impulse. The vague drifting had ceased, and in its place had come a mysterious but regular movement, in which the surrounding mist seemed to participate, until fog and vessel moved together towards some unseen but well-defined bourne. In vain had the boats of the

Excelsior, manned by her crew, endeavored with a towing-line to check or direct the inexplicable movement; in vain had Captain Bunker struggled, with all the skilled weapons of seamanship, against his invincible foe; wrapped in the impenetrable fog, the ship moved ghost-like to what seemed to be her doom.

The anxiety of the officers had not as yet communicated itself to the passengers; those who had been most nervous in the ordinary onset of wind and wave looked upon the fog as a phenomenon whose only disturbance might be delay. To Miss Keene this conveyed no annoyance; rather that placid envelopment of cloud soothed her fancy; she submitted herself to its soft embraces, and to the mysterious onward movement of the ship, as if it were part of a youthful dream. Once she thought of the ship of Sindbad, and that fatal loadstone mountain, with an awe that was, however, half a pleasure.

"You are not frightened, Miss Keene?" said a voice near her.

She started slightly. It was the voice of Mr. Hurlstone. So thick was the fog that his face and figure appeared to come dimly out of it, like a part of her dreaming fancy. Without replying to his question, she said quickly,—

"You are better then, Mr. Hurlstone? We—we were all so frightened for you."

An angry shadow crossed his thin face, and he hesitated. After a pause he recovered himself, and said,—

"I was saying you were taking all this very quietly. I don't think there's much danger myself. And if we should go ashore here"—

"Well?" suggested Miss Keene, ignoring this first intimation of danger in her surprise at the man's manner.

"Well, we should all be separated only a few days earlier, that's all!"

More frightened at the strange bitterness of his voice than by the sense of physical peril, she was vaguely moving away towards the dimly outlined figures of her companions when she was arrested by a voice forward. There was a slight murmur among the passengers.

"What did he say?" asked Miss Keene, "What are 'Breakers ahead'?"

Hurlstone did not reply.

"Where away?" asked a second voice.

The murmur still continuing, Captain Bunker's hoarse voice pierced the gloom,—"Silence fore and aft!"

The first voice repeated faintly,—

"On the larboard bow."

There was another silence. Again the voice repeated, as if mechanically,—

"Breakers!"

"Where away?"

"On the starboard beam."

"We are in some passage or channel," said Hurlstone quietly.

The young girl glanced round her and saw for the first time that, in one of those inexplicable movements she had not understood, the other passengers had been withdrawn into a limited space of the deck, as if through some authoritative orders, while she and her companion had been evidently overlooked. A couple of sailors, who had suddenly taken their positions by the quarter-boats, strengthened the accidental separation.

"Is there some one taking care of you?" he asked, half hesitatingly; "Mr. Brace—Perkins—or"—

"No," she replied quickly. "Why?"

"Well, we are very near the boat in an emergency, and you might allow me to stay here and see you safe in it."

"But the other ladies? Mrs. Markham, and"—

"They'll take their turn after YOU," he said grimly, picking up a wrap from the railing and throwing it over her shoulders.

"But—I don't understand!" she stammered, more embarrassed by the situation than by any impending peril.

"There is very little danger, I think," he added impatiently. "There is scarcely any sea; the ship has very little way on; and these breakers are not over rocks. Listen."

She tried to listen. At first she heard nothing but the occasional low voice of command near the wheel. Then she became conscious of a gentle, soothing murmur through the fog to the right. She had heard such a murmuring accompaniment to her girlish dreams at Newport on a still summer night. There was nothing to frighten her, but it increased her embarrassment.

"And you?" she said awkwardly, raising her soft eyes.

"Oh, if you are all going off in the boats, by Jove, I think I'll stick to the ship!" he returned, with a frankness that would have been rude but for its utter abstraction.

Miss Keene was silent. The ship moved gently onward. The monotonous cry of the leadsman in the chains was the only sound audible. The soundings were indicating shoaler water, although the murmuring of the surf had been left far astern. The almost imperceptible darkening of the mist on either beam seemed to show that the Excelsior was entering some land-locked passage. The movement of the vessel slackened, the tide was beginning to ebb. Suddenly a wave of far-off clamor, faint but sonorous, broke across the ship. There was an interval of breathless silence, and then it broke again, and more distinctly. It was the sound of bells!

The thrill of awe which passed through passengers and crew at this spiritual challenge from the vast and intangible void around them had scarcely subsided when the captain turned to Senor Perkins with a look of surly interrogation. The Senor brushed his hat further back on his head, wiped his brow, and became thoughtful.

"It's too far south for Rosario," he said deprecatingly; "and the only other mission I know of is San Carlos, and that's far inland. But that is the Angelus, and those are mission bells, surely."

The captain turned to Mr. Brooks. The voice of invisible command again passed along the deck, and, with a splash in the water and the rattling of chains, the Excelsior swung slowly round on her anchor on the bosom of what seemed a placid bay.

Miss Keene, who, in her complete absorption, had listened to the phantom bells with an almost superstitious exaltation, had forgotten the presence of her companion, and now turned towards him. But he was gone. The imminent danger he had spoken of, half slightingly, he evidently considered as past. He had taken the opportunity offered by the slight bustle made by the lowering of the quarter-boat and the departure of the mate on a voyage of discovery to mingle with the crowd, and regain his state-room. With the anchoring of the vessel, the momentary restraint was relaxed, the passengers were allowed to pervade the deck, and Mrs. Markham and Mr. Brace simultaneously rushed to Miss Keene's side.

"We were awfully alarmed for you, my dear," said Mrs. Markham, "until we saw you had a protector. Do tell me— what DID he say? He must have thought the danger great to have broken the Senor's orders and come upon deck? What did he talk about?"

With a vivid recollection in her mind of Mr. Hurlstone's contemptuous ignoring of the other ladies, Miss Keene became slightly embarrassed. Her confusion was not removed by the consciousness that the jealous eyes of Brace were fixed upon her.

"Perhaps he thought it was night, and walked upon deck in his sleep," remarked Brace sarcastically. "He's probably gone back to bed."

"He offered me his protection very politely, and begged to remain to put me in the boat in case of danger," said Miss Keene, recovering herself, and directing her reply to Mrs. Markham. "I think that others have made me the same kind

Bret Harte

of offer—who were wide awake," she added mischievously to Brace.

"I wouldn't be too sure that they were not foolishly dreaming too," returned Brace, in a lower voice.

"I should think we all were asleep or dreaming here," said Mrs. Markham briskly. "Nobody seems to know where we are, and the only man who might guess it—Senor Perkins—has gone off in the boat with the mate."

"We're not a mile from shore and a Catholic church," said Crosby, who had joined them. "I just left Mrs. Brimmer, who is very High Church, you know, quite overcome by these Angelus bells. She's been entreating the captain to let her go ashore for vespers. It wouldn't be a bad idea, if we could only see what sort of a place we've got to. It wouldn't do to go feeling round the settlement in the dark—would it? Hallo! what's that? Oh, by Jove, that'll finish Mrs. Brimmer, sure!"

"Hush!" said Miss Keene impulsively.

He stopped. The long-drawn cadence of a chant in thin clear soprano voices swept through the fog from the invisible shore, rose high above the ship, and then fell, dying away with immeasurable sweetness and melancholy. Even when it had passed, a lingering melody seemed to fill the deck. Two or three of the foreign sailors crossed themselves devoutly; the other passengers withheld their speech, and looked at each other. Afraid to break the charm by speech, they listened again, but in vain an infinite repose followed that seemed to pervade everything.

It was broken, at last, by the sound of oars in their rowlocks; the boat was returning. But it was noticed that the fog had slightly lifted from the surface of the water, for the boat was distinctly visible two cables' length from the ship as she approached; and it was seen that besides the first officer and Senor Perkins there were two strangers in the boat. Everybody rushed to the side for a nearer view of those strange inhabitants of the unknown shore; but the boat's crew suddenly ceased rowing, and lay on their oars until an indistinct hail and reply passed between the boat and ship. There was a bustle forward, an unexpected thunder from the Excelsior's eight-pounder at the bow port; Captain Bunker and the second mate ranged themselves at the companion-way, and the passengers for the first time became aware that they were participating at the reception of visitors of distinction, as two strange and bizarre figures stepped upon the deck.

CHAPTER V

TODOS SANTOS

It was evident that the two strangers represented some exalted military and ecclesiastical authority. This was shown in their dress—a long-forgotten, half mediaeval costume, that to the imaginative spectator was perfectly in keeping with their mysterious advent, and to the more practical as startling as a masquerade. The foremost figure wore a broad-brimmed hat of soft felt, with tarnished gold lace, and a dark feather tucked in its recurved flap; a short cloak of fine black cloth thrown over one shoulder left a buff leathern jacket and breeches, ornamented with large round silver buttons, exposed until they were met by high boots of untanned yellow buckskin that reached halfway up the thigh. A broad baldric of green silk hung from his shoulder across his breast, and supported at his side a long sword with an enormous basket hilt, through which somewhat coquettishly peeped a white lace handkerchief. Tall and erect, in spite of the grizzled hair and iron-gray moustaches and wrinkled face of a man of sixty, he suddenly halted on the deck with a military precision that made the jingling chains and bits of silver on his enormous spurs ring again. He was followed by an ecclesiastic of apparently his own age, but smoothly shaven, clad in a black silk sotana and sash, and wearing the old-fashioned oblong, curl-brimmed hat sacred to "Don

Basilo," of the modern opera. Behind him appeared the genial face of Senor Perkins, shining with the benignant courtesy of a master of ceremonies.

"If this is a fair sample of the circus ashore, I'll take two tickets," whispered Crosby, who had recovered his audacity.

"I have the inexpressible honor," said Senor Perkins to Captain Bunker, with a gracious wave of his hand towards the extraordinary figures, "to present you to the illustrious Don Miguel Briones, Comandante of the Presidio of Todos Santos, at present hidden in the fog, and the very reverend and pious Padre Esteban, of the Mission of Todos Santos, likewise invisible. When I state to you," he continued, with a slight lifting of his voice, so as to include the curious passengers in his explanation, "that, with very few exceptions, this is the usual condition of the atmosphere at the entrance to the Mission and Presidio of Todos Santos, and that the last exception took place thirty-five years ago, when a ship entered the harbor, you will understand why these distinguished gentlemen have been willing to waive the formality of your waiting upon them first, and have taken the initiative. The illustrious Comandante has been generous to exempt you from the usual port regulations, and to permit you to wood and to water"—

"What port regulation is he talking of?" asked Captain Bunker testily.

"The Mexican regulations forbidding any foreign vessel to communicate with the shore," returned Senor Perkins deprecatingly.

"Never heard of 'em. When were they given?"

The Senor turned and addressed a few words to the

commander, who stood apart in silent dignity.

"In 1792."

"In what?—Is he mad?" said Bunker. "Does he know what year this is?"

"The illustrious commander believes it to be the year of grace 1854," answered Senor Perkins quietly. "In the case of the only two vessels who have touched here since 1792 the order was not carried out because they were Mexican coasters. The illustrious Comandante explains that the order he speaks of as on record distinctly referred to the ship 'Columbia, which belonged to the General Washington.'"

"General Washington!" echoed Bunker, angrily staring at the Senor. "What's this stuff? Do you mean to say they don't know any history later than our old Revolutionary War? Haven't they heard of the United States among them? Nor California—that we took from them during the late war?"

"Nor how we licked 'em out of their boots, and that's saying a good deal," whispered Crosby, glancing at the Comandante's feet.

Senor Perkins raised a gentle, deprecating hand.

"For fifty years the Presidio and the Mission of Todos Santos have had but this communication with the outer world," he said blandly. "Hidden by impenetrable fogs from the ocean pathway at their door, cut off by burning and sterile deserts from the surrounding country, they have preserved a trust and propagated a faith in enforced but not unhappy seclusion. The wars that have shaken mankind, the dissensions that have even disturbed the serenity of their own nation on the mainland, have never reached them here. Left to themselves, they have created a blameless Arcadia and an ideal community within an extent of twenty square leagues. Why should we disturb their innocent compla-cency and tranquil enjoyment by information which cannot increase and might impair their present felicity? Why should we dwell upon a late political and international episode which, while it has been a benefit to us, has been a humiliation to them as a nation, and which might not only imperil our position as guests, but interrupt our practical relations to the wood and water, with which the country abounds?"

He paused, and before the captain could speak, turned to the silent Commander, addressed him in a dozen phrases of fluent and courteous Spanish, and once more turned to Captain Bunker.

"I have told him you are touched to the heart with his courtesy, which you recognize as coming from the fit representative of the great Mexican nation. He reciprocates your fraternal emotion, and begs you to consider the Presidio and all that it contains, at your disposition and the disposition of your friends—the passengers, particularly those fair ladies," said Senor Perkins, turning with graceful prompti-tude towards the group of lady passengers, and slightly elevating himself on the tips of his neat boots, "whose white hands he kisses, and at whose feet he lays the devotion of a Mexican caballero and officer."

He waved his hand towards the Comandante, who, stepping forward, swept the deck with his plumed hat before each of the ladies in solemn succession. Recovering himself, he bowed more stiffly to the male passengers, picked his handkerchief out of the hilt of his sword, gracefully wiped his lips, pulled the end of his long gray moustache, and became again rigid.

"The reverend father," continued Senor Perkins, turning towards the priest, "regrets that the rules of his order prevent his extending the same courtesy to these ladies at the Mission. But he hopes to meet them at the Presidio, and they will avail themselves of his aid and counsel there and everywhere."

Father Esteban, following the speaker's words with a gracious and ready smile, at once moved forward among the passengers, offering an antique snuff-box to the gentlemen, or passing before the ladies with slightly uplifted benedictory palms and a caressing paternal gesture. Mrs. Brimmer, having essayed a French sentence, was delighted and half frightened to receive a response from the ecclesiastic, and speedily monopolized him until he was summoned by the Commander to the returning boat.

"A most accomplished man, my dear," said Mrs. Brimmer, as the Excelsior's cannon again thundered after the retiring oars, "like all of his order. He says, although Don Miguel does not speak French, that his secretary does; and we shall have no difficulty in making ourselves understood."

"Then you really intend to go ashore?" said Miss Keene timidly.

"Decidedly," returned Mrs. Brimmer potentially. "It would be most unpolite, not to say insulting, if we did not accept the invitation. You have no idea of the strictness of Spanish etiquette. Besides, he may have heard of Mr. Brimmer."

"As his last information was only up to 1792, he might have forgotten it," said Crosby gravely. "So perhaps it would be safer to go on the general invitation."

"As Mr. Brimmer's ancestors came over on the Mayflower,

long before 1792, it doesn't seem so very impossible, if it comes to that," said Mrs. Brimmer, with her usual unanswerable naivete; "provided always that you are not joking, Mr. Crosby. One never knows when you are serious."

"Mrs. Brimmer is quite right; we must all go. This is no mere formality," said Senor Perkins, who had returned to the ladies. "Indeed, I have myself promised the Comandante to bring YOU," he turned towards Miss Keene, "if you will permit Mrs. Markham and myself to act as your escort. It was Don Miguel's express request."

A slight flush of pride suffused the cheek of the young girl, but the next moment she turned diffidently towards Mrs. Brimmer.

"We must all go together," she said; "shall we not?"

"You see your triumphs have begun already," said Brace, with a nervous smile. "You need no longer laugh at me for predicting your fate in San Francisco."

Miss Keene cast a hurried glance around her, in the faint hope—she scarcely knew why—that Mr. Hurlstone had overheard the Senor's invitation; nor could she tell why she was disappointed at not seeing him. But he had not appeared on deck during the presence of their strange visitors; nor was he in the boat which half an hour later conveyed her to the shore. He must have either gone in one of the other boats, or fulfilled his strange threat of remaining on the ship.

The boats pulled away together towards the invisible shore, piloted by Captain Bunker, the first officer, and Senor Perkins in the foremost boat. It had grown warmer, and the fog that stole softly over them touched their faces with the tenderness of caressing fingers. Miss Keene, wrapped up in the stern sheets of the boat, gave way to the dreamy influence of this weird procession through the water, retaining only perception enough to be conscious of the singular illusions of the mist that alternately thickened and lightened before their bow. At times it seemed as if they were driving full upon a vast pier or breakwater of cold gray granite, that, opening to let the foremost boat pass, closed again before them; at times it seemed as if they had diverged from their course, and were once more upon the open sea, the horizon a far-off line of vanishing color; at times, faint lights seemed to pierce the gathering darkness, or to move like will-o'-wisps across the smooth surface, when suddenly the keel grated on the sand. A narrow but perfectly well defined strip of palpable strand appeared before them; they could faintly discern the moving lower limbs of figures whose bodies were still hidden in the mist; then they were lifted from the boats; the first few steps on dry land carried them out of the fog that seemed to rise like a sloping roof from the water's edge, leaving them under its canopy in the full light of actual torches held by a group of picturesquely dressed people before the vista of a faintly lit, narrow, ascending street. The dim twilight of the closing day lingered under this roof of fog, which seemed to hang scarcely a hundred feet above them, and showed a wall or rampart of brown adobe on their right that extended nearly to the water; to the left, at the distance of a few hundred yards, another low brown wall appeared; above it rose a fringe of foliage, and, more distant and indistinct, two white towers, that were lost in the nebulous gray.

One of the figures dressed in green jackets, who seemed to be in authority, now advanced, and, after a moment's parley with Senor Perkins while the Excelsior's passengers were being collected from the different boats, courteously led the way along the wall of the fortification. Presently a low opening or gateway appeared, followed by the challenge of a green-jacketed sentry, and the sentence, "Dios y Libertad" It was repeated in the interior of a dusky courtyard, surrounded by a low corridor, where a dozen green-jacketed men of aboriginal type and complexion, carrying antique flintlocks, were drawn up as a guard of honor.

"The Comandante," said Senor Perkins, "directs me to extend his apologies to the Senor Capitano Bunker for withholding the salute which is due alike to his country, himself, and his fair company; but fifty years of uninterrupted peace and fog have left his cannon inadequate to polite emergencies, and firmly fixed the tampion of his saluting gun. But he places the Presidio at your disposition; you will be pleased to make its acquaintance while it is still light; and he will await you in the guard-room."

Left to themselves, the party dispersed like dismissed school-children through the courtyard and corridors, and in the enjoyment of their release from a month's confinement on shipboard stretched their cramped limbs over the ditches, walls, and parapets, to the edge of the glacis.

Everywhere a ruin that was picturesque, a decay that was refined and gentle, a neglect that was graceful, met the eye; the sharp exterior and reentering angles were softly rounded and obliterated by overgrowths of semitropical creepers; the abatis was filled by a natural brake of scrub-oak and manzanita; the clematis flung its long scaling ladders over the escarpment, until Nature, slowly but securely investing the doomed fortress, had lifted a victorious banner of palm from the conquered summit of the citadel! Some strange convulsions of the earth had completed the victory; the barbette guns of carved and antique bronze commemorating fruitless and long-forgotten triumphs were dismounted; one turned in the cheeks of its carriage had a trunnion raised piteously in the air like an amputated stump; another, sinking through its rotting chassis, had buried itself to its chase in the crumbling adobe wall. But above and beyond this gentle chaos of defense stretched the real ramparts and escarpments of Todos Santos—the impenetrable and unassailable fog! Corroding its brass and iron with saline breath, rotting its wood with unending shadow, sapping its adobe walls with perpetual moisture, and nourishing the obliterating vegetation with its quickening blood, as if laughing to scorn the puny embattlements of men—it still bent around the crumbling ruins the tender grace of an invisible but all-encompassing arm.

Senor Perkins, who had acted as cicerone to the party, pointed out these various mutations with no change from his usual optimism.

"Protected by their peculiar isolation during the late war, there was no necessity for any real fortification of the place. Nevertheless, it affords some occupation and position for our kind friend, Don Miguel, and so serves a beneficial purpose. This little gun," he continued, stopping to attentively examine a small but beautifully carved bronze six-pounder, which showed indications of better care than the others, "seems to be the saluting-gun Don Miguel spoke of. For the last fifty years it has spoken only the language of politeness and courtesy, and yet through want of care the tampion, as you see, has become swollen and choked in its mouth."

"How true in a larger sense," murmured Mrs. Markham, "the habit of courtesy alone preserves the fluency of the heart."

"I know you two are saying something very clever," said Mrs. Brimmer, whose small French slippers and silk stockings were beginning to show their inadequacy to a twilight ramble in the fog; "but I am so slow, and I never catch the point. Do repeat it slowly."

"The Senor was only showing us how they managed to shut up a smooth bore in this country," said Crosby gravely. "I wonder when we're going to have dinner. I suppose old Don Quixote will trot out some of his Senoritas. I want to see those choir girls that sang so stunningly a while ago."

"I suppose you mean the boys—for they're all boys in the Catholic choirs—but then, perhaps you are joking again. Do tell me if you are, for this is really amusing. I may laugh—mayn't I?" As the discomfited humorist fell again to the rear amidst the laughter of the others, Mrs. Brimmer continued naively to Senor Perkins,—"Of course, as Don Miguel is a widower, there must be daughters or sisters-in-law who will meet us. Why, the priest, you know—even he—must have nieces. Really, it's a serious question—if we are to accept his hospitality in a social way. Why don't you ask HIM?" she said, pointing to the green-jacketed subaltern who was accompanying them.

Senor Perkins looked half embarrassed.

"Repeat your question, my dear lady, and I will translate it."

"Ask him if there are any women at the Presidio."

Senor Perkins drew the subaltern aside. Presently he turned to Mrs. Brimmer.

"He says there are four: the wife of the baker, the wife of the saddler, the daughter of the trumpeter, and the niece of the cook."

"Good heavens! we can't meet THEM," said Mrs. Brimmer.

Senor Perkins hesitated.

"Perhaps I ought to have told you," he said blandly, "that the old Spanish notions of etiquette are very strict. The wives of the officials and higher classes do not meet strangers on a first visit, unless they are well known."

"That isn't it," said Winslow, joining them excitedly. "I've heard the whole story. It's a good joke. Banks has been bragging about us all, and saying that these ladies had husbands who were great merchants, and, as these chaps consider that all trade is vulgar, you know, they believe we are not fit to associate with their women, don't you see? All, except one—Miss Keene. She's considered all right. She's to be introduced to the Commander's women, and to the sister of the Alcalde."

"She will do nothing of the kind," said Miss Keene indignantly. "If these ladies are not to be received with me, we'll all go back to the ship together."

She spoke with a quick and perfectly unexpected resolution and independence, so foreign to her usual childlike half dependent character, that her hearers were astounded. Senor Perkins gazed at her thoughtfully; Brace, Crosby, and Winslow admiringly; her sister passengers with doubt and apprehension.

"There must be some mistake," said Senor Perkins gently. "I will inquire."

He was absent but a few moments. When he returned, his face was beaming.

"It's a ridiculous misapprehension. Our practical friend Banks, in his zealous attempts to impress the Comandante's secretary, who knows a little English, with the importance of Mr. Brimmer's position as a large commission merchant, has, I fear, conveyed only the idea that he was a kind of pawnbroker; while Mr. Markham's trade in hides has established him as a tanner; and Mr. Banks' own flour speculations, of which he is justly proud, have been misinterpreted by him as the work of a successful baker!"

"And what idea did he convey about YOU?" asked Crosby audaciously; "it might be interesting to us to know, for our own satisfaction."

"I fear they did not do me the honor to inquire," replied Senor Perkins, with imperturbable good-humor; "there are some persons, you know, who carry all their worldly possessions palpably about with them. I am one of them. Call me a citizen of the world, with a strong leniency towards young and struggling nationalities; a traveler, at home anywhere; a delighted observer of all things, an admirer of brave men, the devoted slave of charming women—and you have, in one word, a passenger of the good ship Excelsior."

For the first time, Miss Keene noticed a slight irony in Senor Perkins' superabundant fluency, and that he did not conceal his preoccupation over the silent saluting gun he was still admiring. The approach of Don Miguel and Padre Esteban with a small bevy of ladies, however, quickly changed her thoughts, and detached the Senor from her side. Her first swift feminine impression of the fair strangers was that they were plain and dowdy, an impression fully shared by the other lady passengers. But her second observation, that they were more gentle, fascinating, child-like, and feminine than her own country-women, was purely her own. Their loose, undulating figures, guiltless of stays; their extravagance of short, white, heavily flounced skirt, which looked like a petticoat; their lightly wrapped, formless, and hooded shoulders and heads, lent a suggestion of dishabille that Mrs. Brimmer at once resented.

"They might, at least, have dressed themselves," she whispered to Mrs. Markham.

"I really believe," returned Mrs. Markham, "they've got no bodices on!"

The introductions over, a polyglot conversation ensued in French by the Padre and Mrs. Brimmer, and in broken English by Miss Chubb, Miss Keene, and the other passengers with the Commander's secretary, varied by occasional scraps of college Latin from Mr. Crosby, the whole aided by occasional appeals to Senor Perkins. The darkness increasing, the party reentered the courtyard, and, passing through the low-studded guard-room, entered another corridor, which looked upon a second court, enclosed on three sides, the fourth opening upon a broad plaza, evidently the public resort of the little town. Encompassing this open space, a few red-tiled roofs could be faintly seen in the gathering gloom. Chocolate and thin spiced cakes were served in the veranda, pending the preparations for a more formal banquet. Already Miss Keene had been singled out from her companions for the special attentions of her hosts, male and female, to her embarrassment and confusion. Already Dona Isabel, the sister of the Alcalde, had drawn her aside, and, with caressing frankness, had begun to question her in broken English,—

"But Miss Keene is no name. The Dona Keene is of nothing."

"Well, you may call me Eleanor, if you like," said Miss Keene, smiling.

"Dona Leonor—so; that is good," said Dona Isabel, clapping her hands like a child. "But how are you?"

"I beg your pardon," said Miss Keene, greatly amused, "but I don't understand."

"Ah, Caramba! What are you, little one?" Seeing that her guest still looked puzzled, she continued,—"Ah! Mother of God! Why are your friends so polite to you? Why does every one love you so?"

"Do they? Well," stammered Miss Keene, with one of her rare, dazzling smiles, and her cheeks girlishly rosy with naive embarrassment, "I suppose they think I am pretty."

"Pretty! Ah, yes, you are!" said Dona Isabel, gazing at her curiously. "But it is not all that."

"What is it, then?" asked Miss Keene demurely.

"You are a—a—Dama de Grandeza!"

CHAPTER VI

"HAIL AND FAREWELL"

Supper was served in the inner room opening from the corridor lit by a few swinging lanterns of polished horn and a dozen wax candles of sacerdotal size and suggestion. The apartment, though spacious, was low and crypt-like, and was not relieved by the two deep oven-like hearths that warmed it without the play of firelight. But when the company had assembled it was evident that the velvet jackets, gold lace, silver buttons, and red sashes of the entertainers not only lost their tawdry and theatrical appearance in the half decorous and thoughtful gloom, but actually seemed more in harmony with it than the modern dresses of the guests. It was the Excelsior party who looked strange and bizarre in these surroundings; to the sensitive fancy of Miss Keene, Mrs. Brimmer's Parisian toilet had an air of provincial assumption; her own pretty Zouave jacket and black silk skirt horrified her with its apparent ostentatious eccentricity; and Mrs. Markham and Miss Chubb seemed dowdy and overdressed beside the satin mantillas and black lace of the Senoritas. Nor were the gentlemen less outres: the stiff correctness of Mr. Banks, and the lighter foppishness of Winslow and Crosby, not to mention Senor Perkins' more pronounced unconven-tionality, appeared as burlesques of their own characters in a play. The crowning contrast was reached by Captain Bunker, who, in accordance with the habits of the mercantile marine of that period when in port, wore a shore-going suit of black broadcloth, with a tall hat, high shirt collar, and diamond pin. Seated next to the Commander, it was no longer Don Miguel who looked old-fashioned, it was Captain Bunker who appeared impossible.

Nevertheless, as the meal progressed, lightened by a sweet native wine made from the Mission grape, and stimulated by champagne—a present of Captain Bunker from the cabin lockers of the Excelsior—this contrast, and much of the restraint that it occasioned, seemed to melt away. The passengers became talkative; the Commander and his friends unbent, and grew sympathetic and inquiring. The temptation to recite the news of the last half century, and to recount the wonderful strides of civilization in that time, was too great to be resisted by the Excelsior party. That some of them—notwithstanding the caution of Senor Perkins—approached dangerously near the subject of the late war between the United States and Mexico, of which Todos Santos was supposed to be still ignorant, or that Crosby in particular seized upon this opportunity for humorous exaggeration, may be readily imagined. But as the translation of the humorist's speech, as well as the indiscretions of his companions, were left to the Senor, in Spanish, and to Mrs. Brimmer and Miss Keene, in French, any imminent danger to the harmony of the evening was averted. Don Ramon Ramirez, the Alcalde, a youngish man of evident distinction, sat next to Miss Keene, and monopolized her conversation with a certain curiosity that was both grave and childish in its frank trustfulness. Some of his questions were so simple and incompatible with his apparent intelligence that she uncons-ciously lowered her voice in answering them, in dread of the ridicule of her companions. She could not resist the impression, which repeatedly obtruded upon her imagi-nation, that the entire population of Todos Santos were a party of lost children, forgotten by their parents, and grown to man and womanhood in utter ignorance of the world.

The Commander had, half informally, drunk the health of Captain Bunker, without rising from his seat, when, to Miss Keene's alarm, Captain Bunker staggered to his feet. He had been drinking freely, as usual; but he was bent on indulging a loquacity which his discipline on shipboard had hitherto precluded, and which had, perhaps, strengthened his solitary habit. His speech was voluble and incoherent, complimentary and tactless, kindly and aggressive, courteous and dogmatic. It was left to Senor Perkins to translate it to the eye and ear of his host without incongruity or offense. This he did so admirably as to elicit not only the applause of the foreigners who did not understand English, but of his own countrymen who did not understand Spanish.

"I feel," said Senor Perkins, in graceful peroration, "that I have done poor justice to the eloquence of this gallant sailor. My unhappy translation cannot offer you that voice, at times trembling with generous emotion, and again inaudible from excessive modesty in the presence of this illustrious assembly—those limbs that waver and bend under the undulations of the chivalrous sentiment which carries him away as if he were still on that powerful element he daily battles with and conquers."

But when coffee and sweets were reached, the crowning triumph of Senor Perkins' oratory was achieved. After an impassioned burst of enthusiasm towards his hosts in their own tongue, he turned towards his own party with bland felicity.

"And how is it with us, dear friends? We find ourselves not in the port we were seeking; not in the goal of our ambition, the haven of our hopes; but on the shores of the decaying past. 'Ever drifting' on one of those—

'Shifting
Currents of the restless main,'

if our fascinating friend Mrs. Brimmer will permit us to use the words of her accomplished fellow-townsman, H. W. Longfellow, of Boston—we find ourselves borne not to the busy hum and clatter of modern progress, but to the soft cadences of a dying crusade, and the hush of ecclesiastical repose. In place of the busy marts of commerce and the towering chimneys of labor, we have the ruined embattlements of a warlike age, and the crumbling church of an ancient Mission. Towards the close of an eventful voyage, during which we have been guided by the skillful hand and watchful eye of that gallant navigator Captain Bunker, we have turned aside from our onward course of progress to look back for a moment upon the faded footprints of those who have so long preceded us, who have lived according to their lights, and whose record is now before us. As I have just stated, our journey is near its end, and we may, in some sense, look upon this occasion, with its sumptuous entertainment, and its goodly company of gallant men and fair women, as a parting banquet. Our voyage has been a successful one. I do not now especially speak of the daring speculations of the distinguished husband of a beautiful lady whose delightful society is known to us all—need I say I refer to Quincy Brimmer, Esq., of Boston" (loud applause)— "whose successful fulfillment of a contract with the Peruvian Government, and the landing of munitions of war at Callao, has checked the uprising of the Quinquinambo insurgents? I do not refer especially to our keen-sighted business friend Mr. Banks" (applause), "who, by buying up all the flour in Callao, and shipping it to California, has virtually starved into submission the revolutionary party of Ariquipa—I do not refer to these admirable illustrations of the relations of commerce and politics, for this, my friends—this is history, and beyond my feeble praise. Let me rather speak of the social and literary triumphs of our little community, of our floating Arcadia—may I say Olympus? Where shall we find another Minerva like Mrs. Markham, another Thalia like Miss Chubb, another Juno like Mrs. Brimmer, worthy of the Jove-like Quincy Brimmer; another Queen of Love and Beauty like—like"—continued the gallant Senor, with an effective oratorical pause, and a profound obeisance to Miss Keene, "like one whose mantling maiden blushes forbid me to name?" (Prolonged applause.) "Where shall we find more worthy mortals to worship them than our young friends, the handsome Brace, the energetic Winslow, the humorous Crosby? When we look back upon our concerts and plays, our minstrel entertainments, with the incomparable performances of our friend Crosby as Brother Bones; our recitations, to which the genius of Mrs. M'Corkle, of Peoria, Illinois, has lent her charm and her manuscript" (a burlesque start of terror from Crosby), "I am forcibly impelled to quote the impassioned words from that gifted woman,—

'When idly Life's barque on the billows of Time,
Drifts hither and yon by eternity's sea;
On the swift feet of verse and the pinions of rhyme
My thoughts, Ulricardo, fly ever to thee!'"

"Who's Ulricardo?" interrupted Crosby, with assumed eagerness, followed by a "hush!" from the ladies.

"Perhaps I should have anticipated our friend's humorous question," said Senor Perkins, with unassailable good-humor. "Ulricardo, though not my own name, is a poetical substitute for it, and a mere figure of apostrophe. The poem is personal to myself," he continued, with a slight increase of color in his smooth cheek which did not escape the attention of the ladies,—"purely as an exigency of verse, and that the inspired authoress might more easily express herself to a friend. My acquaintance with Mrs. M'Corkle has been only epistolary. Pardon this digression, my friends, but an allusion to the muse of poetry did not seem to me to be inconsistent with our gathering here. Let me briefly conclude by saying that the occasion is a happy and memorable one; I think I echo the sentiment of all present when I add that it is one which will not be easily forgotten by either the grateful guests, whose feelings I have tried to express, or the chivalrous hosts, whose kindness I have already so feebly translated."

In the applause that followed, and the clicking of glasses, Senor Perkins slipped away. He mingled a moment with some of the other guests who had already withdrawn to the corridor, lit a cigar, and then passed through a narrow doorway on to the ramparts. Here he strolled to some distance, as if in deep thought, until he reached a spot where the crumbling wall and its fallen debris afforded an easy descent into the ditch. Following the ditch, he turned an angle, and came upon the beach, and the low sound of oars in the invisible offing. A whistle brought the boat to his feet, and without a word he stepped into the stern sheets. A few strokes of the oars showed him that the fog had lifted slightly from the water, and a green light hanging from the side of the Excelsior could be plainly seen. Ten minutes' more steady pulling placed him on her deck, where the second officer stood with a number of the sailors listlessly grouped around him.

"The landing has been completed?" said Senor Perkins interrogatively.

"All except one boat-load more, which waits to take your final instructions," said the mate. "The men have growled a little about it," he added, in a lower tone. "They don't want to lose anything, it seems," he continued, with a half sarcastic laugh.

Senor Perkins smiled peculiarly.

"I am sorry to disappoint them. Who's that in the boat?" he asked suddenly.

The mate followed the Senor's glance.

"It is Yoto. He says he is going ashore, and you will not forbid him."

Senor Perkins approached the ship's side.

"Come here," he said to the man.

The Peruvian sailor rose, but did not make the slightest movement to obey the command.

"You say you are going ashore?" said Perkins blandly.

"Yes, Patrono."

"What for?"

"To follow him—the thief, the assassin—who struck me here;" he pointed to his head. "He has escaped again with his booty."

"You are very foolish, my Yoto; he is no thief, and has no booty. They will put YOU in prison, not him."

"YOU say so," said the man surlily. "Perhaps they will hear me—for other things," he added significantly.

"And for this you would abandon the cause?"

The man shrugged his shoulders.

"Why not?" he glanced meaningly at two of his companions, who had approached the side; "perhaps others would. Who is sending the booty ashore, eh?"

"Come out of that boat," said the Senor, leaning over the bulwarks with folded arms, and his eyes firmly fixed on the man.

The man did not move. But the Senor's hand suddenly flew to the back of his neck, smote violently downwards, and sent eighteen inches of glittering steel hurtling through the air. The bowie-knife entered the upturned throat of the man and buried itself halfway to the hilt. Without a gasp or groan he staggered forward, caught wildly at the side of the ship, and disappeared between the boat and the vessel.

"My lads," said Senor Perkins, turning with a gentle smile towards the faces that in the light of the swinging lantern formed a ghastly circle around him, "when I boarded this ship that had brought aid and succor to our oppressors at Callao, I determined to take possession of it peacefully, without imperiling the peace and property of the innocent passengers who were intrusted to its care, and without endangering your own lives or freedom. But I made no allowance for TRAITORS. The blood that has been shed to-night has not been spilt in obedience to my orders, nor to the cause that we serve; it was from DEFIANCE of it; and the real and only culprit has just atoned for it."

He stopped, and then stepped back from the gangway, as if to leave it open to the men.

"What I have done," he continued calmly, "I do not ask you to consider either as an example or a warning. You are free to do what HE would have done," he repeated, with a wave of his hand towards the open gangway and the empty boat. "You are free to break your contract and leave the ship, and I give you my word that I will not lift a hand to prevent it. But if you stay with me," he said, suddenly turning upon them a face as livid as their own, "I swear by the living God, that, if between this and the accomplishment of my design, you as much as shirk or question any order given by me, you shall die the death of that dog who went before you. Choose as you please—but quickly."

The mate was the first to move. Without a word, he crossed over to the Senor's side. The men hesitated a moment longer, until one, with a strange foreign cry, threw himself on his knees before the Senor, ejaculating, "Pardon! pardon!" The others followed, some impulsively catching at the hand that had just slain their comrade, and covering it with kisses!

"Pardon, Patrono—we are yours."

"You are the State's," said Senor Perkins coldly, with every vestige of his former urbanity gone from his colorless face. "Enough! Go back to your duty." He watched them slink away, and then turned to the mate. "Get the last boat-load ready, and report to me."

From that moment another power seemed to dominate the ship. The men no longer moved listlessly, or slunk along the deck with perfunctory limbs; a feverish haste and eagerness possessed them; the boat was quickly loaded, and the mysterious debarkation completed in rapidity and silence. This done, the fog once more appeared to rise from the water and softly encompass the ship, until she seemed to be obliterated from its face. In this vague obscurity, from time to time, the faint rattling of chains was heard, the soft creaking of blocks, and later on, the regular rise and fall of oars. And then the darkness fell heavier, the sounds became more and more indistinct and were utterly lost.

Ashore, however, the lanterns still glittered brightly in the courtyard of the Presidio; the noise of laughter and revel still came from the supper-room, and, later, the tinkling of guitars and rhythmical clapping hands showed that the festivities were being wound up by a characteristic fandango. Captain Bunker succumbed early to his potations of fiery aguardiente, and was put to bed in the room of the Commander, to whom he had sworn eternal friendship and alliance. It was long past midnight before the other guests were disposed of in the various quarters of the Presidio; but to the ladies were reserved the more ostentatious hospitalities of the Alcalde himself, the walls of whose ambitious hacienda raised themselves across the plaza and overlooked the gardens of the Mission.

It was from one of the deep, quaintly barred windows of the hacienda that Miss Keene gazed thoughtfully on the night, unable to compose herself to sleep. An antique guest-chamber had been assigned to her in deference to her wish to be alone, for which she had declined the couch and vivacious prattle of her new friend, Dona Isabel. The events of the day had impressed her more deeply than they had her companions, partly from her peculiar inexperience of the world, and partly from her singular sensitiveness to external causes. The whole quaint story of the forgotten and isolated settlement, which had seemed to the other passengers as a trivial and half humorous incident, affected her imagination profoundly. When she could escape the attentions of her entertainers, or the frivolities of her companions, she tried to touch the far-off past on the wings of her fancy; she tried to imagine the life of those people, forgetting the world and forgotten by it; she endeavored to picture the fifty years of solitude amidst these decaying ruins, over which even ambition had crumbled and fallen. It seemed to her the true conventual seclusion from the world without the loss of kinship or home influences; she contrasted it with her boarding-school life in the fashionable seminary; she wondered what she would have become had she been brought up here; she thought of the happy ignorance of Dona Isabel, and—shuddered; and yet she felt herself examining the odd furniture of the room with an equally childlike and admiring curiosity. And these people looked upon HER as a superior being!

From the deep embrasure of the window she could see the tops of the pear and olive trees, in the misty light of an invisible moon that suffused the old Mission garden with an ineffable and angelic radiance. To her religious fancy it seemed to be a spiritual effusion of the church itself, enveloping the two gray dome-shaped towers with an atmosphere and repose of its own, until it became the incarnate mystery and passion where it stood.

She was suddenly startled by a moving shadow beside the wall, almost immediately below her—the figure of a man! He was stealing cautiously towards the church, as if to gain the concealment of the shrubbery that grew beside it, and, furtively glancing from side to side, looked towards her window. She unconsciously drew back, forgetting at the moment that her light was extinguished, and that it was impossible for the stranger to see her. But she had seen HIM, and in that instant recognized Mr. Hurlstone!

Then he HAD come ashore, and secretly, for the other passengers believed him still on the ship! But what was he doing there?—and why had he not appeared with the others at the entertainment? She could understand his avoidance of them from what she knew of his reserved and unsocial habits; but when he could so naturally have remained on shipboard, she could not, at first, conceive why he should wish to prowl around the town at the risk of detection. The idea suddenly occurred to her that he had had another attack of his infirmity and was walking in his sleep, and for an instant she thought of alarming the house, that some one might go to his assistance. But his furtive movements had not the serene impassibility of the somnambulist. Another thought withheld her; he had looked up at her window! Did he know she was there? A faint stirring of shame and pleasure sent a slight color to her cheek. But he had gained the corner of the shrubbery and was lost in the shadow. She turned from the window. A gentle sense of vague and half maternal pity suffused her soft eyes as she at last sought her couch and fell into a deep slumber.

Towards daybreak a wind arose over the sleeping town and far outlying waters. It breathed through the leaves of the Mission garden, brushed away the clinging mists from the angles of the towers, and restored the sharp outlines of the ruined fortifications. It swept across the unruffled sea to where the Excelsior, cradled in the softly heaving bay, had peacefully swung at anchor on the previous night, and lifted the snowy curtain of the fog to seaward as far as the fringe of surf, a league away.

But the cradle of the deep was empty—the ship was gone!

Bret Harte

CHAPTER VII

THE GENTLE CASTAWAYS

Miss Keene was awakened from a heavy sleep by a hurried shake of her shoulder and an indefinite feeling of alarm. Opening her eyes, she was momentarily dazed by the broad light of day, and the spectacle of Mrs. Brimmer, pale and agitated, in a half-Spanish dishabille, standing at her bedside.

"Get up and dress yourself, my dear, at once," she said hurriedly, but at the same time attentively examining Miss Keene's clothes, that were lying on the chair: "and thank Heaven you came here in an afternoon dress, and not in an evening costume like mine! For something awful has happened, and Heaven only knows whether we'll ever see a stitch of our clothes again."

"WHAT has happened?" asked Miss Keene impatiently, sitting up in bed, more alarmed at the unusual circumstance of Mrs. Brimmer's unfinished toilet than at her incomplete speech.

"What, indeed! Nobody knows; but it's something awful—a mutiny, or shipwreck, or piracy. But there's your friend, the Commander, calling out the troops; and such a set of Christy Minstrels you never saw before! There's the Alcalde summoning the Council; there's Mr. Banks raving, and running round for a steamboat—as if these people ever heard of such a thing!—and Captain Bunker, what with rage and drink, gone off in a fit of delirium tremens, and locked up in his room! And the Excelsior gone—the Lord knows where!"

"Gone!" repeated Miss Keene, hurrying on her clothes. "Impossible! What does Father Esteban tell you? What does Dona Isabel say?"

"That's the most horrible part of it! Do you know those wretched idiots believe it's some political revolution among ourselves, like their own miserable government. I believe that baby Isabel thinks that King George and Washington have something to do with it; at any rate, they're anxious to know to what side you belong! So; for goodness' sake! if you have to humor them, say we're all on the same side—I mean, don't you and Mrs. Markham go against Miss Chubb and me."

Scarcely knowing whether to laugh or cry at Mrs. Brimmer's incoherent statement, Miss Keene hastily finished dressing as the door flew open to admit the impulsive Dona Isabel and her sister Juanita. The two Mexican girls threw themselves in Miss Keene's arms, and then suddenly drew back with a movement of bashful and diffident respect.

"Do, pray, ask them, for I daren't," whispered Mrs. Brimmer, trying to clasp a mantilla around her, "how this thing is worn, and if they haven't got something like a decent bonnet to lend me for a day or two?"

"The Senora has not then heard that her goods, and all the goods of the Senores and Senoras, have been discovered safely put ashore at the Embarcadero?"

Bret Harte

"No?" said Mrs. Brimmer eagerly.

"Ah, yes!" responded Dona Isabel. "Since the Senora is not of the revolutionary party."

Mrs. Brimmer cast a supplicatory look at Miss Keene, and hastily quitted the room. Miss Keene would have as quickly followed her, but the young Ramirez girls threw themselves again tragically upon her breast, and, with a mysterious gesture of silence, whispered,—

"Fear nothing, Excellencia! We are yours—we will die for you, no matter what Don Ramon, or the Comandante, or the Ayuntamiento, shall decide. Trust us, little one!—pardon— Excellencia, we mean."

"What IS the matter?" said Miss Keene, now thoroughly alarmed, and releasing herself from the twining arms about her. "For Heaven's sake let me go! I must see somebody! Where is—where is Mrs. Markham?"

"The Markham? Is it the severe one?—as thus,"—said Dona Isabel, striking an attitude of infantine portentousness.

"Yes," said Miss Keene, smiling in spite of her alarm.

"She is arrested."

"Arrested!" said Eleanor Keene, her cheeks aflame with indignation. "For what? Who dare do this thing?"

"The Comandante. She has a missive—a despatch from the insurrectionaries."

Without another word, and feeling that she could stand the suspense no longer, Miss Keene forced her way past the young girls, unheeding their cries of consternation and apology, and quickly reached the patio. A single glance showed her that Mrs. Brimmer was gone. With eyes and cheeks still burning, she swept past the astounded peons, through the gateway, into the open plaza. Only one idea filled her mind—to see the Commander, and demand the release of her friend. How she should do it, with what arguments she should enforce her demand, never occurred to her. She did not even think of asking the assistance of Mr. Brace, Mr. Crosby, or any of her fellow-passengers. The consciousness of some vague crisis that she alone could meet possessed her completely.

The plaza was swarming with a strange rabble of peons and soldiery; of dark, lowering faces, odd-looking weapons and costumes, mules, mustangs, and cattle—a heterogeneous mass, swayed by some fierce excitement. That she saw none of the Excelsior party among them did not surprise her; an instinct of some catastrophe more serious than Mrs. Brimmer's vague imaginings frightened but exalted her. With head erect, leveled brows, and bright, determined eyes she walked deliberately into the square. The crowd parted and gave way before this beautiful girl, with her bared head and its invincible crest of chestnut curls. Presently they began to follow her, with a compressed murmur of admiration, until, before she was halfway across the plaza, the sentries beside the gateway of the Presidio were astonished at the vision of a fair-haired and triumphant Pallas, who appeared to be leading the entire population of Todos Santos to victorious attack. In vain a solitary bugle blew, in vain the rolling drum beat an alarm, the sympathetic guard only presented arms as Miss Keene, flushed and excited, her eyes darkly humid with gratified pride, swept past them into the actual presence of the bewildered and indignant Comandante.

The only feminine consciousness she retained was that she

was more relieved at her deliverance from the wild cattle and unbroken horses of her progress than from the Indians and soldiers.

"I want to see Mrs. Markham, and to know by what authority she is arrested," said Miss Keene boldly.

"The Senor Comandante can hold no conference with you until you disperse your party," interpreted the secretary.

She was about to hurriedly reply that she knew nothing of the crowd that had accompanied her; but she was withheld by a newly-born instinct of tact.

"How do I know that I shall not be arrested, like my friend?" she said quickly. "She is as innocent as myself."

"The Comandante pledges himself, as a hidalgo, that you shall not be harmed."

Her first impulse was to advance to the nearest intruders at the gate and say, "Do go away, please;" but she was doubtful of its efficiency, and was already too exalted by the situation to be satisfied with its prosaic weakness. But her newly developed diplomacy again came to her aid. "You may tell them so, if you choose, I cannot answer for them," she said, with apparent dark significance.

The secretary advanced on the corridor and exchanged a few words with her more impulsive followers. Miss Keene, goddess-like and beautiful, remained erect behind him, and sent them a dazzling smile and ravishing wave of her little hand. The crowd roared with an effusive and bovine delight that half frightened her, and with a dozen "Viva la Reyna Americanas!" she was hurried by the Comandante into the guard-room.

"You ask to know of what the Senora Markham is accused," said the Commander, more gently. "She has received correspondence from the pirate—Perkins!"

"The pirate—Perkins?" said Miss Keene, with indignant incredulity.

"The buccaneer who wrote that letter. Read it to her, Manuel."

The secretary took his eyes from the young girl's glowing face, coughed slightly, and then read as follows:—

"ON BOARD THE EXCELSIOR, of the Quinquinambo Independent States Navy, August 8, 1854.

"To Captain Bunker.—Sir," . . .

"But this is not addressed to YOU!" interrupted Miss Keene indignantly.

"The Captain Bunker is a raving madman," said the Commander gravely. "Read on!"

The color gradually faded from the young girl's cheek as the secretary continued, in a monotonous voice:—

"I have the honor to inform you that the barque Excelsior was, on the 8th of July, 1854, and the first year of the Quinquinambo Independence, formally condemned by the Federal Council of Quinquinambo, for having aided and assisted the enemy with munitions of war and supplies, against the law of nations, and the tacit and implied good-will between the Republic of the United States and the struggling Confederacies of South America; and that, in pursuance thereof, and under the law of reprisals and letters of marque, was taken possession of by me yesterday. The goods and personal effects belonging to the passengers and yourself have been safely landed at the Embarcadero of Todos Santos—a neutral port—by my directions; my interpretation of the orders of the Federal Council excepting innocent non-combatants and their official protector from confiscation or amercement.

"I take the liberty of requesting you to hand the inclosed order on the Treasury of the Quinquinambo Confederate States to Don Miguel Briones, in payment of certain stores and provisions, and of a piece of ordnance known as the saluting cannon of the Presidio of Todos Santos. Vigilancia!

"Your obedient servant,

"LEONIDAS BOLIVAR PERKINS,

"Generalissimo Commanding Land and Sea Forces, Quinquinambo Independent States."

In her consternation at this fuller realization of the vague catastrophe, Miss Keene still clung to the idea that had brought her there.

"But Mrs. Markham has nothing to do with all this?"

"Then why does she refuse to give up her secret correspondence with the pirate Perkins?" returned the secretary.

Miss Keene hesitated. Had Mrs. Markham any previous knowledge of the Senor's real character?

"Why don't you arrest the men?" she said scornfully. "There is Mr. Banks, Mr. Crosby, Mr. Winslow, and Mr. Brace."

She uttered the last name more contemptuously, as she thought of that young gentleman's protestations and her present unprotected isolation.

"They are already arrested and removed to San Antonio, a league hence," returned the secretary. "It is fact enough that they have confessed that their Government has seized the Mexican province of California, and that they were on their way to take possession of it."

Miss Keene's heart sank.

"But you knew all this yesterday," she faltered; "and our war with Mexico is all over years ago."

"We did not know it last night at the banquet, Senora; nor would we have known it but for this treason and division in your own party."

A sudden light flashed upon Miss Keene's mind. She now comprehended the advances of Dona Isabel. Extravagant and monstrous as it seemed, these people evidently believed that a revolution had taken place in the United States; that the two opposing parties had been represented by the passengers of the Excelsior; and that one party had succeeded, headed by the indomitable Perkins. If she could be able to convince them of their blunder, would it be wise to do so? She thought of Mrs. Brimmer's supplication to be ranged "on her side," and realized with feminine quickness that the situation might be turned to her countrymen's advantage. But which side had Todos Santos favored? It was left to her woman's wit to discover this, and conceive a plan to rescue her helpless companions.

Her suspense was quickly relieved. The Commander and his secretary exchanged a few words.

"The Comandante will grant Dona Leonora's request," said the secretary, "if she will answer a question."

"What is it?" responded Miss Keene, with inward trepidation.

"The Senora Markham is perhaps beloved by the Pirate Perkins?"

In spite of her danger, in spite of the uncertain fate hanging over her party, Miss Keene could with difficulty repress a half hysterical inclination to laugh. Even then, it escaped in a sudden twinkle of her eye, which both the Commander and his subordinate were quick to notice, as she replied demurely, "Perhaps."

It was enough for the Commander. A gleam of antique archness and venerable raillery lit up his murky, tobacco-colored pupils; a spasm of gallantry crossed the face of the secretary.

"Ah—what would you?—it is the way of the world," said the Commander. "We comprehend. Come!"

He led the way across the corridor, and suddenly opened a small barred door. Whatever preconceived idea Miss Keene may have had of her unfortunate country-woman immured in a noisome cell, and guarded by a stern jailer, was quite dissipated by the soft misty sunshine that flowed in through the open door. The prison of Mrs. Markham was a part of the old glacis which had been allowed to lapse into a wild garden that stretched to the edge of the sea. There was a summer-house built on—and partly from—a crumbling bastion, and here, under the shade of tropical creepers, the melancholy captive was comfortably writing, with her portable desk on her knee, and a traveling-bag at her feet. A Saratoga trunk of obtrusive proportions stood in the centre of the peaceful vegetation, like a newly raised altar to an unknown deity. The only suggestion of martial surveillance was an Indian soldier, whose musket, reposing on the ground near Mrs. Markham, he had exchanged for the rude mattock with which he was quietly digging.

The two women, with a cry of relief, flew into each other's arms. The Commander and his secretary discreetly retired to an angle of the wall.

"I find everything as I left it, my dear, even to my slipper-bag," said Mrs. Markham. "They've forgotten nothing."

"But you are a captive!" said Eleanor. "What does it mean?"

"Nothing, my dear. I gave them a piece of my mind," said Mrs. Markham, looking, however, as if that mental offering had by no means exhausted her capital, "and I have written six pages to the Governor at Mazatlan, and a full account to Mr. Markham."

"And they won't get them in thirty years!" said Miss Keene impetuously. "But where is this letter from Senor Perkins. And, for Heaven's sake, tell me if you had the least suspicion before of anything that has happened."

"Not in the least. The man is mad, my dear, and I really believe driven so by that absurd Illinois woman's poetry. Did you ever see anything so ridiculous—and shameful, too—as the 'Ulricardo' business? I don't wonder he colored so."

Miss Keene winced with annoyance. Was everybody going crazy, or was there anything more in this catastrophe that had only enfeebled the minds of her countrywomen! For here was the severe, strong-minded Mrs. Markham actually preoccupied, like Mrs. Brimmer, with utterly irrelevant particulars, and apparently powerless to grasp the fact that they were abandoned on a half hostile strand, and cut off by half a century from the rest of the world.

"As to the letter," said Mrs. Markham, quietly, "there it is. There's nothing in it that might not have been written by a friend."

Miss Keene took the letter. It was written in a delicate, almost feminine hand. She could not help noticing that in one or two instances corrections had been made and blots carefully removed with an eraser.

"Midnight, on the Excelsior.

"MY FRIEND: When you receive this I shall probably be once more on the bosom of that mysterious and mighty element whose majesty has impressed us, whose poetry we have loved, and whose moral lessons, I trust, have not been entirely thrown away upon us. I go to the deliverance of one of those oppressed nations whose history I have often recited to you, and in whose destiny you have from time to time expressed a womanly sympathy. While it is probable, therefore, that my MOTIVES may not be misunderstood by you, or even other dear friends of the Excelsior, it is by no means impossible that the celerity and unexpectedness of my ACTION may not be perfectly appreciated by the careless mind, and may seem to require some explanation. Let me then briefly say that the idea of debarking your goods and chattels, and parting from your delightful company at Todos Santos, only occurred to me on our unexpected— shall I say PROVIDENTIAL?—arrival at that spot; and the necessity of expedition forbade me either inviting your cooperation or soliciting your confidence. Human intelligence is variously constituted—or, to use a more homely phrase, 'many men have many minds'—and it is not impossible that a premature disclosure of my plans might have jeopardized that harmony which you know it has been my desire to promote. It was my original intention to have landed you at Mazatlan, a place really inferior in climate and natural attractions to Todo Santos, although, perhaps, more easy of access and egress; but the presence of an American steamer in the offing would have invested my enterprise with a certain publicity foreign, I think, to all our tastes. Taking advantage, therefore, of my knowledge of the peninsular coast, and the pardonable ignorance of Captain Bunker, I endeavored, through my faithful subordi-nates, to reach a less known port, and a coast rarely frequented by reason of its prevailing fog. Here occurred one of those dispensations of an overruling power which, dear friend, we have so often discussed. We fell in with an unknown current, and were guided by a mysterious hand into the bay of Todos Santos!

"You know of my belief in the infinite wisdom and benignity of events; you have, dear friend, with certain feminine limitations, shared it with me. Could there have been a more perfect illustration of it than the power that led us here? On a shore, historic in interest, beautiful in climate, hospitable in its people, utterly freed from external influences, and absolutely without a compro-mising future, you are landed, my dear friend, with your youthful companions. From the crumbling ruins of a decaying Past you are called to construct an Arcadia of your own; the rudiments of a new civilization are within your grasp; the cost of existence is comparatively trifling; the various sums you have with you, which even in the chaos of revolution I have succeeded in keeping intact, will more than suffice to your natural wants for years to come. Were I not already devoted to the task of freeing

Bret Harte

Quinquinambo, I should willingly share this Elysium with you all. But, to use the glowing words of Mrs. M'Corkle, slightly altering the refrain—

'Ah, stay me not! With flying feet
O'er desert sands, I rush to greet
My fate, my love, my life, my sweet
Quinquinambo!'

"I venture to intrust to your care two unpublished manuscripts of that gifted woman. The dangers that may environ my present mission, the vicissitudes of battle by sea or land, forbid my imperiling their natural descent to posterity. You, my dear friend, will preserve them for the ages to come, occasionally refreshing yourself, from time to time, from that Parnassian spring.

"Adieu! my friend. I look around the familiar cabin, and miss your gentle faces. I feel as Jason might have felt, alone on the deck of the Argo when his companions were ashore, except that I know of no Circean influences to mar their destiny. In examining the state-rooms to see if my orders for the complete restoration of passengers' property had been carried out, I allowed myself to look into yours. Lying alone, forgotten and overlooked, I saw a peculiar jet hair-pin which I think I have observed in the coils of your tresses. May I venture to keep this gentle instrument as a reminder of the superior intellect it has so often crowned? Adieu, my friend.

"Ever yours, LEONIDAS BOLIVAR PERKINS."

"Well?" said Mrs. Markham impatiently, as Miss Keene remained motionless with the letter in her hand.

"It seems like a ridiculous nightmare! I can't understand it at all. The man that wrote this letter may be mad—but he is neither a pirate nor a thief—and yet"—

"He a pirate?" echoed Mrs. Markham indignantly; "He's nothing of the kind! It's not even his FAULT!"

"Not his fault?" repeated Miss Keene; "are you mad, too?"

"No—nor a fool, my dear! Don't you see? It's all the fault of Banks and Brimmer for compromising the vessel: of that stupid, drunken captain for permitting it. Senor Perkins is a liberator, a patriot, who has periled himself and his country to treat us magnanimously. Don't you see it? It's like that Banks and that Mrs. Brimmer to call HIM a pirate! I've a good mind to give the Commander my opinion of THEM."

"Hush!" said Miss Keene, with a sudden recollection of the Commander's suspicions, "for Heaven's sake; you do not know what you are saying. Look! they were talking with that strange man, and now they are coming this way."

The Commander and his secretary approached them. They were both more than usually grave; but the look of inquiry and suspicion with which they regarded the two women was gone from their eyes.

"The Senor Comandante says you are free, Senoras, and begs you will only decide whether you will remain his guests or the guests of the Alcalde. But for the present he cannot allow you any communication with the prisoners of San Antonio."

"There is further news?" said Miss Keene faintly, with a presentiment of worse complications.

"There is! A body from the Excelsior has been washed on shore."

Bret Harte

The two women turned pale.

"In the pocket of the murdered man is an accusation against one Senor Hurlstone, who was concealed on the ship; who came not ashore openly with the other passengers, but who escaped in secret, and is now hiding somewhere in Todos Santos."

"And you suspect him of this infamous act?" said Eleanor, forgetting all prudence in her indignation. "You are deceiving yourself. He is as innocent as I am!"

The Commander and the secretary smiled sapiently, but gently.

"The Senor Comandante believes you, Dona Leonora: the Senor Hurlstone is innocent of the piracy. He is, of a surety, the leader of the Opposition."

CHAPTER VIII

IN SANCTUARY

When James Hurlstone reached the shelter of the shrubbery he leaned exhaustedly against the adobe wall, and looked back upon the garden he had just traversed. At its lower extremity a tall hedge of cactus reinforced the crumbling wall with a cheval de frise of bristling thorns; it was through a gap in this green barrier that he had found his way a few hours before, as his torn clothes still testified. At one side ran the low wall of the Alcalde's casa, a mere line of dark shadow in that strange diaphanous mist that seemed to suffuse all objects. The gnarled and twisted branches of pear-trees, gouty with old age, bent so low as to impede any progress under their formal avenues; out of a tangled labyrinth of figtrees, here and there a single plume of feathery palm swam in a drowsy upper radiance. The shrubbery around him, of some unknown variety, exhaled a faint perfume; he put out his hand to grasp what appeared to be a young catalpa, and found it the trunk of an enormous passion vine, that, creeping softly upward, had at last invaded the very belfry of the dim tower above him; and touching it, his soul seemed to be lifted with it out of the shadow.

The great hush and quiet that had fallen like a benediction

Bret Harte

on every sleeping thing around him; the deep and passionless repose that seemed to drop from the bending boughs of the venerable trees; the cool, restful, earthy breath of the shadowed mold beneath him, touched only by a faint jessamine-like perfume as of a dead passion, lulled the hurried beatings of his heart and calmed the feverish tremor of his limbs. He allowed himself to sink back against the wall, his hands tightly clasped before him. Gradually, the set, abstracted look of his eyes faded and became suffused, as if moistened by that celestial mist. Then he rose quickly, drew his sleeve hurriedly across his lashes, and began slowly to creep along the wall again.

Either the obscurity of the shrubbery became greater or he was growing preoccupied; but in steadying himself by the wall he had, without perceiving it, put his hand upon a rude door that, yielding to his pressure, opened noiselessly into a dark passage. Without apparent reflection he entered, followed the passage a few steps until it turned abruptly; turning with it, he found himself in the body of the Mission Church of Todos Santos. A swinging-lamp, that burned perpetually before an effigy of the Virgin Mother, threw a faint light on the single rose-window behind the high altar; another, suspended in a low archway, apparently lit the open door of the passage towards the refectory. By the stronger light of the latter Hurlstone could see the barbaric red and tarnished gold of the rafters that formed the straight roof. The walls were striped with equally bizarre coloring, half Moorish and half Indian. A few hangings of dyed and painted cloths with heavy fringes were disposed on either side of the chancel, like the flaps of a wigwam; and the aboriginal suggestion was further repeated in a quantity of colored beads and sea-shells that decked the communion-rails. The Stations of the Cross, along the walls, were commemorated by paintings, evidently by a native artist—to suit the same barbaric taste; while a larger picture of San Francisco d'Assisis, under the choir, seemed to belong to an older and more artistic civilization. But the sombre half-light of the two lamps mellowed and softened the harsh contrast of these details until the whole body of the church appeared filled with a vague harmonious shadow. The air, heavy with the odors of past incense, seemed to be a part of that expression, as if the solemn and sympathetic twilight became palpable in each deep, long-drawn inspiration.

Again overcome by the feeling of repose and peacefulness, Hurlstone sank upon a rude settle, and bent his head and folded arms over a low railing before him. How long he sat there, allowing the subtle influence to transfuse and possess his entire being, he did not know. The faint twitter of birds suddenly awoke him. Looking up, he perceived that it came from the vacant square of the tower above him, open to the night and suffused with its mysterious radiance. In another moment the roof of the church was swiftly crossed and recrossed with tiny and adventurous wings. The mysterious light had taken an opaline color. Morning was breaking.

The slow rustling of a garment, accompanied by a soft but heavy tread, sounded from the passage. He started to his feet as the priest, whom he had seen on the deck of the Excelsior, entered the church from the refectory. The Padre was alone. At the apparition of a stranger, torn and disheveled, he stopped involuntarily and cast a hasty look towards the heavy silver ornaments on the altar. Hurlstone noticed it, and smiled bitterly.

"Don't alarm yourself. I only sought this place for shelter."

He spoke in French—the language he had heard Padre Esteban address to Mrs. Brimmer. But the priest's quick eye had already detected his own mistake. He lifted his hand with a sublime gesture towards the altar, and said,—

Bret Harte

"You are right! Where should you seek shelter but here?"

The reply was so unexpected that Hurlstone was silent. His lips quivered slightly.

"And if it were SANCTUARY I was seeking?" he said.

"You would first tell me why you sought it," said Padre Esteban gently.

Hurlstone looked at him irresolutely for a moment and then said, with the hopeless desperation of a man anxious to anticipate his fate,—

"I am a passenger on the ship you boarded yesterday. I came ashore with the intention of concealing myself somewhere here until she had sailed. When I tell you that I am not a fugitive from justice, that I have committed no offense against the ship or her passengers, nor have I any intention of doing so, but that I only wish concealment from their knowledge for twenty-four hours, you will know enough to understand that you run no risk in giving me assistance. I can tell you no more."

"I did not see you with the other passengers, either on the ship or ashore," said the priest. "How did you come here?"

"I swam ashore before they left. I did not know they had any idea of landing here; I expected to be the only one, and there would have been no need for concealment then. But I am not lucky," he added, with a bitter laugh.

The priest glanced at his garments, which bore the traces of the sea, but remained silent.

"Do you think I am lying?"

The old priest lifted his head with a gesture.

"Not to me—but to God!"

The young man followed the gesture, and glanced around the barbaric church with a slight look of scorn. But the profound isolation, the mystic seclusion, and, above all, the complete obliteration of that world and civilization he shrank from and despised, again subdued and overcame his rebellious spirit. He lifted his eyes to the priest.

"Nor to God," he said gravely.

"Then why withhold anything from Him here?" said the priest gently.

"I am not a Catholic—I do not believe in confession," said Hurlstone doggedly, turning aside.

But Padre Esteban laid his large brown hand on the young man's shoulder. Touched by some occult suggestion in its soft contact, he sank again into his seat.

"Yet you ask for the sanctuary of His house—a sanctuary bought by that contrition whose first expression is the bared and open soul! To the first worldly shelter you sought—the peon's hut or the Alcalde's casa—you would have thought it necessary to bring a story. You would not conceal from the physician whom you asked for balsam either the wound, the symptoms, or the cause? Enough," he said kindly, as Hurlstone was about to reply. "You shall have your request. You shall stay here. I will be your physician, and will salve your wounds; if any poison I know not of rankle there, you will not blame me, son, but perhaps you will assist me to find it. I will give you a secluded cell in the dormitory until the ship has sailed. And then"—

He dropped quietly on the settle, took the young man's hand paternally in his own, and gazed into his eyes as if he read his soul.

And then . . . Ah, yes . . . What then? Hurlstone glanced once more around him. He thought of the quiet night; of the great peace that had fallen upon him since he had entered the garden, and the promise of a greater peace that seemed to breathe with the incense from those venerable walls. He thought of that crumbling barrier, that even in its ruin seemed to shut out, more completely than anything he had conceived, his bitter past, and the bitter world that recalled it. He thought of the long days to come, when, forgetting and forgotten, he might find a new life among these simple aliens, themselves forgotten by the world. He had thought of this once before in the garden; it occurred to him again in this Lethe-like oblivion of the little church, in the kindly pressure of the priest's hand. The ornaments no longer looked uncouth and barbaric—rather they seemed full of some new spiritual significance. He suddenly lifted his eyes to Padre Esteban, and, half rising to his feet, said,—

"Are we alone?"

"We are; it is a half-hour yet before mass," said the priest.

"My story will not last so long," said the young man hurriedly, as if fearing to change his mind. "Hear me, then— it is no crime nor offense to any one; more than that, it concerns no one but myself—it is of"—

"A woman," said the priest softly. "So! we will sit down, my son."

He lifted his hand with a soothing gesture—the movement of a physician who has just arrived at an easy diagnosis of certain uneasy symptoms. There was also a slight suggestion of an habitual toleration, as if even the seclusion of Todos Santos had not been entirely free from the invasion of the primal passion.

Hurlstone waited for an instant, but then went on rapidly.

"It is of a woman, who has cursed my life, blasted my prospects, and ruined my youth; a woman who gained my early affection only to blight and wither it; a woman who should be nearer to me and dearer than all else, and yet who is further than the uttermost depths of hell from me in sympathy or feeling; a woman that I should cleave to, but from whom I have been flying, ready to face shame, disgrace, oblivion, even that death which alone can part us: for that woman is—my wife."

He stopped, out of breath, with fixed eyes and a rigid mouth. Father Esteban drew a snuff-box from his pocket, and a large handkerchief. After blowing his nose violently, he took a pinch of snuff, wiped his lip, and replaced the box.

"A bad habit, my son," he said apologetically, "but an old man's weakness. Go on."

"I met her first five years ago—the wife of another man. Don't misjudge me, it was no lawless passion; it was a friendship, I believed, due to her intellectual qualities as much as to her womanly fascinations; for I was a young student, lodging in the same house with her, in an academic town. Before I ever spoke to her of love, she had confided to me her own unhappiness—the uncongeniality of her married life, the harshness, and even brutality, of her husband. Even a man less in love than I was could have seen the truth of this—the contrast of the coarse, sensual, and vulgar man with an apparently refined and intelligent woman; but any one else except myself would have suspected that such a union was not merely a sacrifice of the woman. I believed her. It was not until long afterwards that I learned that her marriage had been a condonation of her youthful errors by a complaisant bridegroom; that her character had been saved by a union that was a mutual concession. But I loved her madly; and when she finally got a divorce from her uncongenial husband, I believed it less an expression of her love for me than an act of justice. I did not know at the time that they had arranged the divorce together, as they had arranged their marriage, by equal concessions.

"I was the only son of a widowed mother, whose instincts were from the first opposed to my friendship with this woman, and what she prophetically felt would be its result. Unfortunately, both she and my friends were foolish enough to avow their belief that the divorce was obtained solely with a view of securing me as a successor; and it was this argument more than any other that convinced me of my duty to protect her. Enough, I married, not only in spite of all opposition—but BECAUSE of it.

"My mother would have reconciled herself to the marriage, but my wife never forgave the opposition, and, by some hellish instinct divining that her power over me might be weakened by maternal influence, precipitated a quarrel which forever separated us. With the little capital left by my father, divided between my mother and myself, I took my wife to a western city. Our small income speedily dwindled under the debts of her former husband, which she had assumed to purchase her freedom. I endeavored to utilize a good education and some accomplishments in music and the languages by giving lessons and by contributing to the press. In this my wife first made a show of assisting me, but I was not long in discovering that her intelligence was superficial and shallow, and that the audacity of expression, which I had believed to be originality of conviction, was simply shame-lessness, and a desire for notoriety. She had a facility in writing senti-mental poetry, which had been efficacious in her matrimonial confidences, but which editors of magazines and newspapers found to be shallow and insincere. To my astonishment, she remained unaffected by this, as she was equally impervious to the slights and sneers that continually met us in society. At last the inability to pay one of her former husband's claims brought to me a threat and an anonymous letter. I laid them before her, when a scene ensued which revealed the blindness of my folly in all its hideous hopelessness: she accused me of complicity in her divorce, and deception in regard to my own fortune. In a speech, whose language was a horrible revelation of her early habits, she offered to arrange a divorce from me as she had from her former husband. She gave as a reason her preference for another, and her belief that the scandal of a suit would lend her a certain advertisement and prestige. It was a combination of Messalina and Mrs. Jarley"—

"Pardon! I remember not a Madame Jarley," said the priest.

"Of viciousness and commercial calculation," continued Hurlstone hurriedly. "I don't remember what happened; she swore that I struck her! Perhaps—God knows! But she failed, even before a western jury, to convict me of cruelty. The judge that thought me half insane would not believe me brutal, and her application for divorce was lost.

"I need not tell you that the same friends who had opposed my marriage now came forward to implore me to allow her to break our chains. I refused. I swear to you it was from no lingering love for her, for her presence drove me mad; it was from no instinct of revenge or jealousy, for I should have welcomed the man who would have taken her out of my life and memory. But I could not bear the idea of taking her first husband's place in her hideous comedy; I could not purchase my freedom at that price—at any price. I was told that I could get a divorce against HER, and stand forth before the world untrammeled and unstained. But I could not stand before MYSELF in such an attitude. I knew that the shackles I had deliberately forged could not be loosened except by death. I knew that the stains of her would cling to me and become a part of my own sin, even as the sea I plunged into yesterday to escape her, though it has dried upon me, has left its bitter salt behind.

"When she knew my resolve, she took her revenge by dragging my name through the successive levels to which she descended. Under the plea that the hardly-earned sum I gave to her maintenance apart from me was not sufficient, she utilized her undoubted beauty and more doubtful talent in amateur entertainments—and, finally, on the stage. She was openly accompanied by her lover, who acted as her agent, in the hope of goading me to a divorce. Suddenly she disappeared. I thought she had forgotten me. I obtained an honorable position in New York. One night I entered a theater devoted to burlesque opera and the exhibition of a popular actress, known as the Western Thalia, whose beautiful and audaciously draped figure was the talk of the town. I recognized my wife in this star of nudity; more than that, she recognized me. The next day, in addition to the usual notice, the real name of the actress was given in the morning papers, with a sympathizing account of her romantic and unfortunate marriage. I renounced my position, and, taking advantage of an offer from an old friend in California, resolved to join him secretly there. My mother had died broken-hearted; I was alone in the world. But my wife discovered my intention; and when I reached Callao, I heard that she had followed me, by way of the Isthmus of Panama, and that probably she would anticipate me in Mazatlan, where we were to stop. The thought of suicide haunted me during the rest of that horrible voyage; only my belief that she would make it appear as a tacit confession of my guilt saved me from that last act of weakness."

He stopped and shuddered. Padre Esteban again laid his hand softly upon him.

"It was God who spared you that sacrifice of soul and body," he said gently.

"I thought it was God that suggested to me to take the SIMULATION of that act the means of separating myself from her forever. When we neared Mazatlan, I conceived the idea of hiding myself in the hold of the Excelsior until she had left that port, in the hope that it would be believed that I had fallen overboard. I succeeded in secreting myself, but was discovered at the same time that the unexpected change in the ship's destination rendered concealment unnecessary. As we did not put in at Mazatlan, nobody suspected my discovery in the hold to be anything but the accident that I gave it out to be. I felt myself saved the confrontation of the woman at Mazatlan; but I knew she would pursue me to San Francisco.

"The strange dispensation of Providence that brought us into this unknown port gave me another hope of escape and oblivion. While you and the Commander were boarding the Excelsior, I slipped from the cabin-window into the water; I was a good swimmer, and reached the shore in safety. I concealed myself in the ditch of the Presidio until I saw the passengers' boats returning with them, when I sought the safer shelter of this Mission. I made my way through a gap in the hedge and lay under your olive-trees, hearing the voices of my companions, beyond the walls, till past midnight. I then groped my way along the avenue of pear-trees till I came to another wall, and a door that opened to my accidental touch. I entered, and found myself here. You know the rest."

He had spoken with the rapid and unpent fluency of a man who cared more to relieve himself of an oppressive burden than to impress his auditor; yet the restriction of a foreign tongue had checked repetition or verbosity. Without imagination he had been eloquent; without hopefulness he had been convincing. Father Esteban rose, holding both his hands.

"My son, in the sanctuary which you have claimed there is no divorce. The woman who has ruined your life could not be your wife. As long as her first husband lives, she is forever his wife, bound by a tie which no human law can sever!"

CHAPTER IX

AN OPEN-AIR PRISON

An hour after mass Father Esteban had quietly installed Hurlstone in a small cell-like apartment off the refectory. The household of the priest consisted of an old Indian woman of fabulous age and miraculous propriety, two Indian boys who served at mass, a gardener, and a muleteer. The first three, who were immediately in attendance upon the priest, were cognizant of a stranger's presence, but, under instructions from the reverend Padre, were loyally and superstitiously silent; the vocations of the gardener and muleteer made any intrusion from them impossible. A breakfast of fruit, tortillas, chocolate, and red wine, of which Hurlstone partook sparingly and only to please his entertainer, nevertheless seemed to restore his strength, as it did the Padre's equanimity. For the old man had been somewhat agitated during mass, and, except that his early morning congregation was mainly composed of Indians, muleteers, and small venders, his abstraction would have been noticed. With ready tact he had not attempted, by further questioning, to break the taciturnity into which Hurlstone had relapsed after his emotional confession and the priest's abrupt half-absolution. Was it possible he regretted his confidence, or was it possible that his first free and untrammeled expression of his wrongs had left him with a haunting doubt of their real magnitude

"Lie down here, my son," said the old ecclesiastic, pointing to a small pallet in the corner, "and try to restore in the morning what you have taken from the night. Manuela will bring your clothes when they are dried and mended; meantime, shift for yourself in Pepito's serape and calzas. I will betake me to the Comandante and the Alcalde, to learn the dispositions of your party, when the ship will sail, and if your absence is suspected. Peace be with you, son! Manuela, attend to the caballero, and see you chatter not."

Without doubting the substantial truth of his guest's story, the good Padre Esteban was not unwilling to have it corroborated by such details as he thought he could collect among the Excelsior's passengers. His own experience in the confessional had taught him the unreliability of human evidence, and the vagaries of both conscientious and unconscious suppression. That a young, good-looking, and accomplished caballero should have been the victim of not one, but even many, erotic episodes, did not strike the holy father as being peculiar; but that he should have been brought by a solitary unfortunate attachment to despair and renunciation of the world appeared to him marvelous. He was not unfamiliar with the remorse of certain gallants for peccadillos with other men's wives; but this Americano's self-abasement for the sins of his own wife—as he foolishly claimed her to be—whom he hated and despised, struck Father Esteban as a miracle open to suspicion. Was there anything else in these somewhat commonplace details of vulgar and low intrigue than what he had told the priest? Were all these Americano husbands as sensitive and as gloomily self-sacrificing and expiating? It did not appear so from the manners and customs of the others,—from those easy matrons whose complacent husbands had abandoned them to the long companionship of youthful cavaliers on adventurous voyages; from those audacious virgins, who had the freedom of married women. Surely, this was not a pious and sensitive race, passionately devoted to their domestic affections! The young stranger must be either deceiving him—or an exception to his countrymen!

And if he was that exception—what then? An idea which had sprung up in Father Esteban's fancy that morning now took possession of it with the tenacity of a growth on fertile virgin soil. The good Father had been devoted to the conversion of the heathen with the fervor of a one-ideaed man. But his successes had been among the Indians—a guileless, harmless race, who too often confounded the practical benefits of civilization with the abstract benefits of the Church, and their instruction had been simple and coercive. There had been no necessity for argument or controversy; the worthy priest's skill in polemical warfare and disputation had never been brought into play; the Comandante and Alcalde were as punctiliously orthodox as himself, and the small traders and artisans were hopelessly docile and submissive. The march of science, which had been stopped by the local fogs of Todos Santos some fifty years, had not disturbed the simple Aesculapius of the province with heterodox theories: he still purged and bled like Sangrado, and met the priest at the deathbed of his victims with a pious satisfaction that had no trace of skeptical contention. In fact, the gentle Mission of Todos Santos had hitherto presented no field for the good Father's exalted ambition, nor the display of his powers as a zealot. And here was a splendid opportunity.

The conversion of this dark, impulsive, hysterical stranger would be a gain to the fold, and a triumph worthy of his steel. More than that, if he had judged correctly of this young man's mind and temperament, they seemed to contain those elements of courage and sacrificial devotion that indicated the missionary priesthood. With such a subaltern, what might

Bret Harte

not he, Father Esteban, accomplish! Looking further into the future, what a glorious successor might be left to his unfinished work on Todos Santos!

Buried in these reflections, Padre Esteban sauntered leisurely up the garden, that gradually ascended the slight elevation on which the greater part of the pueblo was built. Through a low gateway in the wall he passed on to the crest of the one straggling street of Todos Santos. On either side of him were ranged the low one-storied, deep-windowed adobe fondas and artisans' dwellings, with low-pitched roofs of dull red pipe-like tiles. Absorbed in his fanciful dreams, he did not at first notice that those dwellings appeared deserted, and that even the Posada opposite him, whose courtyard was usually filled with lounging muleteers, was empty and abandoned. Looking down the street towards the plaza, he became presently aware of some undefined stirring in the peaceful hamlet. There was an unusual throng in the square, and afar on that placid surface of the bay from which the fog had lifted, the two or three fishing-boats of Todos Santos were vaguely pulling. But the strange ship was gone.

A feeling of intense relief and satisfaction followed. Father Esteban pulled out his snuff-box and took a long and complacent pinch. But his relief was quickly changed to consternation as an armed cavalcade rapidly wheeled out of the plaza and cantered towards him, with the unmistakable spectacle of the male passengers of the Excelsior riding two and two, and guarded by double files of dragoons on each side.

At a sign from the priest the subaltern reined in his mustang, halted the convoy, and saluted respectfully, to the astonishment of the prisoners. The clerical authority of Todos Santos evidently dominated the military. Renewed hope sprang up in the hearts of the Excelsior party.

"What have we here?" asked Padre Esteban.

"A revolution, your Reverence, among the Americanos, with robbery of the Presidio saluting-gun; a grave affair. Your Reverence has been sent for by the Comandante. I am taking these men to San Antonio to await the decision of the Council."

"And the ship?"

"Gone, your Reverence. One of the parties has captured it."

"And these?"

"Are the Legitimists, your Reverence: at least they have confessed to have warred with Mexico, and invaded California—the brigands."

The priest remained lost for a moment in blank and bitter amazement. Banks took advantage of the pause to edge his way to the front.

"Ask him, some of you," he said, turning to Brace and Crosby, "when this d—d farce will be over, and where we can find the head man—the boss idiot of this foolery."

"Let him put it milder," whispered Winslow. "You got us into trouble enough with your tongue already."

Crosby hesitated a moment.

"Quand finira ce drole representation?—et—et—qui est ce qui est l'entrepreneur?" he said dubiously.

The priest stared. These Americans were surely cooler and less excitable than his strange guest. A thought struck him.

Bret Harte

"How many are still in the ship?" he asked gently.

"Nobody but Perkins and that piratical crew of niggers."

"And that infernal Hurlstone," added Winslow.

The priest pricked up his ears.

"Hurlstone?" he repeated.

"Yes—a passenger like ourselves, as we supposed. But we are satisfied now he was in the conspiracy from the beginning," translated Crosby painfully.

"Look at his strange disappearance—a regular put-up job," broke in Brace, in English, without reference to the Padre's not comprehending him; "so that he and Perkins could shut themselves up together without suspicion."

"Never mind Hurlstone now; he's GONE, and we're HERE," said Banks angrily. "Ask the parson, as a gentle-man and a Christian, what sort of a hole we've got into, anyhow. How far is the next settlement?"

Crosby put the question. The subaltern lit a cigarette.

"There is no next settlement. The pueblo ends at San Antonio."

"And what's beyond that?"

"The ocean."

"And what's south?"

"The desert—one cannot pass it."

"And north?"

"The desert."

"And east?"

"The desert too."

"Then how do you get away from here?"

"We do not get away."

"And how do you communicate with Mexico—with your Government?"

"When a ship comes."

"And when does a ship come?"

"Quien sabe?"

The officer threw away his cigarette.

"I say, you'll tell the Commander that all this is illegal; and that I'm going to complain to our Government," continued Banks hurriedly.

"I go to speak to the Comandante," responded the priest gravely.

"And tell him that if he touches a hair of the ladies' heads we'll have his own scalp," interrupted Brace impetuously.

Even Crosby's diplomatic modification of this speech did not appear entirely successful.

"The Mexican soldier wars not with women," said the priest coldly. "Adieu, messieurs!"

The cavalcade moved on. The Excelsior passengers at once resumed their chorus of complaint, tirade, and aggressive suggestion, heedless of the soldiers who rode stolidly on each side.

"To think we haven't got a single revolver among us," said Brace despairingly.

"We might each grab a carbine from these nigger fellows," said Crosby, eying them contemplatively.

"And if they didn't burst, and we weren't shot by the next patrol, and if we'd calculated to be mean enough to run away from the women—where would we escape to?" asked Banks curtly. "Hold on at least until we get an ultimatum from that commodious ass at the Presidio! Then we'll anticipate the fool-killer, if you like. My opinion is, they aren't in any great hurry to try ANYTHING on us just yet."

"And I say, lie low and keep dark until they show their hand," added Winslow, who had no relish for an indiscriminate scrimmage, and had his own ideas of placating their captors.

Nevertheless, by degrees they fell into a silence, partly the effect of the strangely enervating air. The fog had completely risen from the landscape, and hung high in mid-air, through which an intense sun, shorn of its fierceness, diffused a lambent warmth, and a yellowish, unctuous light, as if it had passed through amber. The bay gleamed clearly and distinctly; not a shadow flecked its surface to the gray impenetrable rampart of fog that stretched like a granite wall before its entrance. On one side of the narrow road billows of monstrous grain undulated to the crest of the low hills, that looked like larger undulations of the soil, furrowed by bosky canadas or shining arroyos. Banks was startled into a burst of professional admiration.

"There's enough grain there to feed a thousand Todos Santos; and raised, too, with tools like that," he continued, pointing to a primitive plow that lay on the wayside, formed by a single forked root. A passing ox-cart, whose creaking wheels were made of a solid circle of wood, apparently sawn from an ordinary log, again plunged him into cogitation. Here and there little areas of the rudest cultivation broke into a luxuriousness of orange, lime, and fig trees. The joyous earth at the slightest provocation seemed to smile and dimple with fruit and flowers. Everywhere the rare beatitudes of Todos Santos revealed and repeated its simple story. The fructifying influence of earth and sky; the intervention of a vaporous veil between a fiery sun and fiery soil; the combination of heat and moisture, purified of feverish exhalations, and made sweet and wholesome by the saline breath of the mighty sea, had been the beneficent legacy of their isolation, the munificent compensation of their oblivion.

A gradual and gentle ascent at the end of two hours brought the cavalcade to a halt upon a rugged upland with semi-tropical shrubbery, and here and there larger trees from the tierra templada in the evergreens or madrono. A few low huts and corrals, and a rambling hacienda, were scattered along the crest, and in the midst arose a little votive chapel, flanked by pear-trees. Near the roadside were the crumbling edges of some long-forgotten excavation. Crosby gazed at it curiously. Touching the arm of the officer, he pointed to it.

"Una mina de plata," said the officer sententiously.

"A mine of some kind—silver, I bet!" said Crosby, turning to the others. "Is it good—bueno—you know?" he conti-nued to the officer, with vague gesticulations.

"En tiempos pasados," returned the officer gravely.

"I wonder what that means?" said Winslow.

But before Crosby could question further, the subaltern signaled to them to dismount. They did so, and their horses were led away to a little declivity, whence came the sound of running water. Left to themselves, the Americans looked around them. The cavalcade seemed to have halted near the edge of a precipitous ridge, the evident termination of the road. But the view that here met their eyes was unexpected and startling.

The plateau on which they stood seemed to drop suddenly away, leaving them on the rocky shore of a monotonous and far-stretching sea of waste and glittering sand. Not a vestige nor trace of vegetation could be seen, except an occasional ridge of straggling pallid bushes, raised in hideous simulation of the broken crest of a ghostly wave. On either side, as far as the eye could reach, the hollow empty vision extended—the interminable desert stretched and panted before them.

"It's the jumping-off place, I reckon," said Crosby, "and they've brought us here to show us how small is our chance of getting away. But," he added, turning towards the plateau again, "what are they doing now? 'Pon my soul! I believe they're going off—and leaving us."

The others turned as he spoke. It was true. The dragoons were coolly galloping off the way they came, taking with them the horses the Americans had just ridden.

"I call that cool," said Crosby. "It looks deuced like as if we were to be left here to graze, like cattle."

"Perhaps that's their idea of a prison in this country," said Banks. "There's certainly no chance of our breaking jail in that direction," he added, pointing to the desert; "and we can't follow them without horses."

"And I dare say they've guarded the pass in the road lower down," said Winslow.

"We ought to be able to hold our own here until night," said Brace, "and then make a dash into Todos Santos, get hold of some arms, and join the ladies."

"The women are all right," said Crosby impatiently, "and are better treated than if we were with them. Suppose, instead of maundering over them, we reconnoitre and see what WE can do here. I'm getting devilishly hungry; they can't mean to starve us, and if they do, I don't intend to be starved as long as there is anything to be had by buying or stealing. Come along. There's sure to be fruit near that old chapel, and I saw some chickens in the bush near those huts. First, let's see if there's any one about. I don't see a soul."

The little plateau, indeed, seemed deserted. In vain they shouted; their voices were lost in the echoless air. They examined one by one the few thatched huts: they were open, contained one or two rude articles of furniture—a bed, a bench, and table—were scrupulously clean—and empty. They next inspected the chapel; it was tawdry and barbaric in ornament, but the candlesticks and crucifix and the basin for holy water were of heavily beaten silver. The same thought crossed their minds—the abandoned mine at the roadside!

Bananas, oranges, and prickly-pears growing within the

cactus-hedge of the chapel partly mollified their thirst and hunger, and they turned their steps towards the long, rambling, barrack-looking building, with its low windows and red-tiled roof, which they had first noticed. Here, too, the tenement was deserted and abandoned; but there was evidence of some previous and more ambitious preparation: in a long dormitory off the corridor a number of scrupulously clean beds were ranged against the whitewashed walls, with spotless benches and tables. To the complete astonishment and bewilderment of the party another room, fitted up as a kitchen, with the simpler appliances of housekeeping, revealed a larder filled with provisions and meal. A shout from Winslow, who had penetrated the inner courtyard, however, drew them to a more remarkable spectacle. Their luggage and effects from the cabins of the Excelsior were there, carefully piled in the antique ox-cart that had evidently that morning brought them from Todos Santos!

"There's no mistake," said Brace, with a relieved look, after a hurried survey of the trunks. "They have only brought our baggage. The ladies have evidently had the opportunity of selecting their own things."

"Crosby told you they'd be all right," said Banks; "and as for ourselves, I don't see why we can't be pretty comfor-table here, and all the better for our being alone. I shall take an opportunity of looking around a bit. It strikes me that there are some resources in this country that might pay to develop."

"And I shall have a look at that played-out mine," said Crosby; "if it's been worked as they work the land, they've left about as much in it as they've taken out."

"That's all well enough," said Brace, drawing a dull vermilion-colored stone from his pocket; "but here's something I picked up just now that ain't 'played out,' nor even the value of it suspected by those fellows. That's cinnabar—quicksilver ore—and a big per cent. of it too; and if there's as much of it here as the indications show, you could buy up all your SILVER mines in the country with it."

"If I were you, I'd put up a notice on a post somewhere, as they do in California, and claim discovery," said Banks seriously. "There's no knowing how this thing may end. We may not get away from here for some time yet, and if the Government will sell the place cheap, it wouldn't be a bad spec' to buy it. Form a kind of 'Excelsior Company' among ourselves, you know, and go shares."

The four men looked earnestly at each other. Already the lost Excelsior and her mutinous crew were forgotten; even the incidents of the morning—their arrest, the uncertainty of their fate, and the fact that they were in the hands of a hostile community—appeared but as trivial preliminaries to the new life that opened before them! They suddenly became graver than they had ever been—even in the moment of peril.

"I don't see why we shouldn't," said Brace quickly. "We started out to do that sort of thing in California, and I reckon if we'd found such a spot as this on the Sacramento or American River we'd have been content. We can take turns at housekeeping, prospect a little, and enter into negotiations with the Government. I'm for offering them a fair sum for this ridge and all it contains at once."

"The only thing against that," said Crosby slowly, "is the probability that it is already devoted to some other use by the Government. Ever since we've been here I've been thinking —I don't know why—that we've been put in a sort of quarantine. The desertion of the place, the half hospital arrangements of this building, and the means they have taken to isolate us from themselves, must mean something. I've read somewhere that in these out-of-the-way spots in the tropics they have a place where they put the fellows with malarious or contagious diseases. I don't want to frighten you boys: but I've an idea that we're in a sort of lazaretto, and the people outside won't trouble us often."

CHAPTER X

TODOS SANTOS SOLVES THE MYSTERY

Notwithstanding his promise, and the summons of the Council, Father Esteban, on parting with the Excelsior prisoners in the San Antonio Road, did not proceed immediately to the presence of the Comandante. Partly anxious to inform himself more thoroughly regarding Hurlstone's antecedents before entering upon legislative functions that might concern him, partly uneasy at Brace's allusion to any possible ungentleness in the treatment of the fair Americanas, and partly apprehensive that Mrs. Brimmer might seek him at the Mission in the present emergency, the good Father turned his steps towards the Alcalde's house.

Mrs. Brimmer, in a becoming morning wrapper, half reclining in an Indian hammock in the corridor, supported by Miss Chubb, started at his approach. So did the young Alcalde, sympathetically seated at her side. Padre Esteban for an instant was himself embarrassed; Mrs. Brimmer quickly recovered her usual bewildering naivete.

"I knew you would come; but if you hadn't, I should have mustered courage enough to go with Miss Chubb to find you at the Mission," she said, half coquettishly. "Not but that Don Ramon has been all kindness and consideration, but you know one always clings to one's spiritual adviser in such an emergency; and although there are differences of opinion between us, I think I may speak to you as freely as I would speak to my dear friend Dr. Potts, of Trinity Chapel. Of course you don't know HIM; but you couldn't have helped liking him, he's so gentle, so tactful, so refined! But do tell me the fullest particulars of this terrible calamity that has happened so awkwardly. Tell me all! I fear that Don Ramon, out of kindness, has not told me everything. I have been perfectly frank, I told him everything—who I am, who Mr. Brimmer is, and given him even the connections of my friend Miss Chubb. I can do no more; but you will surely have no difficulty in finding some one in Todos Santos who has heard of the Quincys and Brimmers. I've no doubt that there are books in your library that mention them. Of course I can say nothing of the other passengers, except that Mr. Brimmer would not have probably permitted me to associate with any notorious persons. I confess now—I think I told you once before, Clarissa—that I greatly doubted Captain Bunker's ability"—

"Ah," murmured Don Ramon.

"—To make a social selection," continued Mrs. Brimmer. "He may have been a good sailor, and boxed his compass, but he lacked a knowledge of the world. Of the other passengers I can truly say I know nothing; I cannot think that Mr. Crosby's sense of humor led him into bad associations, or that he ever went beyond verbal impropriety. Certainly nothing in Miss Keene's character has led me to believe she could so far forget what was due to herself and to us as to address a lawless mob in the streets as she did just now; although her friend Mrs. Markham, as I just told Don Ramon, is an advocate of Women's Rights and Female Suffrage, and I believe she contemplates addressing the public from the lecturer's platform."

"It isn't possible!" interrupted Don Ramon excitedly, in mingled horror of the masculinely rampant Mrs. Markham and admiration of the fascinatingly feminine Mrs. Brimmer; "a lady cannot be an orator—a haranguer of men!"

"Not in society," responded Mrs. Brimmer, with a sigh, "and I do not remember to have met the lady before. The fact is, she does not move in our circle—in the upper classes."

The Alcalde exchanged a glance with the Padre.

"Ah! you have classes? and she is of a distinct class, perhaps?"

"Decidedly," said Mrs. Brimmer promptly.

"Pardon me," said Padre Esteban, with gentle persuasiveness, "but you are speaking of your fellow-passengers. Know you not, then, of one Hurlstone, who is believed to be still in the ship Excelsior, and perhaps of the party who seized it?"

"Mr. Hurlstone?—it is possible; but I know really nothing of him," said Mrs. Brimmer carelessly. "I don't think Clarissa did, either—did you, dear? Even in our enforced companionship we had to use some reserve, and we may have drawn the line at him! He was a friend of Miss Keene's; indeed, she was the only one who seemed to know him."

"And she is now here?" asked the Padre eagerly.

"No. She is with her friend the Senora Markham, at the Presidio. The Comandante has given her the disposition of his house," said Don Ramon, with a glance of grave archness at Mrs. Brimmer; "it is not known which is the most favored, the eloquent orator or the beautiful and daring leader!"

"Mrs. Markham is a married woman," said Mrs. Brimmer severely, "and, of course, she can do as she pleases; but it is far different with Miss Keene. I should scarcely consider it proper to expose Miss Chubb to the hospitality of a single man, without other women, and I cannot understand how she could leave the companionship and protection of your lovely sisters."

The priest here rose, and, with formal politeness, excused himself, urging the peremptory summons of the Council.

"I scarcely expected, indeed, to have had the pleasure of seeing my colleague here," he added with quiet suavity, turning to the Alcalde.

"I have already expressed my views to the Comandante," said the official, with some embarrassment, "and my attendance will hardly be required."

The occasional misleading phosphorescence of Mrs. Brimmer's quiet eyes, early alluded to in these pages, did not escape Father Esteban's quick perception at that moment; however, he preferred to leave his companion to follow its aberrations rather than to permit that fair ignis fatuus to light him on his way by it.

"But my visit to you, Father Esteban," she began sweetly, "is only postponed."

"Until I have the pleasure of anticipating it here," said the priest, with paternal politeness bending before the two ladies; "but for the present, au revoir!"

"It would be an easy victory to win this discreetly emotional Americana to the Church," said Father Esteban to himself, as he crossed the plaza; "but, if I mistake not, she would not cease to be a disturbing element even there. However, she is not such as would give this Hurlstone any trouble. It seems I must look elsewhere for the brains of this party, and to find a solution of this young man's mystery; and, if I judge correctly, it is with this beautiful young agitator of revolutions and her oratorical duenna I must deal."

He entered the low gateway of the Presidio unchallenged, and even traversed the courtyard without meeting a soul. The guard and sentries had evidently withdrawn to their habitual peaceful vocations, and the former mediaeval repose of the venerable building had returned. There was no one in the guard-room; but as the priest turned back to the corridor, his quick ear was suddenly startled by the unhallowed and inconsistent sounds of a guitar. A mono-tonous voice also— the Comandante's evidently—was raised in a thin, high recitative.

The Padre passed hastily through the guard-room, and opened the door of the passage leading to the garden slope. Here an extraordinary group presented itself to his astonished eyes. In the shadow of a palm-tree, Mrs. Markham, seated on her Saratoga trunk as on a throne, was gazing blandly down upon the earnest features of the Commander, who, at her feet, guitar in hand, was evidently repeating some musical composition. His subaltern sat near him, divided in admiration of his chief and the guest. Miss Keene, at a little distance, aided by the secretary, was holding an animated conversation with a short, stout, Sancho Panza-looking man, whom the Padre recognized as the doctor of Todos Santos.

At the apparition of the reverend Father, the Commander started, the subaltern stared, and even the secretary and the doctor looked discomposed.

"I am decidedly de trop this morning," soliloquized the ecclesiastic; but Miss Keene cut short his reflection by running to him frankly, with outstretched hand.

"I am so glad that you have come," she said, with a youthful, unrestrained earnestness that was as convincing as it was fascinating, "for you will help me to persuade this gentleman that poor Captain Bunker is suffering more from excitement of mind than body, and that bleeding him is more than folly."

"The man's veins are in a burning fever and delirium from aguardiente," said the little doctor excitedly, "and the fire must first be put out by the lancet."

"He is only crazy with remorse for having lost his ship through his own carelessness and the treachery of others," said Miss Keene doughtily.

"He is a maniac and will kill himself, unless his fever is subdued," persisted the doctor.

"And you would surely kill him by your way of subduing it," said the young girl boldly. "Better for him, a disgraced man of honor, to die by his own hand, than to be bled like a calf into a feeble and helpless dissolution. I would, if I were in his place—if I had to do it by tearing off the bandages."

She made a swift, half unconscious gesture of her little hand, and stopped, her beautiful eyes sparkling, her thin pink nostrils dilated, her red lips parted, her round throat lifted in the air, and one small foot advanced before her. The men glanced hurriedly at each other, and then fixed their eyes upon her with a rapt yet frightened admiration. To their simple minds it was Anarchy and Revolution personified, beautiful, and victorious.

"Ah!" said the secretary to Padre Esteban, in Spanish, "it is true! she knows not fear! She was in the room alone with the madman; he would let none approach but her! She took a knife from him—else the medico had suffered!"

"He recognized her, you see! Ah! they know her power," said the Comandante, joining the group.

"You will help me, Father Esteban?" said the young girl, letting the fire of her dark eyes soften to a look of almost childish appeal—"you will help me to intercede for him? It is the restraint only that is killing him—that is goading him to madness! Think of him, Father—think of him: ruined and disgraced, dying to retrieve himself by any reckless action, any desperate chance of recovery, and yet locked up where he can do nothing—attempt nothing—not even lift a hand to pursue the man who has helped to bring him to this!"

"But he CAN do nothing! The ship is gone!" remonstrated the Comandante.

"Yes, the ship is gone; but the ocean is still there," said Miss Keene.

"But he has no boat."

"He will find or make one."

"And the fog conceals the channel."

"He can go where THEY have gone, or meet their fate. You do not know my countrymen, Senor Comandante," she said proudly.

"Ah, yes—pardon! They are at San Antonio—the baker, the buffoon, the two young men who dig. They are already baking and digging and joking. We have it from my officer, who has just returned."

Miss Keene bit her pretty lips.

"They think it is a mistake; they cannot believe that any intentional indignity is offered them," she said quietly. "Perhaps it is well they do not."

"They desired me to express their condolences to the Senora," said the Padre, with exasperating gentleness, "and were relieved to be assured by me of your perfect security in the hands of these gentlemen."

Miss Keene raised her clear eyes to the ecclesiastic. That accomplished diplomat of Todos Santos absolutely felt confused under the cool scrutiny of this girl's unbiased and unsophisticated intelligence.

"Then you HAVE seen them," she said, "and you know their innocence, and the utter absurdity of this surveillance?"

"I have not seen them ALL," said the priest softly. "There is still another—a Senor Hurlstone—who is missing? Is he not?"

It was not in the possibility of Eleanor Keene's truthful blood to do other than respond with a slight color to this question. She had already concealed from every one the fact of having seen the missing man in the Mission garden the evening before. It did not, however, prevent her the next moment from calmly meeting the glance of the priest as she answered gravely,—

"I believe so. But I cannot see what that has to do with the detention of the others."

"Much, perhaps. It has been said that you alone, my child, were in the confidence of this man."

"Who dared say that?" exclaimed Miss Keene in English, forgetting herself in her indignation.

"If it's anything mean—it's Mrs. Brimmer, I'll bet a cooky," said Mrs. Markham, whose linguistic deficiencies had debarred her from the previous conversation.

"You have only," continued the priest, without noticing the interruption, "to tell us what you know of this Hurlstone's plans,—of his complicity with Senor Perkins, or," he added significantly, "his opposition to them—to insure that perfect justice shall be done to all."

Relieved that the question involved no disclosure of her only secret regarding Hurlstone, Miss Keene was about to repeat the truth that she had no confidential knowledge of him, or of his absurd alleged connection with Senor Perkins, when, with an instinct of tact, she hesitated. Might she not serve them all—even Hurlstone himself—by saying nothing, and leaving the burden of proof to their idiotic accusers? Was she altogether sure that Hurlstone was entirely ignorant of Senor Perkins' plans, or might he not have refused, at the last moment, to join in the conspiracy, and so left the ship?

"I will not press you for your answer now," said the priest gently. "But you will not, I know, keep back anything that may throw a light on this sad affair, and perhaps help to reinstate your friend Mr. Hurlstone in his REAL position."

"If you ask me if I believe that Mr. Hurlstone had anything to do with this conspiracy, I should say, unhesitatingly, that I do NOT. And more, I believe that he would have jumped overboard rather than assent to so infamous an act," said the young girl boldly.

"Then you think he had no other motive for leaving the ship?" said the priest slowly.

"Decidedly not." She stopped; a curious anxious look in the Padre's persistent eyes both annoyed and frightened her. "What other motive could he have?" she said coldly.

Father Esteban's face lightened.

"I only ask because I think you would have known it. Thank you for the assurance all the same, and in return I promise you I will use my best endeavors with the Comandante for your friend the Captain Bunker. Adieu, my daughter. Adieu, Madame Markham," he said, as, taking the arm of Don Miguel, he turned with him and the doctor towards the guard-room. The secretary lingered behind for a moment.

"Fear nothing," he said, in whispered English to Miss Keene. "I, Ruy Sanchez, shall make you free of Capitano Bunker's cell," and passed on.

"Well," said Mrs. Markham, when the two women were alone again. "I don't pretend to fathom the befogged brains of Todos Santos; but as far as I can understand their grown-up child's play, they are making believe this unfortunate Mr. Hurlstone, who may be dead for all we know, is in revolt against the United States Government, which is supposed to be represented by Senor Perkins and the Excelsior—think of that!"

"But Perkins signed himself of the Quinquinambo navy!" said Miss Keene wonderingly.

"That is firmly believed by those idiots to be one of OUR

States. Remember they know nothing of what has happened anywhere in the last fifty years. I dare say they never heard of filibusters like Perkins, and they couldn't comprehend him if they had. I've given up trying to enlighten them, and I think they're grateful for it. It makes their poor dear heads ache."

"And it is turning mine! But, for Heaven's sake, tell me what part I am supposed to act in this farce!" said Miss Keene.

"You are the friend and colleague of Hurlstone, don't you see?" said Mrs. Markham. "You are two beautiful young patriots—don't blush, my dear!—endeared to each other and a common cause, and ready to die for your country in opposition to Perkins, and the faint-heartedness of such neutrals as Mrs. Brimmer, Miss Chubb, the poor Captain, and all the men whom they have packed off to San Antonio."

"Impossible!" said Miss Keene, yet with an uneasy feeling that it not only was possible, but that she herself had contributed something to the delusion. "But how do they account for my friendship with YOU—you, who are supposed to be a correspondent—an accomplice of Perkins?"

"No, no," returned Mrs. Markham, with a half serious smile, "I am not allowed that honor. I am presumed to be only the disconsolate Dulcinea of Perkins, abandoned by HIM, pitied by you, and converted to the true faith—at least, that is what I make out from the broken English of that little secretary of the Commander."

Miss Keene winced.

"That's all my fault, dear," she said, suddenly entwining her arms round Mrs. Markham, and hiding her half embarrassed smile on the shoulder of her strong-minded friend; "they

Bret Harte

suggested it to me, and I half assented, to save you. Please forgive me."

"Don't think I am blaming you, my dear Eleanor," said Mrs. Markham. "For Heaven's sake assent to the wildest and most extravagant hypothesis they can offer, if it will leave us free to arrange our own plans for getting away. I begin to think we were not a very harmonious party on the Excelsior, and most of our troubles here are owing to that. We forget we have fallen among a lot of original saints, as guileless and as unsophisticated as our first parents, who know nothing of our customs and antecedents. They have accepted us on what they believe to be our own showing. From first to last we've underrated them, forgetting they are in the majority. We can't expect to correct the ignorance of fifty years in twenty-four hours, and I, for one, sha'n't attempt it. I'd much rather trust to the character those people would conceive of me from their own consciousness than to one Mrs. Brimmer or Mr. Winslow would give of me. From this moment I've taken a firm resolve to leave my reputation and the reputation of my friends entirely in their hands. If you are wise you will do the same. They are inclined to worship you—don't hinder them. My belief is, if we only take things quietly, we might find worse places to be stranded on than Todos Santos. If Mrs. Brimmer and those men of ours, who, I dare say, have acted as silly as the Mexicans themselves, will only be quiet, we can have our own way here yet."

"And poor Captain Bunker?" said Miss Keene.

"It seems hard to say it, but, in my opinion, he is better under lock and key, for everybody's good, at present. He'd be a firebrand in the town if he got away. Meantime, let us go to our room. It is about the time when everybody is taking a siesta, and for two hours, thank Heaven! we're certain nothing more can happen."

"I'll join you in a moment," said Miss Keene.

Her quick ear had caught the sound of voices approaching. As Mrs. Markham disappeared in the passage, the Commander and his party reappeared from the guard-room, taking leave of Padre Esteban. The secretary, as he passed Miss Keene, managed to add to his formal salutation the whispered words,—"When the Angelus rings I will await you before the grating of his prison."

Padre Esteban was too preoccupied to observe this incident. As soon as he quitted the Presidio, he hastened to the Mission with a disquieting fear that his strange guest might have vanished. But, crossing the silent refectory, and opening the door of the little apartment, he was relieved to find him stretched on the pallet in a profound slumber. The peacefulness of the venerable walls had laid a gentle finger on his weary eyelids.

The Padre glanced round the little cell, and back again at the handsome suffering face that seemed to have found surcease and rest in the narrow walls, with a stirring of regret. But the next moment he awakened the sleeper, and in the briefest, almost frigid, sentences, related the events of the morning.

The young man rose to his feet with a bitter laugh.

"You see," he said, "God is against me! And yet a few hours ago I dared to think that He had guided me to a haven of rest and forgetfulness!

"Have you told the truth to him and to me?" said the priest sternly, "or have you—a mere political refugee—taken advantage of an old man's weakness to forge a foolish lie of sentimental passion?"

Bret Harte

"What do you mean?" said Hurlstone, turning upon him almost fiercely.

The priest rose, and drawing a folded paper from his bosom, opened it before the eyes of his indignant guest.

"Remember what you told me last night in the sacred confidences of yonder holy church, and hear what you really are from the lips of the Council of Todos Santos."

Smoothing out the paper, he read slowly as follows:—

"Whereas, it being presented to an Emergency Council, held at the Presidio of Todos Santos, that the foreign barque Excelsior had mutinied, discharged her captain and passengers, and escaped from the waters of the bay, it was, on examination, found and decreed that the said barque was a vessel primarily owned by a foreign Power, then and there confessed and admitted to be at war with Mexico and equipped to invade one of her northern provinces. But that the God of Liberty and Justice awakening in the breasts of certain patriots—to wit, the heroic Senor Diego Hurlstone and the invincible Dona Leonor—the courage and discretion to resist the tyranny and injustice of their oppressors, caused them to mutiny and abandon the vessel rather than become accomplices, in the company of certain neutral and non-combatant traders and artisans, severally known as Brace, Banks, Winslow, and Crosby; and certain aristocrats, known as Senoras Brimmer and Chubb. In consideration thereof, it is decreed by the Council of Todos Santos that asylum, refuge, hospitality, protection, amity, and alliance be offered and extended to the patriots, Senor Diego Hurlstone, Dona Leonor, and a certain Duenna Susana Markham, particularly attached to Dona Leonor's person; and that war, reprisal, banishment, and death be declared against Senor Perkins, his unknown aiders and abettors. And that for the purposes of probation, and in the interests of clemency, provisional parole shall be extended to the alleged neutrals—Brace, Banks, Crosby, and Winslow—within the limits and boundaries of the lazaretto of San Antonio, until their neutrality shall be established, and pending the further pleasure of the Council. And it is further decreed and declared that one Capitano Bunker, formerly of the Excelsior, but now a maniac and lunatic—being irresponsible and visited of God, shall be exempted from the ordinances of this decree until his reason shall be restored; and during that interval subjected to the ordinary remedial and beneficent restraint of civilization and humanity. By order of the Council,—

"The signatures and rubrics of—

"DON MIGUEL BRIONES,

Comandante.

"PADRE ESTEBAN,

of the Order of San Francisco d'Assisis.

"DON RAMON RAMIREZ,

Alcalde of the Pueblo of Todos Santos."

CHAPTER XI

THE CAPTAIN FOLLOWS HIS SHIP

When Padre Esteban had finished reading the document he laid it down and fixed his eyes on the young man. Hurlstone met his look with a glance of impatient disdain.

"What have you to say to this?" asked the ecclesiastic, a little impressed by his manner.

"That as far as it concerns myself it is a farrago of absurdity. If I were the person described there, why should I have sought you with what you call a lie of 'sentimental passion,' when I could have claimed protection openly with my SISTER PATRIOT," he added, with a bitter laugh.

"Because you did not know THEN the sympathy of the people nor the decision of the Council," said the priest.

"But I know it NOW, and I refuse to accept it."

"You refuse—to—to accept it?" echoed the priest.

"I do." He walked towards the door. "Before I go, let me thank you for the few hours' rest and security that you have given to one who may be a cursed man, yet is no impostor.

But I do not blame you for doubting one who talks like a desperate man, yet lacks the courage of desperation. Good-by!"

"Where are you going?"

"What matters? There is a safer protection and security to be found than even that offered by the Council of Todos Santos."

His eyes were averted, but not before the priest had seen them glaze again with the same gloomy absorption that had horrified him in the church the evening before. Father Esteban stepped forward and placed his soft hand on Hurlstone's shoulder.

"Look at me. Don't turn your face aside, but hear me; for I believe your story."

Without raising his eyes, the young man lifted Father Esteban's hand from his shoulder, pressed it lightly, and put it quietly aside.

"I thank you," he said, "for keeping at least that unstained memory of me. But it matters little now. Good-by!"

He had his hand upon the door, but the priest again withheld him.

"When I tell you I believe your story, it is only to tell you more. I believe that God has directed your wayward, wandering feet here to His house, that you may lay down the burden of your weak and suffering manhood before His altar, and become once more a child of His. I stand here to offer you, not a refuge of a day or a night, but for all time; not a hiding-place from man or woman, but from yourself, my son—yourself, your weak and mortal self, more fatal to you than all. I stand here to open for you not only the door of this humble cell, but that of His yonder blessed mansion. You shall share my life with me; you shall be one of my disciples; you shall help me strive for other souls as I have striven for yours; the protection of the Church, which is all-powerful, shall be around you if you wish to be known; you shall hide yourself in its mysteries if you wish to be forgotten. You shall be my child, my companion, my friend; all that my age can give you shall be yours while I live, and it shall be your place one day to take up my unfinished work when it falls from these palsied hands forever."

"You are mistaken," said the young man coldly. "I came to you for human aid, and thank you for what you have granted me: I have not been presumptuous enough to ask more, nor to believe myself a fitting subject for conversion. I am weak, but not weak enough to take advantage of the mistaken kindness of either the temporal Council of Todos Santos or its spiritual head." He opened the door leading into the garden. "Forget and forgive me, Father Esteban, and let me say farewell."

"Stop!" said the ecclesiastic, raising himself to his full height and stepping before Hurlstone. "Then if you will not hear me in the name of your Father who lives, in the name of your father who is dead I command you to stay! I stand here to-day in the place of that man I never knew—to hold back his son from madness and crime. Think of me as of him whom you loved, and grant to an old man who might have had a son as old as you the right of throwing a father's protecting arm around you."

There was a moment's silence.

"What do you want me to do?" said Hurlstone, suddenly

lifting his now moist and glistening eyes upon the old man.

"Give me your word of honor that for twenty-four hours you will remain as you are—pledging yourself to nothing—only promising to commit no act, take no step, without consulting me. You will not be sought here, nor yet need you keep yourself a prisoner in these gloomy walls—except that, by exposing yourself to the people now, you might be compromised to some course that you are not ready to take."

"I promise," said Hurlstone.

He turned and held out both his hands; but Father Esteban anticipated him with a paternal gesture of uplifted and opened arms, and for an instant the young man's forehead was bowed on the priest's shoulder.

Father Esteban gently raised the young man's head.

"You will take a pasear in the garden until the Angelus rings, my son, while the air is sweet and wholesome, and think this over. Remember that you may accept the hospitality of the Council without sin of deception. You were not in sympathy with either the captors of the Excelsior or their defeated party; for you would have flown from both. You, of all your party now in Todos Santos, are most in sympathy with us. You have no cause to love your own people; you have abandoned them for us. Go, my son; and meditate upon my words. I will fetch you from yonder slope in time for the evening refection."

Hurlstone bowed his head and turned his irresolute feet towards the upper extremity of the garden, indicated by the priest, which seemed to offer more seclusion and security than the avenue of pear-trees. He was dazed and benumbed. The old dogged impulses of self-destruction—revived by the priest's reproaches, but checked by the vision of his dead and forgotten father, which the priest's words had called up— gave way, in turn, to his former despair. With it came a craving for peace and rest so insidious that in some vague fear of yielding to it he quickened his pace, as if to increase his distance from the church and its apostle. He was almost out of breath when he reached the summit, and turned to look back upon the Mission buildings and the straggling street of the pueblo, which now for the first time he saw skirted the wall of the garden in its descent towards the sea. He had not known the full extent of Todos Santos before; when he swam ashore he had landed under a crumbling outwork of the fort; he gazed now with curious interest over the hamlet that might have been his home. He looked over the red-tiled roofs, and further on to the shining bay, shut in by the impenetrable rampart of fog. He might have found rest and oblivion here but for the intrusion of those fellow-passengers to share his exile and make it intolerable. How he hated and loathed them all! Yet the next moment he found himself scrutinizing the street and plaza below him for a glimpse of his countrywomen, whom he knew were still in the town or vainly endeavoring to locate their habitation among the red-tiled roofs. And that frank, clear-eyed girl— Miss Keene!—she who had seemed to vaguely pity him— she was somewhere here too—selected by the irony of fate to be his confederate! He could not help thinking of her beauty and kindness now, with a vague curiosity that was half an uneasiness. It had not struck him before, but if he were to accept the ridiculous attitude forced upon him by Todos Santos, its absurdity, as well as its responsibility, would become less odious by sharing it with another. Perhaps it might be to HER advantage—and if so, would he be justified in exposing its absurdity? He would have to see her first—and if he did, how would he explain his real position? A returning wave of bitterness threw him back into his old despair.

The twilight had slowly gathered over the view as he gazed—or, rather a luminous concentration above the pueblo and bay had left the outer circle of fog denser and darker. Emboldened by the apparent desertion of the Embarcadero, he began to retrace his steps down the slope, keeping close to the wall so as to avoid passing before the church again, or a closer contact with the gardener among the vines. In this way he reached the path he had skirted the night before, and stopped almost under the shadow of the Alcalde's house. It was here he had rested and hidden,—here he had tasted the first sweets of isolation and oblivion in the dreamy garden,—here he had looked forward to peace with the passing of the ship,—and now? The sound of voices and laughter suddenly grated upon his ear. He had heard those voices before. Their distinctness startled him until he became aware that he was standing before a broken, half-rotting door that permitted a glimpse of the courtyard of the neighboring house. He glided quickly past it without pausing, but in that glimpse beheld Mrs. Brimmer and Miss Chubb half reclining in the corridor—in the attitude he had often seen them on the deck of the ship—talking and laughing with a group of Mexican gallants. A feeling of inconceivable loathing and aversion took possession of him. Was it to THIS he was returning after his despairing search for oblivion? Their empty, idle laughter seemed to ring mockingly in his ears as he hurried on, scarce knowing whither, until he paused before the broken cactus hedge and crumbling wall that faced the Embarcadero. A glance over the hedge showed him that the strip of beach was deserted. He looked up the narrow street; it was empty. A few rapid strides across it gained him the shadow of the sea-wall of the Presidio, unchecked and unhindered. The ebbing tide had left a foot or two of narrow shingle between the sea and the wall. He crept along this until, a hundred yards distant, the sea-wall reentered inland around a bastion at the entrance of a moat half filled at high tide by the waters of the bay, but now a ditch of shallow

Bret Harte

pools, sand, and debris. He leaned against the bastion, and looked over the softly darkening water.

How quiet it looked, and, under that vaporous veil, how profound and inscrutable! How easy to slip into its all-embracing arms, and sink into its yielding bosom, leaving behind no stain, trace, or record! A surer oblivion than the Church, which could not absolve memory, grant forget-fulness, nor even hide the ghastly footprints of its occupants. Here was obliteration. But was he sure of that? He thought of the body of the murdered Peruvian, laid out at the feet of the Council by this same fickle and uncertain sea; he thought of his own distorted face subjected to the cold curiosity of these aliens or the contemptuous pity of his countrymen. But that could be avoided. It was easy for him—a good swimmer—to reach a point far enough out in the channel for the ebbing tides to carry him past that barrier of fog into the open and obliterating ocean. And then, at least, it might seem as if he had attempted to ESCAPE—indeed, if he cared, he might be able to keep afloat until he was picked up by some passing vessel, bound to a distant land! The self-delusion pleased him, and seemed to add the clinching argument to his resolution. It was not suicide; it was escape—certainly no more than escape—he intended! And this miserable sophism of self-apology, the last flashes of expiring conscience, helped to light up his pale, determined face with satisfaction. He began coolly to divest himself of his coat.

What was that?—the sound of some dislodged stones splashing in one of the pools further up! He glanced hurrie-dly round the wall of the bastion. A figure crouching against the side of the ditch, as if concealing itself from observation on the glacis above, was slowly approaching the sea. Suddenly, when within a hundred yards of Hurlstone, it turned, crossed the ditch, rapidly mounted its crumbling sides, and disappeared over the crest. But in that hurried glimpse he had recognized Captain Bunker!

The sudden and mysterious apparition of this man produced on Hurlstone an effect that the most violent opposition could not have created. Without a thought of the terrible purpose it had interrupted, and obeying some stronger instinct that had seized him, he dashed down into the ditch and up to the crest again after Captain Bunker. But he had completely disappeared. A little lagoon, making in from the bay, on which a small fishing-boat was riding, and a solitary fisherman mending his nets on the muddy shore a few feet from it, were all that was to be seen.

He was turning back, when he saw the object of his search creeping from some reeds, on all fours, with a stealthy, panther-like movement towards the unconscious fisherman. Before Hurlstone could utter a cry, Bunker had sprung upon the unfortunate man, thrown him to the earth, rapidly rolled him over and over, enwrapping him hand and foot in his own net, and involving him hopelessly in its meshes. Tossing the helpless victim—who was apparently too stupefied to call out—to one side, he was rushing towards the boat when, with a single bound, Hurlstone reached his side and laid his hand upon his shoulder.

"Captain Bunker, for God's sake! what are you doing?"

Captain Bunker turned slowly and without apparent concern towards his captor. Hurlstone fell back before the vacant, lack-lustre eyes that were fixed upon him.

"Captain Bunker's my name," said the madman, in a whisper. "Lemuel Bunker, of Nantucket! Hush! don't waken him," pointing to the prostrate fisherman; "I've put him to sleep. I'm Captain Bunker—old drunken Bunker—who stole one ship from her owners, and disgraced himself, and now is going to steal another—ha, ha! Let me go."

"Captain Bunker," said Hurlstone, recovering himself in time to prevent the maniac from dashing into the water. "Look at me. Don't you know me?"

"Yes, yes; you're one of old Bunker's dogs kicked overboard by Perkins. I'm one of Perkins' dogs gone mad, and locked up by Perkins! Ha, ha! But I got out! Hush! SHE let me out. SHE thought I was going to see the boys at San Antonio. But I'm going off to see the old barque out there in the fog. I'm going to chuck Perkins overboard and the two mates. Let me go."

He struggled violently. Hurlstone, fearful of quitting his hold to release the fisherman, whom Captain Bunker no longer noticed, and not daring to increase the Captain's fury by openly calling to him, beckoned the pinioned man to make an effort. But, paralyzed by fear, the wretched captive remained immovable, staring at the struggling men. With the strength of desperation Hurlstone at last forced the Captain down upon his knees.

"Listen, Captain! We'll go together—you understand. I'll help you—but we must get a larger boat first—you know."

"But they won't give it," said Captain Bunker mysteriously. "Didn't you hear the Council—the owners—the underwriters say: 'He lost his ship, he's ruined and disgraced, for rum, all for rum!' And we want rum, you know, and it's all over there, in the Excelsior's locker!"

"Yes, yes," said Hurlstone soothingly; "but there's more in the bigger boat. Come with me. We'll let the man loose, and we'll make him show us his bigger boat."

It was an unfortunate suggestion; for the Captain, who had listened with an insane chuckle, and allowed himself to be taken lightly by the hand, again caught sight of the prostrate fisherman. A yell broke from him—his former frenzy returned. With a cry of "Treachery! all hands on deck!" he threw off Hurlstone and rushed into the water.

"Help!" cried the young man, springing after him, "It is madness. He will kill himself!"

The water was shallow, they were both wading, they both reached the boat at the same time; but the Captain had scrambled into the stern-sheets, and cast loose the painter, as Hurlstone once more threw his arms about him.

"Hear me, Captain. I'll go with you. Listen! I know the way through the fog. You understand: I'll pilot you!" He was desperate, but no longer from despair of himself, but of another; he was reckless, but only to save a madman from the fate that but a moment before he had chosen for himself.

Captain Bunker seemed to soften. "Get in for'ard," he said, in a lower voice. Hurlstone released his grasp, but still clinging to the boat, which had now drifted into deeper water, made his way to the bow. He was climbing over the thwarts when a horrified cry from the fisherman ashore and a jarring laugh in his ear caused him to look up. But not in time to save himself! The treacherous maniac had suddenly launched a blow from an oar at the unsuspecting man as he was rising to his knees. It missed his head, but fell upon his arm and shoulder, precipitating him violently into the sea.

Stunned by the shock, he sank at first like lead to the bottom. When he rose again, with his returning conscious-ness, he could see that Captain Bunker had already hoisted sail, and, with the assistance of his oars, was rapidly increasing his distance from the shore. With his returning desperation he turned to strike out after him, but groaned as his one arm sank powerless to his side. A few strokes showed him the madness of the attempt; a few more convinced him that he himself could barely return to the shore. A sudden torpor had taken possession of him—he was sinking!

With this thought, a struggle for life began; and this man who had just now sought death so eagerly—with no feeling of inconsistency, with no physical fear of dissolution, with only a vague, blind, dogged determination to live for some unknown purpose—a determination as vague and dogged as his former ideas of self-destruction—summoned all his energies to reach the shore. He struck out wildly, desperately; once or twice he thought he felt his feet touch the bottom, only to find himself powerlessly dragged back towards the sea. With a final superhuman effort he gained at last a foothold on the muddy strand, and, half scrambling, half crawling, sank exhaustedly beside the fisherman's net. But the fisherman was gone! He attempted again to rise to his feet, but a strange dizziness attacked him. The darkening landscape, with its contracting wall of fog; the gloomy flat; the still, pale sea, as yet unruffled by the faint land breeze that was slowly wafting the escaping boat into the shadowy offing—all swam round him! Through the roaring in his ears he thought he heard drumbeats, and the fanfare of a trumpet, and voices. The next moment he had lost all consciousness.

When he came to, he was lying in the guard-room of the Presidio. Among the group of people who surrounded him he recognized the gaunt features of the Commander, the sympathetic eyes of Father Esteban, and the fisherman who had disappeared. When he rose on his elbow, and attempted to lift himself feebly, the fisherman, with a cry of gratitude, threw himself on his knees, and kissed his helpless hand.

"He lives, he lives! your Excellencies! Saints be praised, he lives! The hero—the brave Americano—the noble caballero who delivered me from the madman."

"Who are you? and whence come you?" demanded the Commander of Hurlstone, with grave austerity.

Hurlstone hesitated; the priest leaned forward with a half anxious, half warning gesture. There was a sudden rustle in the passage; the crowd gave way as Miss Keene, followed by Mrs. Markham, entered. The young girl's eyes caught those of the prostrate man. With an impulsive cry she ran towards him.

"Mr. Hurlstone!"

"Hurlstone," echoed the group, pressing nearer the astonished man.

The Comandante lifted his hand gravely with a gesture of silence, and then slowly removed his plumed hat. Every head was instantly uncovered.

"Long live our brave and noble ally, Don Diego! Long live the beautiful Dona Leonor!"

A faint shade of sadness passed over the priest's face. He glanced from Hurlstone to Miss Keene.

"Then you have consented?" he whispered.

Hurlstone cast a rapid glance at Eleanor Keene.

"I consent!"

PART II

FREED

CHAPTER I

THE MOURNERS AT SAN FRANCISCO

The telegraph operator at the Golden Gate of San Francisco had long since given up hope of the Excelsior. During the months of September and October, 1854, stimulated by the promised reward, and often by the actual presence of her owners, he had shown zeal and hope in his scrutiny of the incoming ships. The gaunt arms of the semaphore at Fort Point, turned against the sunset sky, had regularly recorded the smallest vessel of the white-winged fleet which sought the portal of the bay during that eventful year of immigration; but the Excelsior was not amongst them. At the close of the year 1854 she was a tradition; by the end of January, 1855, she was forgotten. Had she been engulfed in her own element she could not have been more completely swallowed up than in the changes of that shore she never reached. Whatever interest or hope was still kept alive in solitary breasts the world never knew. By the significant irony of Fate, even the old-time semaphore that should have signaled her was abandoned and forgotten.

The mention of her name—albeit in a quiet, unconcerned voice—in the dress-circle of a San Francisco theatre, during the performance of a popular female star, was therefore so peculiar that it could only have come from the lips of some one personally interested in the lost vessel. Yet the speaker was a youngish, feminine-looking man of about thirty, notable for his beardlessness, in the crowded circle of bearded and moustachioed Californians, and had been one of the most absorbed of the enthusiastic audience. A weak smile of vacillating satisfaction and uneasiness played on his face during the plaudits of his fellow-admirers, as if he were alternately gratified and annoyed. It might have passed for a discriminating and truthful criticism of the performance, which was a classical burlesque, wherein the star displayed an unconventional frankness of shapely limbs and unrestrained gestures and glances; but he applauded the more dubious parts equally with the audience. He was evidently familiar with the performance, for a look of eager expectation greeted most of the "business." Either he had not come for the entire evening, or he did not wish to appear as if he had, as he sat on one of the back benches near the passage, and frequently changed his place. He was well, even foppishly, dressed for the period, and appeared to be familiarly known to the loungers in the passage as a man of some social popularity.

He had just been recognized by a man of apparently equal importance and distinction, who had quietly and unconsciously taken a seat by his side, and the recognition appeared equally unexpected and awkward. The new-comer was the older and more decorous-looking, with an added formality of manner and self-assertion that did not, however, conceal a certain habitual shrewdness of eye and lip. He wore a full beard, but the absence of a moustache left the upper half of his handsome and rather satirical mouth uncovered. His dress was less pronounced than his companion's, but of a type of older and more established gentility.

"I was a little late coming from the office to-night," said the younger man, with an embarrassed laugh, "and I thought I'd drop in here on my way home. Pretty rough outside, ain't it?"

"Yes, it's raining and blowing; so I thought I wouldn't go up to the plaza for a cab, but wait here for the first one that dropped a fare at the door, and take it on to the hotel."

"Hold on, and I'll go with you," said the young man carelessly. "I say, Brimmer," he added, after a pause, with a sudden assumption of larger gayety, "there's nothing mean about Belle Montgomery, eh? She's a whole team and the little dog under the wagon, ain't she? Deuced pretty woman! —no make-up there, eh?"

"She certainly is a fine woman," said Brimmer gravely, borrowing his companion's lorgnette. "By the way, Markham, do you usually keep an opera-glass in your office in case of an emergency like this?"

"I reckon it was forgotten in my overcoat pocket," said Markham, with an embarrassed smile.

"Left over from the last time," said Brimmer, rising from his seat. "Well, I'm going now—I suppose I'll have to try the plaza."

"Hold on a moment. She's coming on now—there she is!" He stopped, his anxious eyes fixed upon the stage. Brimmer turned at the same moment in no less interested absorption. A quick hush ran through the theatre; the men bent eagerly forward as the Queen of Olympus swept down to the footlights, and, with a ravishing smile, seemed to envelop the whole theatre in a gracious caress.

"You know, 'pon my word, Brimmer, she's a very superior woman," gasped Markham excitedly, when the goddess had temporarily withdrawn. "These fellows here," he said, indicating the audience contemptuously, "don't know her,—think she's all that sort of thing, you know,—and come here just to LOOK at her. But she's very accomplished—in fact, a kind of literary woman. Writes devilish good poetry—only took up the stage on account of domestic trouble: drunken husband that beat her—regular affecting story, you know. These sap-headed fools don't, of course, know THAT. No, sir; she's a remarkable woman! I say, Brimmer, look here! I"—he hesitated, and then went on more boldly, as if he had formed a sudden resolution. "What have you got to do to-night?"

Brimmer, who had been lost in abstraction, started slightly, and said,—

"I—oh! I've got an appointment with Keene. You know he's off by the steamer—day after to-morrow?"

"What! He's not going off on that wild-goose chase, after all? Why, the man's got Excelsior on the brain!" He stopped as he looked at Brimmer's cold face, and suddenly colored. "I mean his plan—his idea's all nonsense—you know that!"

"I certainly don't agree with him," began Brimmer gravely; "but"—

"The idea," interrupted Markham, encouraged by Brimmer's beginning, "of his knocking around the Gulf of California, and getting up an expedition to go inland, just because a mail-steamer saw a barque like the Excelsior off Mazatlan last August. As if the Excelsior wouldn't have gone into Mazatlan if it had been her! I tell you what it is, Brimmer: it's mighty rough on you and me, and it ain't the square thing at all—after all we've done, and the money we've spent, and the nights we've sat up over the Excelsior—to have this young fellow Keene always putting up the bluff of his lost sister on us! His lost sister, indeed! as if WE hadn't any feelings."

The two men looked at each other, and each felt it incumbent to look down and sigh deeply—not hypo-critically, but per-functorily, as over a past grief, although anger had been the dominant expression of the speaker.

"I was about to remark," said Brimmer practically, "that the insurance on the Excelsior having been paid, her loss is a matter of commercial record; and that, in a business point of view, this plan of Keene's ain't worth looking at. As a private matter of our own feelings—purely domestic—there's no question but that we must sympathize with him, although he refuses to let us join in the expenses."

"Oh, as to that," said Markham hurriedly, "I told him to draw on me for a thousand dollars last time I saw him. No, sir; it ain't that. What gets me is this darned nagging and simpering around, and opening old sores, and putting on sentimental style, and doing the bereaved business generally. I reckon he'd be even horrified to see you and me here—though it was just a chance with both of us."

"I think not," said Brimmer dryly. "He knows Miss Montgomery already. They're going by the same steamer."

Markham looked up quickly.

"Impossible! She's going by the other line to Panama; that is"—he hesitated—"I heard it from the agent."

"She's changed her mind, so Keene says," returned Brimmer. "She's going by way of Nicaragua. He stops at San Juan to reconnoitre the coast up to Mazatlan. Good-night. It's no use waiting here for a cab any longer, I'm off."

"Hold on!" said Markham, struggling out of a sudden uneasy reflection. "I say, Brimmer," he resumed, with an enforced smile, which he tried to make playful, "your engagement with Keene won't keep you long. What do you say to having a little supper with Miss Montgomery, eh?—perfectly proper, you know—at our hotel? Just a few friends, eh?"

Brimmer's eyes and lips slightly contracted.

"I believe I am already invited," he said quietly. "Keene asked me. In fact, that's the appointment. Strange he didn't speak of you," he added dryly.

"I suppose it's some later arrangement," Markham replied, with feigned carelessness. "Do you know her?"

"Slightly."

"You didn't say so!"

"You didn't ask me," said Brimmer. "She came to consult me about South American affairs. It seems that filibuster General Leonidas, alias Perkins, whose little game we stopped by that Peruvian contract, actually landed in Quinquinambo and established a government. It seems she knows him, has a great admiration for him as a Liberator, as she calls him. I think they correspond!"

"She's a wonderful woman, by jingo, Brimmer! I'd like to hear whom she don't know," said Markham, beaming with a patronizing vanity. "There's you, and there's that filibuster, and old Governor Pico, that she's just snatched bald-headed—I mean, you know, that he recognizes her worth, don't you see? Not like this cattle you see here."

"Are you coming with me?" said Brimmer, gravely buttoning up his coat, as if encasing himself in a panoply of impervious respectability.

"I'll join you at the hotel," said Markham hurriedly. "There's a man over there in the parquet that I want to say a word to; don't wait for me."

With a slight inclination of the head Mr. Brimmer passed out into the lobby, erect, self-possessed, and impeccable. One or two of his commercial colleagues of maturer age, who were loitering leisurely by the wall, unwilling to compromise themselves by actually sitting down, took heart of grace at this correct apparition. Brimmer nodded to them coolly, as if on 'Change, and made his way out of the theatre. He had scarcely taken a few steps before a furious onset of wind and rain drove him into a doorway for shelter. At the same moment a slouching figure, with a turned-up coat-collar, slipped past him and disappeared in a passage at his right. Partly hidden by his lowered umbrella, Mr. Brimmer himself escaped notice, but he instantly recognized his late companion, Markham. As he resumed his way up the street he glanced into the passage. Halfway down, a light flashed upon the legend "Stage Entrance." Quincy Brimmer, with a faint smile, passed on to his hotel.

It was striking half-past eleven when Mr. Brimmer again issued from his room in the Oriental and passed down a long corridor. Pausing a moment before a side hall that opened from it, he cast a rapid look up and down the corridor, and then knocked hastily at a door. It was opened sharply by a lady's maid, who fell back respectfully before Mr. Brimmer's all-correct presence.

Half reclining on a sofa in the parlor of an elaborate suite of apartments was the woman whom Mr. Brimmer had a few hours before beheld on the stage of the theatre. Lifting her eyes languidly from a book that lay ostentatiously on her lap, she beckoned her visitor to approach. She was a woman still young, whose statuesque beauty had but slightly suffered from cosmetics, late hours, and the habitual indulgence of certain hysterical emotions that were not only inconsistent with the classical suggestions of her figure, but had left traces not unlike the grosser excitement of alcoholic stimulation. She looked like a tinted statue whose slight mutations through stress of time and weather had been unwisely repaired by freshness of color.

"I am such a creature of nerves," she said, raising a superb neck and extending a goddess-like arm, "that I am always perfectly exhausted after the performance. I fly, as you see, to my first love—poetry—as soon as Rosina has changed my dress. It is not generally known—but I don't mind telling YOU—that I often nerve myself for the effort of acting by reading some well-remembered passage from my favorite poets, as I stand by the wings. I quaff, as one might say, a single draught of the Pierian spring before I go on."

The exact relations between the humorous "walk round," in which Miss Montgomery usually made her first entrance, and the volume of Byron she held in her hand, did not trouble Mr. Brimmer so much as the beautiful arm with which she emphasized it. Neither did it strike him that the distinguishing indications of a poetic exaltation were at all unlike the effects of a grosser stimulant known as "Champagne cocktail" on the less sensitive organization of her colleagues. Touched by her melancholy but fascinating smile, he said gallantly that he had observed no sign of exhaustion, or want of power in her performance that evening.

"Then you were there!" she said, fixing her eyes upon him

with an expression of mournful gratitude. "You actually left your business and the calls of public duty to see the poor mountebank perform her nightly task."

"I was there with a friend of yours," answered Brimmer soberly, "who actually asked me to the supper to which Mr. Keene had already invited me, and which YOU had been kind enough to suggest to me a week ago."

"True, I had forgotten," said Miss Montgomery, with a large goddess-like indifference that was more effective with the man before her than the most elaborate explanation. "You don't mind them—do you?—for we are all friends together. My position, you know," she added sadly, "prevents my always following my own inclinations or preferences. Poor Markham, I fear the world does not do justice to his gentle, impressible nature. I sympathize with him deeply; we have both had our afflictions, we have both—lost. Good heavens!" she exclaimed, with a sudden exaggerated start of horror, "what have I done? Forgive my want of tact, dear friend; I had forgotten, wretched being that I am, that YOU, too"—

She caught his hand in both hers, and bowed her head over it as if unable to finish her sentence.

Brimmer, who had been utterly mystified and amazed at this picture of Markham's disconsolate attitude to the world, and particularly to the woman before him, was completely finished by this later tribute to his own affliction. His usually composed features, however, easily took upon themselves a graver cast as he kept, and pressed, the warm hands in his own.

"Fool that I was," continued Miss Montgomery; "in thinking of poor Markham's childlike, open grief, I forgot the deeper sorrow that the more manly heart experiences under an exterior that seems cold and impassible. Yes," she said, raising her languid eyes to Brimmer, "I ought to have felt the throb of that volcano under its mask of snow. You have taught me a lesson."

Withdrawing her hands hastily, as if the volcano had shown some signs of activity, she leaned back on the sofa again.

"You are not yet reconciled to Mr. Keene's expedition, then?" she asked languidly.

"I believe that everything has been already done," said Brimmer, somewhat stiffly; "all sources of sensible inquiry have been exhausted by me. But I envy Keene the eminently practical advantages his impractical journey gives him," he added, arresting himself, gallantly; "he goes with you."

"Truly!" said Miss Montgomery, with the melancholy abstraction of a stage soliloquy. "Beyond obeying the dictates of his brotherly affection, he gains no real advantage in learning whether his sister is alive or dead. The surety of her death would not make him freer than he is now—freer to absolutely follow the dictates of a new affection; free to make his own life again. It is a sister, not a wife, he seeks."

Mr. Brimmer's forehead slightly contracted. He leaned back a little more rigidly in his chair, and fixed a critical, half supercilious look upon her. She did not seem to notice his almost impertinent scrutiny, but sat silent, with her eyes bent on the carpet, in gloomy abstraction.

"Can you keep a secret?" she said, as if with a sudden resolution.

"Yes," said Brimmer briefly, without changing his look.

Bret Harte

"You know I am a married woman. You have heard the story of my wrongs?"

"I have heard them," said Brimmer dryly.

"Well, the husband who abused and deserted me was, I have reason to believe, a passenger on the Excelsior."

"M'Corkle!—impossible. There was no such name on the passenger list."

"M'Corkle!" repeated Miss Montgomery, with a dissonant tone in her voice and a slight flash in her eyes. "What are you thinking of? There never was a Mr. M'Corkle; it was one of my noms de plume. And where did YOU hear it?"

"I beg your pardon, I must have got it from the press notices of your book of poetry. I knew that Montgomery was only a stage name, and as it was necessary that I should have another in making the business investments you were good enough to charge me with, I used what I thought was your real name. It can be changed, or you can sign M'Corkle."

"Let it go," said Miss Montgomery, resuming her former manner. "What matters? I wish there was no such thing as business. Well," she resumed, after a pause, "my husband's name is Hurlstone."

"But there was no Hurlstone on the passenger list either," said Brimmer. "I knew them all, and their friends."

"Not in the list from the States; but if he came on board at Callao, you wouldn't have known it. I knew that he arrived there on the Osprey a few days before the Excelsior sailed."

Mr. Brimmer's eyes changed their expression.

"And you want to find him?"

"No," she said, with an actress's gesture. "I want to know the truth. I want to know if I am still tied to this man, or if I am free to follow the dictates of my own conscience,—to make my life anew,—to become—you see I am not ashamed to say it—to become the honest wife of some honest man."

"A divorce would suit your purpose equally," said Brimmer coldly. "It can be easily obtained."

"A divorce! Do you know what that means to a woman in my profession? It is a badge of shame,—a certificate of disgrace,—an advertisement to every miserable wretch who follows me with his advances that I have no longer the sanctity of girlhood, nor the protection of a wife."

There was tragic emotion in her voice, there were tears in her eyes. Mr. Brimmer, gazing at her with what he firmly thought to be absolute and incisive penetration, did not believe either. But like most practical analysts of the half-motived sex, he was only half right. The emotion and the tears were as real as anything else in the woman under criticism, notwithstanding that they were not as real as they would have been in the man who criticised. He, however, did her full justice on a point where most men and all women misjudged her: he believed that, through instinct and calculation, she had been materially faithful to her husband; that this large goddess-like physique had all the impeccability of a goddess; that the hysterical dissipation in which she indulged herself was purely mental, and usurped and preoccupied all other emotions. In this public exposition of her beauty there was no sense of shame, for there was no sense of the passion it evoked. And he was right. But there he should have stopped. Unfortunately, his masculine logic forced him to supply a reason for her coldness in the existence of some more absorbing passion. He believed her ambitious and calculating: she was neither. He believed she might have made him an admirable copartner and practical helpmeet: he was wrong.

"You know my secret now," she continued. "You know why I am anxious to know my fate. You understand now why I sympathize with"—she stopped, and made a half contemptuous gesture—"with these men Markham and Keene. THEY do not know it; perhaps they prefer to listen to their own vanity—that's the way of most men; but you do know it, and you have no excuse for misjudging me, or undeceiving them." She stopped and looked at the clock. "They will be here in five minutes; do you wish them to find you already here?"

"It is as YOU wish," stammered Brimmer, completely losing his self-possession.

"I have no wish," she said, with a sublime gesture of indifference. "If you wait you can entertain them here, while Rosina is dressing me in the next room. We sup in the larger room across the hall."

As she disappeared, Quincy Brimmer rose irresolutely from his seat and checked a half uttered exclamation. Then he turned nervously to the parlor-door. What a senseless idiot he had become! He had never for an instant conceived the idea of making this preliminary confidential visit known to the others; he had no wish to suggest the appearance of an assignation with the woman, who, rightly or wrongly, was notorious; he had nothing to gain by this voluntary assumption of a compromising attitude; yet here he was, he —Mr. Brimmer—with the appearance of being installed in her parlor, receiving her visitors, and dispensing her courtesies. Only a man recklessly in love would be guilty of such an indiscretion—even Markham's feebleness had never reached this absurdity. In the midst of his uneasiness there was a knock at the door; he opened it himself nervously and sharply. Markham's self-satisfied face drew back in alarm and embarrassment at the unexpected apparition. The sight restored Brimmer's coolness and satirical self-possession.

"I—I—didn't know you were here," stammered Markham. "I left Keene in your room."

"Then why didn't you bring him along with you?" said Brimmer maliciously. "Go and fetch him."

"Yes; but he said you were to meet him there," continued Markham, glancing around the empty room with a slight expression of relief.

"My watch was twenty minutes fast, and I had given him up," said Brimmer, with mendacious effrontery. "Miss Montgomery is dressing. You can bring him here before she returns."

Markham flew uneasily down the corridor and quickly returned with a handsome young fellow of five-and-twenty, whose frank face was beaming with excitement and youthful energy. The two elder men could not help regarding him with a mingled feeling of envy and compassion.

"Did you tell Brimmer yet?" said Keene, with animation.

"I haven't had time," hesitated Markham. "The fact is, Brimmer, I think of going with Keene on this expedition."

"Indeed!" said Brimmer superciliously.

"Yes," said Markham, coloring slightly. "You see, we've got

news. Tell him, Dick."

"The Storm Cloud got in yesterday from Valparaiso and Central American ports," said Keene, with glowing cheeks. "I boarded her, as usual, last night, for information. The mate says there is a story of a man picked up crazy, in an open fishing-boat, somewhere off the peninsula, and brought into hospital at San Juan last August. He recovered enough lately to tell his story and claim to be Captain Bunker of the Excelsior, whose crew mutinied and ran her ashore in a fog. But the boat in which he was picked up was a Mexican fishing-boat, and there was something revolu-tionary and political about the story, so that the authorities detained him. The consul has just been informed of the circumstances, and has taken the matter in hand."

"It's a queer story," said Brimmer, gazing from the one to the other, "and I will look into it also to-morrow. If it is true," he added slowly, "I will go with you."

Richard Keene extended his hand impulsively to his two elders.

"You'll excuse me for saying it, Brimmer—and you, too, Markham—but this is just what I've been looking forward to. Not but what I'd have found Nell without your assistance; but you see, boys, it DID look mighty mean in me to make more fuss about a sister than you would for your wives! But now that it's all settled"—

"We'll go to supper," said Miss Montgomery theatrically, appearing at the door. "Dick will give me his arm."

CHAPTER II

THE MOURNERS AT TODOS SANTOS

There was a breath of spring in the soft morning air of Todos Santos—a breath so subtle and odorous that it penetrated the veil of fog beyond the bay, and for a moment lingered on the deck of a passing steamer like an arresting memory. But only for an instant; the Ometepe, bound from San Francisco to San Juan del Norte, with its four seekers of the Excelsior, rolled and plunged on its way unconsciously.

Within the bay and over the restful pueblo still dwelt the golden haze of its perpetual summer; the two towers of the old Mission church seemed to dissolve softly into the mellow upper twilight, and the undulating valleys rolled their green waves up to the wooded heights of San Antonio, that still smiled down upon the arid, pallid desert. But although Nature had not changed in the months that had passed since the advent of the Excelsior, there appeared some strange mutations in the town and its inhabitants. On the beach below the Presidio was the unfinished skeleton of a small sea-going vessel on rude stocks; on the plaza rose the framed walls and roofless rafters of a wooden building; near the Embarcadero was the tall adobe chimney of some inchoate manufactory whose walls had half risen from their foundations; but all of these objects had evidently succumbed to the

Bret Harte

drowsy influence of the climate, and already had taken the appearances of later and less pictures-que ruins of the past. There were singular innovations in the costumes: one or two umbrellas, used as sunshades, were seen upon the square; a few small chip hats had taken the place of the stiff sombreros, with an occasional tall white beaver; while linen coat and nankeen trousers had, at times, usurped the short velvet jacket and loose calzas of the national costume.

At San Antonio the change was still more perceptible. Beside the yawning pit of the abandoned silver mine a strag-gling building arose, filled with rude machinery, bearing the legend, painted in glowing letters, "Excelsior Silver Mining Co., J. Crosby, Superintendent;" and in the midst of certain excavations assailing the integrity of the cliff itself was another small building, scarcely larger than a sentry-box, with the inscription, "Office: Eleanor Quicksilver Smelting Works."

Basking in that yellow morning sunlight, with his back against his office, Mr. Brace was seated on the ground, rolling a cigarette. A few feet from him Crosby, extended on his back on the ground, was lazily puffing rings of smoke into the still air. Both of these young gentlemen were dressed in exaggerated Mexican costumes; the silver buttons fringing the edge of Crosby's calza, open from the knee down to show a glimpse of the snowy under-trouser, were richer and heavier than those usually worn; while Brace, in addition to the crimson silk sash round his waist, wore a crimson handkerchief around his head, under his sombrero.

"Pepe's falling off in his tobacco," said Brace. "I think I'll have to try some other Fonda."

"How's Banks getting on with his crop?" asked Crosby. "You know he was going to revolutionize the business, and cut out

Cuba on that hillside."

"Oh, the usual luck! He couldn't get proper cultivators, and the Injins wouldn't work regular. I must try and get hold of some of the Comandante's stock; but I'm out of favor with the old man since Winslow and I wrecked that fishing-boat on the rocks off yonder. He always believed we were trying to run off, like Captain Bunker. That's why he stopped our shipbuilding, I really believe."

"All the same, we might have had it built and ready now but for our laziness. We might have worked on it nights without their knowing it, and slipped off some morning in the fog."

"And we wouldn't have got one of the women to go with us! If we are getting shiftless here—and I don't say we're not—these women have just planted themselves and have taken root. But that ain't all: there's the influence of that infernal sneak Hurlstone! He's set the Comandante against us, you know; he, and the priest, the Comandante, and Nelly Keene make up the real Council of Todos Santos. Between them they've shoved out the poor little Alcalde, who's ready to give up everything to dance attendance on Mrs. Brimmer. They run the whole concern, and they give out that it's owing to them that we're given parole of the town, and the privilege of spending our money and working these mines. Who'd have thought that sneak Hurlstone would have played his cards so well? It makes me regularly sick to hear him called 'Don Diego.'"

"Yet you're mightily tickled when that black-eyed sister of the Alcalde calls you 'Don Carlos,'" said Crosby, yawning.

"Dona Isabel," said Brace, with some empressement, "is a lady of position, and these are only her national courtesies."

"She just worships Miss Keene, and I reckon she knows by this time all about your old attentions to her friend," said Crosby, with lazy mischief.

"My attentions to Miss Keene were simply those of an ordinary acquaintance, and were never as strongly marked as yours to Mrs. Brimmer."

"Who has deserted ME as Miss Keene did YOU," rejoined Crosby.

Brace's quick color had risen again, and he would have made some sharp retort, but the jingling of spurs caught his ear. They both turned quickly, and saw Banks approaching. He was dressed as a vaquero, but with his companions' like exaggeration of detail; yet, while his spurs were enormous, and his sombrero unusually expansive, he still clung to his high shirt-collars and accurately tied check cravat.

"Well?" he said, approaching them.

"Well?" said Crosby.

"Well?" repeated Brace.

After this national salutation, the three Americans regarded each other silently.

"Knocked off cultivating to-day?" queried Crosby, lighting a fresh cigarette.

"The peons have," said Banks; "it's another saint's day. That's the fourth in two weeks. Leaves about two clear working days in each week, counting for the days off, when they're getting over the effects of the others. I tell you what, sir, the Catholic religion is not suited to a working civilization, or else the calendar ought to be overhauled and a lot of these saints put on the retired list. It's hard enough to have all the Apostles on your pay-roll, so to speak, but to have a lot of fellows run in on you as saints, and some of them not even men or women, but IDEAS, is piling up the agony! I don't wonder they call the place 'All Saints.' The only thing to do," continued Banks severely, "is to open communication with the desert, and run in some of the heathen tribes outside. I've made a proposition to the Council offering to take five hundred of them in the raw, unregenerate state, and turn 'em over after a year to the Church. If I could get Hurlstone to do some log-rolling with that Padre, his friend, I might get the bill through. But I'm always put off till to-morrow. Everything here is 'Hasta manana; hasta manana,' always. I believe when the last trump is sounded, they'll say, 'Hasta manana.' What are YOU doing?" he said, after a pause.

"Waiting for your ship," answered Crosby sarcastically.

"Well, you can laugh, gentlemen—but you won't have to wait long. According to my calculations that Mexican ship is about due now. And I ain't basing my figures on anything the Mexican Government is going to do, or any commercial speculation. I'm reckoning on the Catholic Church."

The two men languidly looked towards him. Banks continued gravely,—

"I made the proper inquiries, and I find that the stock of rosaries, scapularies, blessed candles, and other ecclesiastical goods, is running low. I find that just at the nick of time a fresh supply always comes from the Bishop of Guadalajara, with instructions from the Church. Now, gentlemen, my opinion is that the Church, and the Church only, knows the secret of the passage through the foggy channel, and keeps it to itself. I look at this commercially, as a question of demand and supply. Well, sir; the only real trader here at Todos Santos is the Church."

"Then you don't take in account the interests of Brimmer, Markham, and Keene," said Brace. "Do you suppose they're doing nothing?"

"I don't say they're not; but you're confounding interests with INSTINCTS. They haven't got the instinct to find this place, and all that they've done and are doing is blind calculation. Just look at the facts. As the filibuster who captured the Excelsior of course changed her name, her rig-out, and her flag, and even got up a false register for her, she's as good as lost, as far as the world knows, until she lands at Quinquinambo. Then supposing she's found out, and the whole story is known—although everything's against such a proposition—the news has got to go back to San Francisco before the real search will be begun. As to any clue that might come from Captain Bunker, that's still more remote. Allowing he crossed the bar and got out of the channel, he wasn't at the right time for meeting a passing steamer; and the only coasters are Mexican. If he didn't die of delirium tremens or exposure, and was really picked up in his senses by some other means, he would have been back with succor before this, if only to get our evidence to prove the loss of the vessel. No, sir sooner or later, of course, the San Francisco crowd are bound to find us here. And if it wasn't for my crops and our mine, I wouldn't be in a hurry for them; but our FIRST hold is the Church."

He stopped. Crosby was asleep. Brace arose lazily, lounged into his office, and closed his desk.

"Going to shut for the day?" said Banks, yawning.

"I reckon," said Brace dubiously; "I don't know but I'd take a little pasear into the town if I had my horse ready."

"Take mine, and I'll trapse over on foot to the Ranche with Crosby—after a spell. You'll find him under that big madrono, if he has not already wound himself up with his lariat by walking round it. Those Mexican horses can't go straight even when they graze—they must feed in a circle. He's a little fresh, so look out for him!"

"All the better. I'd like to get into town just after the siesta."

"Siesta!" echoed Banks, lying comfortably down in the shade just vacated by Brace; "that's another of their shiftless practices. Two hours out of every day—that's a day out of the week—spent in a hammock; and during business hours too! It's disgraceful, sir, simply disgraceful."

He turned over and closed his eyes, as if to reflect on its enormity.

Brace had no difficulty in finding the mare, although some trouble in mounting her. But, like his companions, having quickly adopted the habits of the country, he had become a skillful and experienced horseman, and the mustang, after a few springless jumps, which failed to unseat him, submitted to his rider. The young man galloped rapidly towards Todos Santos; but when within a few miles of the pueblo he slackened his pace. From the smiles and greetings of wayfarers—among whom were some pretty Indian girls and mestizas—it was evident that the handsome young foreigner, who had paid them the compliment of extravagantly adopting their national costume, was neither an unfamiliar nor an unpleasing spectacle. When he reached the posada at the top of the hilly street, he even carried his simulation of the local customs to the point of charging the veranda at full speed, and pulling up suddenly at the threshold, after the usual fashion of vaqueros. The impetuous apparition brought a short stout man to the door, who, welcoming him with effusive politeness, conducted him to an inner room that gave upon a green grass courtyard. Seated before a rude table, sipping aguardiente, was his countryman Winslow and two traders of the pueblo. They were evidently of the number already indicated who had adopted the American fashions. Senor Ruiz wore a linen "duster" in place of his embroidered jacket, and Senor Martinez had an American beard, or "goatee," in imitation of Mr. Banks. The air was yellow with the fumes of tobacco, through which the shrewd eyes of Winslow gleamed murkily.

"This," he said to his countryman, in fluent if not elegant Spanish, indicating the gentleman who had imitated Banks, "is a man of ideas, and a power in Todos Santos. He would control all the votes in his district if there were anything like popular suffrage here, and he understands the American policy."

Senor Martinez here hastened to inform Mr. Brace that he had long cherished a secret and enthusiastic admiration for that grand and magnanimous nation of which his friend was such a noble representative; that, indeed, he might say it was an inherited taste, for had not his grandfather once talked with the American whaling Capitano Coffino and partaken of a subtle spirit known as "er-r-rum" on his ship at Acapulco

"There's nothing mean about Martinez," said Winslow to Brace confidentially, in English. "He's up to anything, and ready from the word 'Go.' Don't you think he's a little like Banks, you know—a sort of Mexican edition. And there is Ruiz, he's a cattle dealer; he'd be a good friend of Banks if Banks wasn't so infernally self-opinionated. But Ruiz ain't a fool, either. He's picked up a little English—good American,

I mean—from me already."

Senor Ruiz here smiled affably, to show his compre-hension; and added slowly, with great gravity,—

"It is of twenty-four year I have first time the Amencano of your beautiful country known. He have buy the hides and horns of the cattle—for his ship—here."

"Here?" echoed Brace. "I thought no American ship—no ship at all—had been in here for fifty years."

Ruiz shrugged his shoulders, and cast a glance at his friend Martinez, lowered his voice and lifted his eyelashes at the same moment, and, jerking his yellow, tobacco-stained thumb over his arm, said,—

"Ah—of a verity—on the beach—two leagues away."

"Do you hear that?" said Winslow, turning complacently to Brace and rising to his feet. "Don't you see now what hogwash the Commander, Alcalde, and the priest have been cramming down our throats about this place being sealed up for fifty years. What he says is all Gospel truth. That's what I wanted you fellows to hear, and you might have heard before, only you were afraid of compromising yourselves by talking with the people. You get it into your heads—and the Comandante helped you to get it there—that Todos Santos was a sort of Sleepy Hollow, and that no one knew anything of the political changes for the last fifty years. Well, what's the fact? Ask Ruiz there, and Martinez, and they'll both tell you they know that Mexico got her independence in 1826, and that the Council keep it dark that they may perpetuate themselves. They know," he continued, lowering his voice, "that the Commander's commission from the old Viceroy isn't worth the paper it is stamped upon."

Bret Harte

"But what about the Church?" asked Brace hesitatingly, remembering Banks' theory.

"The Church—caramba! the priests were ever with the Escossas, the aristocrats, and against the Yorkenos, the men of the Republic—the people," interrupted Martinez vehemently; "they will not accept, they will not proclaim the Republic to the people. They shut their eyes, so—. They fold their hands, so—. They say, 'Sicut era principio et nunc et semper in secula seculorum!' Look you, Senor, I am not of the Church—no, caramba! I snap my fingers at the priests. Ah! what they give one is food for the bull's horns, believe me—I have read 'Tompano,' the American 'Tompano.'"

"Who's he?" asked Brace.

"He means Tom Paine! 'The Age of Reason'—you know," said Winslow, gazing with a mixture of delight and patronizing pride at the Radicals of Todos Santos. "Oh! he's no fool—is Martinez, nor Ruiz either! And while you've been flirting with Dona Isabel, and Banks has been trying to log-roll the Padre, and Crosby going in for siestas, I'VE found them out. And there are a few more—aren't there, Ruiz?"

Ruiz darted a mysterious glance at Brace, and apparently not trusting himself to speak, checked off his ten fingers dramatically in the air thrice.

"As many of a surety! God and liberty!"

"But, if this is so, why haven't they DONE something?"

Senor Martinez glanced at Senor Ruiz.

"Hasta manana!" he said slowly.

"Oh, this is a case of 'Hasta manana!'" said Brace, somewhat relieved.

"They can wait," returned Winslow hurriedly. "It's too big a thing to rush into without looking round. You know what it means? Either Todos Santos is in rebellion against the present Government of Mexico, or she is independent of any. Her present Government, in any event, don't represent either the Republic of Mexico or the people of Todos Santos— don't you see? And in that case WE'VE got as good a right here as any one."

"He speaks the truth," said Ruiz, grasping a hand of Brace and Winslow each; "in this we are—as brothers."

"God and liberty!" ejaculated Martinez, in turn seizing the other disengaged hands of the Americans, and completing the mystic circle.

"God and liberty!" echoed a thin chorus from their host and a few loungers who had entered unperceived.

Brace felt uneasy. He was not wanting in the courage or daring of youth, but it struck him that his attitude was by no means consistent with his attentions to Dona Isabel. He managed to get Winslow aside.

"This is all very well as a 'free lunch' conspiracy; but you're forgetting your parole," he said, in a low voice.

"We gave our parole to the present Government. When it no longer exists, there will be no parole—don't you see?"

"Then these fellows prefer waiting"—

"Until we can get OUTSIDE help, you understand. The first

American ship that comes in here—eh?"

Brace felt relieved. After all, his position in regard to the Alcalde's sister would not be compromised; he might even be able to extend some protection over her; and it would be a magnanimous revenge if he could even offer it to Miss Keene.

"I see you don't swear anybody to secrecy," he said, with a laugh; "shall I speak to Crosby, or will you?"

"Not yet; he'll only see something to laugh at. And Banks and Martinez would quarrel at once, and go back on each other. No; my idea is to let some outsider do for Todos Santos what Perkins did for Quinquinambo. Do you take?"

His long, thin, dyspeptic face lit up with a certain small political cunning and shrewdness that struck Brace with a half-respect.

"I say, Winslow; you'd have made a first-class caucus leader in San Francisco."

Winslow smiled complacently. "There's something better to play on here than ward politics," he replied. "There's a material here that—like the mine and the soil—ain't half developed. I reckon I can show Banks something that beats lobbying and log-rolling for contracts. I've let you into this thing to show you a sample of my prospecting. Keep it to yourself if you want it to pay. Dat's me, George! Good-by! I'll be out to the office to-morrow!"

He turned back towards his brother politicians with an expression of satisfied conceit that Brace for a moment envied. The latter even lingered on the veranda, as if he would have asked Winslow another question; but, looking at his watch, he suddenly recollected himself, and, mounting his horse, cantered down towards the plaza.

The hour of siesta was not yet over, and the streets were still deserted—probably the reason why the politicians of Todos Santos had chosen that hour for their half secret meeting. At the corner of the plaza he dismounted and led his horse to the public hitching-post—gnawn and nibbled by the teeth of generations of mustangs—and turned into the narrow lane flanked by the walls of the Alcalde's garden. Halfway down he stopped before a slight breach in the upper part of the adobe barrier, and looked cautiously around. The long, shadowed vista of the lane was unobstructed by any moving figure as far as the yellow light of the empty square beyond. With a quick leap he gained the top of the wall and disappeared on the other aide.

Bret Harte

CHAPTER III

INTERNATIONAL COURTESIES

The garden over whose wall Brace had mysteriously vanished was apparently as deserted as the lane and plaza without. But its solitude was one of graceful shadow and restful loveliness. A tropical luxuriance, that had perpetuated itself year after year, until it was half suffocated in its own overgrowth and strangled with its own beauty, spread over a variegated expanse of starry flowers, shimmering leaves, and slender inextricable branches, pierced here and there by towering rigid cactus spikes or the curved plumes of palms. The repose of ages lay in its hushed groves, its drooping vines, its lifeless creepers; the dry dust of its decaying leaves and branches mingled with the living perfumes like the spiced embalmings of a forgotten past.

Nevertheless, this tranquillity, after a few moments, was singularly disturbed. There was no breeze stirring, and yet the long fronds of a large fan palm, that stood near the breach in the wall, began to move gently from right to left, like the arms of some graceful semaphore, and then as suddenly stopped. Almost at the same moment a white curtain, listlessly hanging from a canopied balcony of the Alcalde's house, began to exhibit a like rhythmical and regular agitation. Then everything was motionless again; an interval of perfect peace settled upon the garden. It was broken by the apparition of Brace under the balcony, and the black-veiled and flowered head of Dona Isabel from the curtain above.

"Crazy boy!"

"Senorita!"

"Hush! I am coming down!"

"You? But Dona Ursula!"

"There is no more Dona Ursula!"

"Well—your duenna, whoever she is!"

"There is no duenna!"

"What?"

"Hush up your tongue, idiot boy!" (this in English.)

The little black head and the rose on top of it disappeared. Brace drew himself up against the wall and waited. The time seemed interminable. Impatiently looking up and down, he at last saw Dona Isabel at a distance, quietly and unconcernedly moving among the roses, and occasionally stooping as if to pick them. In an instant he was at her side.

"Let me help you," he said.

She opened her little brownish palm,—

"Look!" In her hand were a few leaves of some herb. "It is for you."

Brace seized and kissed the hand.

"Is it some love-test?"

"It is for what you call a julep-cocktail," she replied gravely. "He will remain in a glass with aguardiente; you shall drink him with a straw. My sister has said that ever where the Americans go they expect him to arrive."

"I prefer to take him straight," said Brace, laughing, as he nibbled a limp leaf bruised by the hand of the young girl. "He's pleasanter, and, on the whole, more wildly intoxicating this way! But what about your duenna? and how comes this blessed privilege of seeing you alone?"

Dona Isabel lifted her black eyes suddenly to Brace.

"You do not comprehend, then? Is it not, then, the custom of the Americans? Is it not, then, that there is no duenna in your country?"

"There are certainly no duennas in my country. But who has changed the custom here?"

"Is it not true that in your country any married woman shall duenna the young senorita?" continued Dona Isabel, without replying; "that any caballero and senorita shall see each other in the patio, and not under a balcony?—that they may speak with the lips, and not the fan?"

"Well—yes," said Brace.

"Then my brother has arranged it as so. He have much hear the Dona Barbara Brimmer when she make talk of these things frequently, and he is informed and impressed much. He will truly have that you will come of the corridor, and not the garden, for me, and that I shall have no duenna but the Dona Barbara. This does not make you happy, you American idiot boy!"

It did not. The thought of carrying on a flirtation under the fastidious Boston eye of Mrs. Brimmer, instead of under the discreet and mercenarily averted orbs of Dona Ursula, did not commend itself pleasantly to Brace.

"Oh, yes," he returned quickly. "We will go into the corridor, in the fashion of my country"—

"Yes," said Dona Isabel dubiously.

"AFTER we have walked in the garden in the fashion of YOURS. That's only fair, isn't it?"

"Yes," said Dona Isabel gravely; "that's what the Comandante will call 'internation-al courtesy.'"

The young man slipped his arm around the young diplomatist's waist, and they walked on in decorous silence under the orange-trees.

"It seems to me," said Brace presently, "that Mrs. Brimmer has a good deal to say up your way?"

"Ah, yes; but what will you? It is my brother who has love for her."

"But," said Brace, stopping suddenly, "doesn't he know that she has a husband living?"

Dona Isabel lifted her lashes in childlike wonder.

"Always! you idiot American boy. That is why. Ah, Mother

Bret Harte

of God! my brother is discreet. He is not a maniac, like you, to come after a silly muchacha like me."

The response which Brace saw fit to make to this statement elicited a sharp tap upon the knuckles from Dona Isabel.

"Tell to me," she said suddenly, "is not that a custom of your country?"

"What? THAT?"

"No, insensate. To attend a married senora?"

"Not openly."

"Ah, that is wrong," said Dona Isabel meditatively, moving the point of her tiny slipper on the gravel. "Then it is the young girl that shall come in the corridor and the married lady on the balcony?"

"Well, yes."

"Good-by, ape!"

She ran swiftly down the avenue of palms to a small door at the back of the house, turned, blew a kiss over the edge of her fan to Brace, and disappeared. He hesitated a moment or two, then quickly rescaling the wall, dropped into the lane outside, followed it to the gateway of the casa, and entered the patio as Dona Isabel decorously advanced from a darkened passage to the corridor. Although the hour of siesta had passed, her sister, Miss Chubb, the Alcalde, and Mrs. Brimmer were still lounging here on sofas and hammocks.

It would have been difficult for a stranger at a first glance to discover the nationality of the ladies. Mrs. Brimmer and her friend Miss Chubb had entirely succumbed to the extreme dishabille of the Spanish toilet—not without a certain languid grace on the part of Mrs. Brimmer, whose easy contour lent itself to the stayless bodice; or a certain bashful, youthful naivete on the part of Miss Chubb, the rounded dazzling whiteness of whose neck and shoulders half pleased and half frightened her in her low, white, plain camisa— under the lace mantilla.

"It is SUCH a pleasure to see you again, Mr. Brace," said Mrs. Brimmer, languidly observing the young man through the sticks of her fan; "I was telling Don Ramon that I feared Dona Ursula had frightened you away. I told him that your experience of American society might have caused you to misinterpret the habitual reserve of the Castilian," she continued with the air of being already an alien of her own country, "and I should be only too happy to undertake the chaperoning of both these young ladies in their social relations with our friends. And how is dear Mr. Banks? and Mr. Crosby? whom I so seldom see now. I suppose, however, business has its superior attractions."

But Don Ramon, with impulsive gallantry, would not—nay, COULD not—for a moment tolerate a heresy so alarming. It was simply wildly impossible. For why? In the presence of Dona Barbara—it exists not in the heart of man!

"YOU cannot, of course, conceive it, Don Ramon," said Mrs. Brimmer, with an air of gentle suffering; "but I fear it is sadly true of the American gentlemen. They become too absorbed in their business. They forget their duty to our sex in their selfish devotion to affairs in which we are debarred from joining them, and yet they wonder that we prefer the society of men who are removed by birth, tradition, and position from this degrading kind of selfishness."

Bret Harte

"But that was scarcely true of your own husband. HE was not only a successful man in business, but we can see that he was equally successful in his relations to at least one of the fastidious sex," said Brace, maliciously glancing at Don Ramon.

Mrs. Brimmer received the innuendo with invulnerable simplicity.

"Mr. Brimmer is, I am happy to say, NOT a business man. He entered into certain contracts having more or less of a political complexion, and carrying with them the genius but not the material results of trade. That he is not a business man—and a successful one—my position here at the present time is a sufficient proof," she said triumphantly. "And I must also protest," she added, with a faint sigh, "against Mr. Brimmer being spoken of in the past tense by anybody. It is painfully premature and ominous!"

She drew her mantilla across her shoulders with an expression of shocked sensitiveness which completed the humiliation of Brace and the subjugation of Don Ramon. But, unlike most of her sex, she was wise in the moment of victory. She cast a glance over her fan at Brace, and turned languidly to Dona Isabel.

"Mr. Brace must surely want some refreshment after his long ride. Why don't you seize this opportunity to show him the garden and let him select for himself the herbs he requires for that dreadful American drink; Miss Chubb and your sister will remain with me to receive the Comandante's secretary and the Doctor when they come."

"She's more than my match," whispered Brace to Dona Isabel, as they left the corridor together. "I give in. I don't understand her: she frightens me."

"That is of your conscience! It is that you would understand the Dona Leonor—your dear Miss Keene—better! Ah! silence, imbecile! this Dona Barbara is even as thou art—a talking parrot. She will have that the Comandante's secretary, Manuel, shall marry Mees Chubb, and that the Doctor shall marry my sister. But she knows not that Manuel—listen so that you shall get sick at your heart and swallow your moustachio!—that Manuel loves the beautiful Leonor, and that Leonor loves not him, but Don Diego; and that my sister loathes the little Doctor. And this Dona Barbara, that makes your liver white, would be a feeder of chickens with such barley as this! Ah! come along!"

The arrival of the Doctor and the Comandante's secretary created another diversion, and the pairing off of the two couples indicated by Dona Isabel for a stroll in the garden, which was now beginning to recover from the still heat of mid-day. This left Don Ramon and Mrs. Brimmer alone in the corridor; Mrs. Brimmer's indefinite languor, generally accepted as some vague aristocratic condition of mind and body, not permitting her to join them.

There was a moment of dangerous silence; the voices of the young people were growing fainter in the distance. Mrs. Brimmer's eyes, in the shadow of her fan, were becoming faintly phosphorescent. Don Ramon's melancholy face, which had grown graver in the last few moments, approached nearer to her own.

"You are unhappy, Dona Barbara. The coming of this young cavalier, your countryman, revives your anxiety for your home. You are thinking of this husband who comes not. Is it not so?"

"I am thinking," said Mrs. Brimmer, with a sudden revulsion of solid Boston middle-class propriety, shown as much in the

Bret Harte

dry New England asperity of voice that stung even through her drawling of the Castilian speech, as in anything she said,—"I am thinking that, unless Mr. Brimmer comes soon, I and Miss Chubb shall have to abandon the hospitality of your house, Don Ramon. Without looking upon myself as a widow, or as indefinitely separated from Mr. Brimmer, the few words let fall by Mr. Brace show me what might be the feelings of my countrymen on the subject. However charming and consi-derate your hospitality has been—and I do not deny that it has been MOST grateful to ME—I feel I cannot continue to accept it in those equivocal circums-tances. I am speaking to a gentleman who, with the instincts and chivalrous obligations of his order, must sympathize with my own delicacy in coming to this conclusion, and who will not take advantage of my confession that I do it with pain."

She spoke with a dry alacrity and precision so unlike her usual languor and the suggestions of the costume, and even the fan she still kept shading her faintly glowing eyes, that the man before her was more troubled by her manner than her words, which he had but imperfectly understood.

"You will leave here—this house?" he stammered.

"It is necessary," she returned.

"But you shall listen to me first!" he said hurriedly. "Hear me, Dona Barbara—I have a secret—I will to you confess"—

"You must confess nothing," said Mrs. Brimmer, dropping her feet from the hammock, and sitting up primly, "I mean—nothing I may not hear."

The Alcalde cast a look upon her at once blank and imploring.

"Ah, but you will hear," he said, after a pause. "There is a ship coming here. In two weeks she will arrive. None know it but myself, the Comandante, and the Padre. It is a secret of the Government. She will come at night; she will depart in the morning, and no one else shall know. It has ever been that she brings no one to Todos Santos, that she takes no one from Todos Santos. That is the law. But I swear to you that she shall take you, your children, and your friend to Acapulco in secret, where you will be free. You will join your husband; you will be happy. I will remain, and I will die."

It would have been impossible for any woman but Mrs. Brimmer to have regarded the childlike earnestness and melancholy simplicity of this grown-up man without a pang. Even this superior woman experienced a sensible awkwardness as she slipped from the hammock and regained an upright position.

"Of course," she, began, "your offer is exceedingly generous; and although I should not, perhaps, take a step of this kind without the sanction of Mr. Brimmer, and am not sure that he would not regard it as rash and premature, I will talk it over with Miss Chubb, for whom I am partially responsible. Nothing," she continued, with a sudden access of feeling, "would induce me, for any selfish consideration, to take any step that would imperil the future of that child, towards whom I feel as a sister." A slight suffusion glistened under her pretty brown lashes. "If anything should happen to her, I would never forgive myself; if I should be the unfortunate means of severing any ties that SHE may have formed, I could never look her in the face again. Of course, I can well understand that our presence here must be onerous to you, and that you naturally look forward to any sacrifice—even that of the interests of your country, and the defiance of its laws—to relieve you from a position so embarrassing as yours has become. I only trust, however, that the ill effects you allude to as likely to occur to yourself after our departure may be exaggerated by your sensitive nature. It would be an obligation added to the many that we owe you, which Mr. Brimmer would naturally find he could not return—and that, I can safely say, he would not hear of for a single moment."

While speaking, she had unconsciously laid aside her fan, lifted her mantilla from her head with both hands, and, drawing it around her shoulders and under her lifted chin, had crossed it over her bosom with a certain prim, automatic gesture, as if it had been the starched kerchief of some remote Puritan ancestress. With her arms still unconsciously crossed, she stooped rigidly, picked up her fan with three fingers, as if it had been a prayer-book, and, with a slight inclination of her bared head, with its accurately parted brown hair, passed slowly out of the corridor.

Astounded, bewildered, yet conscious of some vague wound, Don Ramon remained motionless, staring after her straight, retreating figure. Unable to follow closely either the meaning of her words or the logic of her reasoning, he nevertheless comprehended the sudden change in her manner, her voice, and the frigid resurrection of a nature he had neither known nor suspected. He looked blankly at the collapsed hammock, as if he expected to find in its depths those sinuous graces, languid fascinations, and the soft, half sensuous contour cast off by this vanishing figure of propriety.

In the eight months of their enforced intimacy and platonic seclusion he had learned to love this naive, insinuating woman, whose frank simplicity seemed equal to his own, without thought of reserve, secrecy, or deceit. He had gradually been led to think of the absent husband with what he believed to be her own feelings—as of some impalpable, fleshless ancestor from whose remote presence she derived power, wealth, and importance, but to whom she owed only respect and certain obligations of honor equal to his own. He had never heard her speak of her husband with love, with sympathy, with fellowship, with regret. She had barely spoken of him at all, and then rather as an attractive factor in her own fascinations than a bar to a free indulgence in them. He was as little in her way as—his children. With what grace she had adapted herself to his—Don Ramon's—life—she who frankly confessed she had no sympathy with her husband's! With what languid enthusiasm she had taken up the customs of HIS country, while deploring the habits of her own! With what goddess-like indifference she had borne this interval of waiting! And yet this woman—who had seemed the embodiment of romance—had received the announcement of his sacrifice—the only revelation he allowed himself to make of his hopeless passion—with the frigidity of a duenna! Had he wounded her in some other unknown way? Was she mortified that he had not first declared his passion—he who had never dared to speak to her of love before? Perhaps she even doubted it! In his ignorance of the world he had, perhaps, committed some grave offense! He should not have let her go! He should have questioned, implored her—thrown himself at her feet! Was it too late yet.

He passed hurriedly into the formal little drawing-room, whose bizarre coloring was still darkened by the closed blinds and dropped awnings that had shut out the heat of day. She was not there. He passed the open door of her room; it was empty. At the end of the passage a faint light stole from a door opening into the garden that was still ajar. She must have passed out that way. He opened it, and stepped out into the garden.

The sound of voices beside a ruined fountain a hundred yards away indicated the vicinity of the party; but a single glance showed him that she was not among them. So much the better—he would find her alone. Cautiously slipping beside the wall of the house, under the shadow of a creeper, he gained the long avenue without attracting attention. She was not there. Had she effectively evaded contact with the others by leaving the garden through the little gate in the wall that entered the Mission enclosure? It was partly open, as if some one had just passed through. He followed, took a few steps, and stopped abruptly. In the shadow of one of the old pear-trees a man and woman were standing. An impulse of wild jealousy seized him; he was about to leap forward, but the next moment the measured voice of the Comandante, addressing Mrs. Markham, fell upon his ear. He drew back with a sudden flush upon his face. The Comandante of Todos Santos, in grave, earnest accents, was actually offering to Mrs. Markham the same proposal that he, Don Ramon, had made to Mrs. Brimmer but a moment ago!

"No one," said the Comandante sententiously, "will know it but myself. You will leave the ship at Acapulco; you will rejoin your husband in good time; you will be happy, my child; you will forget the old man who drags out the few years of loneliness still left to him in Todos Santos."

Forgetting himself, Don Ramon leaned breathlessly forward to hear Mrs. Markham's reply. Would she answer the Comandante as Dona Barbara had answered HIM? Her words rose distinctly in the evening air.

"You're a gentleman, Don Miguel Briones; and the least respect I can show a man of your kind is not to pretend that I don't understand the sacrifice you're making. I shall always remember it as about the biggest compliment I ever received, and the biggest risk that any man—except one—ever ran for me. But as the man who ran that bigger risk isn't here to speak for himself, and generally trusts his wife, Susan Markham, to speak for him—it's all the same as if HE

thanked you. There's my hand, Don Miguel: shake it. Well—
if you prefer it—kiss it then. There—don't be a fool—but
let's go back to Miss Keene."

Bret Harte

CHAPTER IV

A GLEAM OF SUNSHINE

While these various passions had been kindled by her compatriots in the peaceful ashes of Todos Santos, Eleanor Keene had moved among them indifferently and, at times, unconsciously. The stranding of her young life on that unknown shore had not drawn her towards her fellow-exiles, and the circumstances which afterwards separated her from daily contact with them completed the social estrangement. She found herself more in sympathy with the natives, to whom she had shown no familiarity, than with her own people, who had mixed with them more or less contemptuously. She found the naivete of Dona Isabel more amusing than the doubtful simplicity of that married ingenue Mrs. Brimmer, although she still met the young girl's advances with a certain reserve. She found herself often pained by the practical brusqueness with which Mrs. Markham put aside the Comandante's delicate attentions, and she was moved with a strange pity for his childlike trustfulness, which she knew was hopeless. As the months passed, on the few occasions that she still met the Excelsior's passengers she was surprised to find how they had faded from her memory, and to discover in them the existence of qualities that made her wonder how she could have ever been familiar with them. She reproached herself with this fickleness; she wondered if she would have felt thus if they had completed their voyage to San Francisco together; and she recalled, with a sad smile, the enthusiastic plans they had formed during the passage to perpetuate their fellowship by anniversaries and festivals. But she, at last, succumbed, and finally accepted their open alienation as preferable to the growing awkwardness of their chance encounters.

For a few weeks following the flight of Captain Bunker and her acceptance of the hospitality and protection of the Council, she became despondent. The courage that had sustained her, and the energy she had shown in the first days of their abandonment, suddenly gave way, for no apparent reason. She bitterly regretted the brother whom she scarcely remembered; she imagined his suspense and anguish on her account, and suffered for both; she felt the dumb pain of homesickness for a home she had never known. Her loneliness became intolerable. Her condition at last affected Mrs. Markham, whose own idleness had been beguiled by writing to her husband an exhaustive account of her captivity, which had finally swelled to a volume on Todos Santos, its resources, inhabitants, and customs. "Good heavens!" she said, "you must do something, child, to occupy your mind—if it is only a flirtation with that conceited Secretary." But this terrible alternative was happily not required. The Comandante had still retained as part of the old patriarchal government of the Mission the Presidio school, for the primary instruction of the children of the soldiers,— dependants of the garrison. Miss Keene, fascinated by several little pairs of beady black eyes that had looked up trustingly to hers from the playground on the glacis, offered to teach English to the Comandante's flock. The offer was submitted to the spiritual head of Todos Santos, and full permission given by Padre Esteban to the fair heretic. Singing was added to the Instruction, and in a few months the fame of the gracious Dona Leonor's pupils stirred to emulation even the boy choristers of the Mission.

Her relations with James Hurlstone during this interval were at first marked by a strange and unreasoning reserve. Whether she resented the singular coalition forced upon them by the Council and felt the awkwardness of their unintentional imposture when they met, she did not know, but she generally avoided his society. This was not difficult, as he himself had shown no desire to intrude his confidences upon her; and even in her shyness she could not help thinking that if he had treated the situation lightly or humorously—as she felt sure Mr. Brace or Mr. Crosby would have done—it would have been less awkward and unpleasant. But his gloomy reserve seemed to the high-spirited girl to color their innocent partnership with the darkness of conspiracy.

"If your conscience troubles you, Mr. Hurlstone, in regard to the wretched infatuation of those people," she had once said, "undeceive them, if you can, and I will assist you. And don't let that affair of Captain Bunker worry you either. I have already confessed to the Comandante that he escaped through my carelessness."

"You could not have done otherwise without sacrificing the poor Secretary, who must have helped you," Hurlstone returned quietly.

Miss Keene bit her lip and dropped the subject. At their next meeting Hurlstone himself resumed it.

"I hope you don't allow that absurd decree of the Council to disturb you; I imagine they're quite convinced of their folly. I know that the Padre is; and I know that he thinks you've earned a right to the gratitude of the Council in your gracious task at the Presidio school that is far beyond any fancied political service."

"I really haven't thought about it at all," said Miss Keene coolly. "I thought it was YOU who were annoyed."

"I? not at all," returned Hurlstone quickly. "I have been able to assist the Padre in arranging the ecclesiastical archives of the church, and in suggesting some improve-ment in codifying the ordinances of the last forty years. No; I believe I'm earning my living here, and I fancy they think so."

"Then it isn't THAT that troubles you?" said Miss Keene carelessly, but glancing at him under the shade of her lashes.

"No," he said coldly, turning away.

Yet unsatisfactory as these brief interviews were, they revived in Miss Keene the sympathizing curiosity and interest she had always felt for this singular man, and which had been only held in abeyance at the beginning of their exile; in fact, she found herself thinking of him more during the interval when they seldom saw each other, and apparently had few interests in common, than when they were together on the Excelsior. Gradually she slipped into three successive phases of feeling towards him, each of them marked with an equal degree of peril to her peace of mind. She began with a profound interest in the mystery of his secluded habits, his strange abstraction, and a recognition of the evident superiority of a nature capable of such deep feeling—uninfluenced by those baser distrac-tions which occupied Brace, Crosby, and Winslow. This phase passed into a settled conviction that some woman was at the root of his trouble, and responsible for it. With an instinctive distrust of her own sex, she was satisfied that it must be either a misplaced or unworthy attachment, and that the unknown woman was to blame. This second phase—which hovered between compassion and resent-ment—suddenly changed to the latter—the third phase of her feelings. Miss Keene became convinced that Mr. Hurlstone had a settled aversion to HERSELF. Why and wherefore, she did not attempt to reason, yet she was satisfied that from the first he disliked her. His studious reserve on the Excelsior, compared with the attentions of the others, ought then to have convinced her of the fact; and there was no doubt now that his present discontent could be traced to the unfortunate circumstances that brought them together. Having given herself up to that idea, she vacillated between a strong impulse to inform him that she knew his real feelings and an equally strong instinct to avoid him hereafter entirely. The result was a feeble compromise. On the ground that Mr. Hurlstone could "scarcely be expected to admire her inferior performances," she declined to invite him with Father Esteban to listen to her pupils. Father Esteban took a huge pinch of snuff, examined Miss Keene attentively, and smiled a sad smile. The next day he begged Hurlstone to take a volume of old music to Miss Keene with his compliments. Hurlstone did so, and for some reason exerted himself to be agreeable. As he made no allusion to her rudeness, she presumed he did not know of it, and speedily forgot it herself. When he suggested a return visit to the boy choir, with whom he occasionally practiced, she blushed and feared she had scarcely the time. But she came with Mrs. Markham, some consciousness, and a visible color!

And then, almost without her knowing how or why, and entirely unexpected and unheralded, came a day so strangely and unconsciously happy, so innocently sweet and joyous, that it seemed as if all the other days of her exile had only gone before to create it, and as if it—and it alone—were a sufficient reason for her being there. A day full of gentle intimations, laughing suggestions, childlike surprises and awakenings; a day delicious for the very incompleteness of its vague happiness. And this remarkable day was simply marked in Mrs. Markham's diary as follows:—"Went with E. to Indian village; met Padre and J. H. J. H. actually left shell and crawled on beach with E. E. chatty."

The day itself had been singularly quiet and gracious, even for that rare climate of balmy days and recuperating nights. At times the slight breath of the sea which usually stirred the morning air of Todos Santos was suspended, and a hush of expectation seemed to arrest land and water. When Miss Keene and Mrs. Markham left the Presidio, the tide was low, and their way lay along the beach past the Mission walls. A walk of two or three miles brought them to the Indian village—properly a suburban quarter of Todos Santos—a collection of adobe huts and rudely cultivated fields. Padre Esteban and Mr. Hurlstone were awaiting them in the palm-thatched veranda of a more pretentious cabin, that served as a school-room. "This is Don Diego's design," said the Padre, beaming with a certain paternal pride on Hurlstone, "built by himself and helped by the heathen; but look you: my gentleman is not satisfied with it, and wishes now to bring his flock to the Mission school, and have them mingle with the pure-blooded races on an equality. That is the revolutionary idea of this sans culotte reformer," continued the good Father, shaking his yellow finger with gentle archness at the young man. "Ah, we shall yet have a revolution in Todos Santos unless you ladies take him in hand. He has already brought the half-breeds over to his side, and those heathens follow him like dumb cattle anywhere. There, take him away and scold him, Dona Leonor, while I speak to the Senora Markham of the work that her good heart and skillful fingers may do for my poor muchachos."

Eleanor Keene lifted her beautiful eyes to Hurlstone with an artless tribute in their depths that brought the blood faintly into his cheek. She was not thinking of the priest's admonishing words; she was thinking of the quiet, unselfish work that this gloomy misanthrope had been doing while his companions had been engaged in lower aims and listless pleasures, and while she herself had been aimlessly fretting and diverting herself. What were her few hours of applauded instruction with the pretty Murillo-like children of the Fort compared to his silent and unrecognized labor! Yet even at this moment an uneasy doubt crossed her mind.

"I suppose Mrs. Brimmer and Miss Chubb interest themselves greatly in your—in the Padre's charities?"

The first playful smile she had seen on Hurlstone's face lightened in his eyes and lips, and was becoming.

"I am afraid my barbarians are too low and too near home for Mrs. Brimmer's missionary zeal. She and Miss Chubb patronize the Mexican school with cast-off dresses, old bonnets retrimmed, flannel petticoats, some old novels and books of poetry—of which the Padre makes an auto-da-fe—and their own patronizing presence on fete days. Providence has given them the vague impression that leprosy and contagious skin-disease are a peculiarity of the southern aborigine, and they have left me severely alone."

"I wish you would prevail upon the Padre to let ME help you," said Miss Keene, looking down.

"But you already have the Commander's chickens—which you are bringing up as swans, by the way," said Hurlstone mischievously. "You wouldn't surely abandon the nest again?"

"You are laughing at me," said Miss Keene, putting on a slight pout to hide the vague pleasure that Hurlstone's gayer manner was giving her. "But, really, I've been thinking that the Presidio children are altogether too pretty and picturesque for me, and that I enjoy them too much to do them any good. It's like playing with them, you know!"

Hurlstone laughed, but suddenly looking down upon her face he was struck with its youthfulness. She had always impressed him before—through her reserve and indepen-dence—as older, and more matured in character. He did not know how lately she was finding her lost youth as he asked her, quite abruptly, if she ever had any little brothers and sisters.

The answer to this question involved the simple story of Miss Keene's life, which she gave with naive detail. She told him of her early childhood, and the brother who was only an indistinct memory; of her school days, and her friendships up to the moment of her first step into the great world that was so strangely arrested at Todos Santos. He was touched with the almost pathetic blankness of this virgin page. Encouraged by his attention, and perhaps feeling a sympathy she had lately been longing for, she confessed to him the thousand little things which she had reserved from even Mrs. Markham during her first apathetic weeks at Todos Santos.

"I'm sure I should have been much happier if I had had any one to talk to," she added, looking up into his face with a naivete of faint reproach; "it's very different for men, you know. They can always distract themselves with something. Although," she continued hesitatingly, "I've sometimes thought YOU would have been happier if you had had somebody to tell your troubles to—I don't mean the Padre; for, good as he is, he is a foreigner, you know, and wouldn't look upon things as WE do—but some one in sympathy with you."

She stopped, alarmed at the change of expression in his face.

Bret Harte

A quick flush had crossed his cheek; for an instant he had looked suspiciously into her questioning eyes. But the next moment the idea of his quietly selecting this simple, unsophisticated girl as the confidant of his miserable marriage, and the desperation that had brought him there, struck him as being irresistibly ludicrous and he smiled. It was the first time that the habitual morbid intensity of his thoughts on that one subject had ever been disturbed by reaction; it was the first time that a clear ray of reason had pierced the gloom in which he had enwrapped it. Seeing him smile, the young girl smiled too. Then they smiled together vaguely and sympathetically, as over some unspoken confidence. But, unknown and unsuspected by himself, that smile had completed his emancipation and triumph. The next moment, when he sought with a conscientious sigh to reenter his old mood, he was half shocked to find it gone. Whatever gradual influence—the outcome of these few months of rest and repose—may have already been at work to dissipate his clouded fancy, he was only vaguely conscious that the laughing breath of the young girl had blown it away forever.

The perilous point passed, unconsciously to both of them, they fell into freer conversation, tacitly avoiding the subject of Mr. Hurlstone's past reserve only as being less interesting. Hurlstone did not return Miss Keene's confidences—not because he wished to deceive her, but that he preferred to entertain her; while she did not care to know his secret now that it no longer affected their sympathy in other things. It was a pleasant, innocent selfishness, that, however, led them along, step by step, to more uncertain and difficult ground.

In their idle, happy walk they had strayed towards the beach, and had come upon a large stone cross with its base half hidden in sand, and covered with small tenacious, sweet-scented creepers, bearing a pale lilac blossom that exhaled a mingled odor of sea and shore. Hurlstone pointed out the cross as one of the earliest outposts of the Church on the edge of the unclaimed heathen wilderness. It was hung with strings of gaudy shells and feathers, which Hurlstone explained were votive offerings in which their pagan superstitions still mingled with their new faith.

"I don't like to worry that good old Padre," he continued, with a light smile, "but I'm afraid that they prefer this cross to the chapel for certain heathenish reasons of their own. I am quite sure that they still hold some obscure rites here under the good Father's very nose, and that, in the guise of this emblem of our universal faith, they worship some deity we have no knowledge of."

"It's a shame," said Miss Keene quickly.

To her surprise, Hurlstone did not appear so shocked as she, in her belief of his religious sympathy with the Padre, had imagined.

"They're a harmless race," he said carelessly. "The place is much frequented by the children—especially the young girls; a good many of these offerings came from them."

The better to examine these quaint tributes, Miss Keene had thrown herself, with an impulsive, girlish abandonment, on the mound by the cross, and Hurlstone sat down beside her. Their eyes met in an innocent pleasure of each other's company. She thought him very handsome in the dark, half official Mexican dress that necessity alone had obliged him to assume, and much more distinguished-looking than his companions in their extravagant foppery; he thought her beauty more youthful and artless than he had imagined it to be, and with his older and graver experiences felt a certain protecting superiority that was pleasant and reassuring.

Bret Harte

Nevertheless, seated so near each other, they were very quiet. Hurlstone could not tell whether it was the sea or the flowers, but the dress of the young girl seemed to exhale some subtle perfume of her own freshness that half took away his breath. She had scraped up a handful of sand, and was allowing it to escape through her slim fingers in a slender rain on the ground. He was watching the operation with what he began to fear was fatuous imbecility.

"Miss Keene?—I beg your pardon"—

"Mr. Hurlstone?—Excuse me, you were saying"—

They had both spoken at the same moment, and smiled forgivingly at each other. Hurlstone gallantly insisted upon the precedence of her thought—the scamp had doubted the coherency of his own.

"I used to think," she began—"you won't be angry, will you?"

"Decidedly not."

"I used to think you had an idea of becoming a priest."

"Why?"

"Because—you are sure you won't be angry—because I thought you hated women!"

"Father Esteban is a priest," said Hurlstone, with a faint smile, "and you know he thinks kindly of your sex."

"Yes; but perhaps HIS life was never spoiled by some wicked woman like—like yours."

For an instant he gazed intently into her eyes.

"Who told you that?"

"No one."

She was evidently speaking the absolute truth. There was no deceit or suppression in her clear gaze; if anything, only the faintest look of wonder at his astonishment. And he—this jealously guarded secret, the curse of his whole wretched life, had been guessed by this simple girl, without comment, without reserve, without horror! And there had been no scene, no convulsion of Nature, no tragedy; he had not thrown himself into yonder sea; she had not fled from him shrinking, but was sitting there opposite to him in gentle smiling expectation, the golden light of Todos Santos around them, a bit of bright ribbon shining in her dark hair, and he, miserable, outcast, and recluse, had not even changed his position, but was looking up without tremulousness or excitement, and smiling, too.

He raised himself suddenly on his knee.

"And what if it were all true?" he demanded.

"I should be very sorry for you, and glad it were all over now," she said softly.

A faint pink flush covered her cheek the next moment, as if she had suddenly become aware of another meaning in her speech, and she turned her head hastily towards the village. To her relief she discerned that a number of Indian children had approached them from behind and had halted a few paces from the cross. Their hands were full of flowers and shells as they stood hesitatingly watching the couple.

"They are some of the school-children," said Hurlstone, in answer to her inquiring look; "but I can't understand why they come here so openly."

"Oh, don't scold them!" said Eleanor, forgetting her previous orthodox protest; "let us go away, and pretend we don't notice them."

But as she was about to rise to her feet the hesitation of the little creatures ended in a sudden advance of the whole body, and before she comprehended what they were doing they had pressed the whole of their floral tributes in her lap. The color rose again quickly to her laughing face as she looked at Hurlstone.

"Do you usually get up this pretty surprise for visitors?" she said hesitatingly.

"I assure you I have nothing to do with it," he answered, with frank amazement; "it's quite spontaneous. And look—they are even decorating ME."

It was true; they had thrown a half dozen strings of shells on Hurlstone's unresisting shoulders, and, unheeding the few words he laughingly addressed them in their own dialect, they ran off a few paces, and remained standing, as if gravely contemplating their work. Suddenly, with a little outcry of terror, they turned, fled wildly past them, and disappeared in the bushes.

Miss Keene and Hurlstone rose at the same moment, but the young girl, taking a step forward, suddenly staggered, and was obliged to clasp one of the arms of the cross to keep herself from falling. Hurlstone sprang to her side.

"Are you ill?" he asked hurriedly. "You are quite white.

What is the matter?"

A smile crossed her colorless face.

"I am certainly very giddy; everything seems to tremble."

"Perhaps it is the flowers," he said anxiously. "Their heavy perfume in this close air affects you. Throw them away, for Heaven's sake!"

But she clutched them tighter to her heart as she leaned for a moment, pale yet smiling, against the cross.

"No, no!" she said earnestly; "it was not that. But the children were frightened, and their alarm terrified me. There, it is over now."

She let him help her to her seat again as he glanced hurriedly around him. It must have been sympathy with her, for he was conscious of a slight vertigo himself. The air was very close and still. Even the pleasant murmur of the waves had ceased.

"How very low the tide is!" said Eleanor Keene, resting her elbow on her knees and her round chin upon her hand. "I wonder if that could have frightened those dear little midgets?" The tide, in fact, had left the shore quite bare and muddy for nearly a quarter of a mile to seaward.

Hurlstone arose, with grave eyes, but a voice that was unchanged.

"Suppose we inquire? Lean on my arm, and we'll go up the hill towards the Mission garden. Bring your flowers with you."

The color had quite returned to her cheek as she leant on his proffered arm. Yet perhaps she was really weaker than she knew, for he felt the soft pressure of her hand and the gentle abandonment of her figure against his own as they moved on. But for some preoccupying thought, he might have yielded more completely to the pleasure of that innocent contact and have drawn her closer towards him; yet they moved steadily on, he contenting himself from time to time with a hurried glance at the downcast fringes of the eyes beside him. Presently he stopped, his attention disturbed by what appeared to be the fluttering of a black-winged, red-crested bird, in the bushes before him. The next moment he discovered it to be the rose-covered head of Dona Isabel, who was running towards them. Eleanor withdrew her arm from Hurlstone's.

"Ah, imbecile!" said Dona Isabel, pouncing upon Eleanor Keene like an affectionate panther. "They have said you were on the seashore, and I fly for you as a bird. Tell to me quick," she whispered, hastily putting her own little brown ear against Miss Keene's mouth, "immediatamente, are you much happy?"

"Where is Mr. Brace?" said Miss Keene, trying to effect a diversion, as she laughed and struggled to get free from her tormentor.

"He, the idiot boy! Naturally, when he is for use, he comes not. But as a maniac—ever! I would that I have him no more. You will to me presently give your—brother! I have since to-day a presentimiento that him I shall love! Ah!"

She pressed her little brown fist, still tightly clutching her fan, against her low bodice, as if already transfixed with a secret and absorbing passion.

"Well, you shall have Dick then," said Miss Keene, laughing;

"but was it for THAT you were seeking me?"

"Mother of God! you know not then what has happened? You are a blind—a deaf—to but one thing all the time? Ah!" she said quickly, unfolding her fan and modestly diving her little head behind it, "I have ashamed for you, Miss Keene."

"But WHAT has happened?" said Hurlstone, interposing to relieve his companion. "We fancied something"—

"Something! he says something!—ah, that something was a temblor! An earthquake! The earth has shaken himself. Look!"

She pointed with her fan to the shore, where the sea had suddenly returned in a turbulence of foam and billows that was breaking over the base of the cross they had just quitted.

Miss Keene drew a quick sigh. Dona Isabel had ducked again modestly behind her fan, but this time dragging with her other arm Miss Keene's head down to share its discreet shadow as she whispered,—

"And—infatuated one!—you two never noticed it!"

CHAPTER V

CLOUDS AND CHANGE

The earthquake shock, although the first experienced by the Americans, had been a yearly phenomenon to the people of Todos Santos, and was so slight as to leave little impression upon either the low adobe walls of the pueblo or the indolent population. "If it's a provision of Nature for shaking up these Rip Van Winkle Latin races now and then, it's a dead failure, as far as Todos Santos is concerned," Crosby had said, with a yawn. "Brace, who's got geology on the brain ever since he struck cinnabar ore, says he isn't sure the Injins ain't right when they believe that the Pacific Ocean used to roll straight up to the Presidio, and there wasn't any channel—and that reef of rocks was upheaved in their time. But what's the use of it? it never really waked them up." "Perhaps they're waiting for another kind of earthquake," Winslow had responded sententiously.

In six weeks it had been forgotten, except by three people— Miss Keene, James Hurlstone, and Padre Esteban. Since Hurlstone had parted with Miss Keene on that memorable afternoon he had apparently lapsed into his former reserve. Without seeming to avoid her timid advances, he met her seldom, and then only in the presence of the Padre or Mrs. Markham. Although uneasy at the deprivation of his society, his present shyness did not affect her as it had done at first: she knew it was no longer indifference; she even fancied she understood it from what had been her own feelings. If he no longer raised his eyes to hers as frankly as he had that day, she felt a more delicate pleasure in the consciousness of his lowered eyelids when they met, and the instinct that told her when his melancholy glance followed her unobserved. The sex of these lovers—if we may call them so who had never exchanged a word of love—seemed to be changed. It was Miss Keene who now sought him with a respectful and frank admiration; it was Hurlstone who now tried to avoid it with a feminine dread of reciprocal display. Once she had even adverted to the episode of the cross. They were standing under the arch of the refectory door, waiting for Padre Esteban, and looking towards the sea.

"Do you think we were ever in any real danger, down there, on the shore—that day?" she said timidly.

"No; not from the sea," he replied, looking at her with a half defiant resolution.

"From what then?" she asked, with a naivete that was yet a little conscious.

"Do you remember the children giving you their offerings that day?" he asked abruptly.

"I do," she replied, with smiling eyes.

"Well, it appears that it is the custom for the betrothed couples to come to the cross to exchange their vows. They mistook us for lovers."

All the instinctive delicacy of Miss Keene's womanhood resented the rude infelicity of this speech and the flippant manner of its utterance. She did not blush, but lifted her clear eyes calmly to his.

"It was an unfortunate mistake," she said coldly, "the more so as they were your pupils. Ah! here is Father Esteban," she added, with a marked tone of relief, as she crossed over to the priest's side.

When Father Esteban returned to the refectory that evening, Hurlstone was absent. When it grew later, becoming uneasy, the good Father sought him in the garden. At the end of the avenue of pear-trees there was a break in the sea-wall, and here, with his face to the sea, Hurlstone was leaning gloomily. Father Esteban's tread was noiseless, and he had laid his soft hand on the young man's shoulder before Hurlstone was aware of his presence. He started slightly, his gloomy eyes fell before the priest's.

"My son," said the old man gravely, "this must go on no longer."

"I don't understand you," Hurlstone replied coldly.

"Do not try to deceive yourself, nor me. Above all, do not try to deceive HER. Either you are or are not in love with this countrywoman of yours. If you are not, my respect for her and my friendship for you prompts me to save you both from a foolish intimacy that may ripen into a misplaced affection; if you are already in love with her"—

"I have never spoken a word of love to her!" interrupted Hurlstone quickly. "I have even tried to avoid her since"—

"Since you found that you loved her! Ah, foolish boy! and you think that because the lips speak not, the passions of the heart are stilled! Do you think your silence in her presence is not a protestation that she, even she, child as she is, can read, with the cunning of her sex?"

"Well—if I am in love with her, what then?" said Hurlstone doggedly. "It is no crime to love a pure and simple girl. Am I not free? You yourself, in yonder church, told me"—

"Silence, Diego," said the priest sternly. "Silence, before you utter the thought that shall disgrace you to speak and me to hear!"

"Forgive me, Father Esteban," said the young man hurriedly, grasping both hands of the priest. "Forgive me—I am mad—distracted—but I swear to you I only meant"—

"Hush!" interrupted the priest more gently. "So; that will do." He stopped, drew out his snuff-box, rapped the lid, and took a pinch of snuff slowly. "We will not recur to that point. Then you have told her the story of your life?"

"No; but I will, She shall know all—everything—before I utter a word of love to her."

"Ah! bueno! muy bueno!" said the Padre, wiping his nose ostentatiously. "Ah! let me see! Then, when we have shown her that we cannot possibly marry her, we will begin to make love to her! Eh, eh! that is the American fashion. Ah, pardon!" he continued, in response to a gesture of protestation from Hurlstone; "I am wrong. It is when we have told her that we cannot marry her as a Protestant, that we will make love as a Catholic. Is that it?"

"Hear me," said Hurlstone passionately. "You have saved me from madness and, perhaps, death. Your care—your kindness—your teachings have given me life again. Don't blame me, Father Esteban, if, in casting off my old self, you have given me hopes of a new and fresher life—of"—

"A newer and fresher love, you would say," said the Padre, with a sad smile. "Be it so. You will at least do justice to the old priest, when you remember that he never pressed you to take vows that would have prevented this forever."

"I know it," said Hurlstone, taking the old man's hand. "And you will remember, too, that I was happy and contented before this came upon me. Tell me what I shall do. Be my guide—my friend, Father Esteban. Put me where I was a few months ago—before I learned to love her."

"Do you mean it, Diego?" said the old man, grasping his hand tightly, and fixing his eyes upon him.

"I do."

"Then listen to me, for it is my turn to speak. When, eight months ago, you sought the shelter of that blessed roof, it was for refuge from a woman that had cursed your life. It was given you. You would leave it now to commit an act that would bring another woman, as mad as yourself, clamoring at its doors for protection from YOU. For what you are proposing to this innocent girl is what you accepted from the older and wickeder woman. You have been cursed because a woman divided for you what was before God an indivisible right; and you, Diego, would now redivide that with another, whom you dare to say you LOVE! You would use the opportunity of her helplessness and loneliness here to convince her; you would tempt her with sympathy, for she is unhappy; with companionship, for she has no longer the world to choose from—with everything that should make her sacred from your pursuit."

"Enough," said Hurlstone hoarsely; "say no more. Only I implore you tell me what to do now to save her. I will—if you tell me to do it—leave her forever."

"Why should YOU go?" said the priest quietly. "HER absence will be sufficient."

"HER absence?" echoed Hurlstone.

"Hers alone. The conditions that brought YOU here are unchanged. You are still in need of an asylum from the world and the wife you have repudiated. Why should you abandon it? For the girl, there is no cause why she should remain—beyond yourself. She has a brother whom she loves—who wants her—who has the right to claim her at any time. She will go to him."

"But how?"

"That has been my secret, and will be my sacrifice to you, Diego, my son. I have foreseen all this; I have expected it from the day that girl sent you her woman's message, that was half a challenge, from her school—I have known it from the day you walked together on the sea-shore. I was blind before that—for I am weak in my way, too, and I had dreamed of other things. God has willed it otherwise." He paused, and returning the pressure of Hurlstone's hand, went on. "My secret and my sacrifice for you is this. For the last two hundred years the Church has had a secret and trusty messenger from the See at Guadalajara—in a ship that touches here for a few hours only every three years. Her arrival and departure is known only to myself and my brothers of the Council. By this wisdom and the provision of God, the integrity of the Holy Church and the conversion of the heathen have been maintained without interruption and interference. You know now, my son, why your comrades were placed under surveillance; why it was necessary that the people should believe in a political conspiracy among yourselves, rather than the facts as they existed, which might have bred a dangerous curiosity among them. I have given you our secret, Diego—that is but a part of my sacrifice. When that ship arrives, and she is expected daily, I will secretly place Miss Keene and her friend on board, with explanatory letters to the Archbishop, and she will be assisted to rejoin her brother. It will be against the wishes of the Council; but my will," continued the old man, with a gesture of imperiousness, "is the will of the Church, and the law that overrides all."

He had stopped, with a strange fire in his eyes. It still continued to burn as he went on rapidly,—

"You will understand the sacrifice I am making in telling you this, when you know that I could have done all that I propose without your leave or hindrance. Yes, Diego; I had but to stretch out my hand thus, and that foolish fire-brand of a heretic muchacha would have vanished from Todos Santos forever. I could have left you in your fool's paradise, and one morning you would have found her gone. I should have condoled with you, and consoled you, and you would have forgotten her as you did the other. I should not have hesitated; it is the right of the Church through all time to break through those carnal ties without heed of the suffering flesh, and I ought to have done so. This, and this alone, would have been worthy of Las Casas and Junipero Serra! But I am weak and old—I am no longer fit for His work. Far better that the ship which takes her away should bring back my successor and one more worthy Todos Santos than I."

He stopped, his eyes dimmed, he buried his face in his hands.

"You have done right, Father Esteban," said Hurlstone, gently putting his arm round the priest's shoulders, "and I swear to you your secret is as safe as if you had never revealed it to me. Perhaps," he added, with a sigh, "I should have been happier if I had not known it—if she had passed out of my life as mysteriously as she had entered it; but you will try to accept my sacrifice as some return for yours. I shall see her no more."

"But will you swear it?" said the priest eagerly. "Will you swear that you will not even seek her to say farewell; for in that moment the wretched girl may shake your resolution?"

"I shall not see her," repeated the young man slowly.

"But if she asks an interview," persisted the priest, "on the pretense of having your advice?"

"She will not," returned Hurlstone, with a half bitter recollection of their last parting. "You do not know her pride."

"Perhaps," said the priest musingly. "But I have YOUR word, Diego. And now let us return to the Mission, for there is much to prepare, and you shall assist me."

Meantime, Hurlstone was only half right in his estimate of Miss Keene's feelings, although the result was the same. The first shock to her delicacy in his abrupt speech had been succeeded by a renewal of her uneasiness concerning his past life or history. While she would, in her unselfish attachment for him, have undoubtingly accepted any explanation he might have chosen to give her, his continued reserve and avoidance of her left full scope to her imaginings. Rejecting any hypothesis of his history except that of some unfortunate love episode, she began to think that perhaps he still loved this nameless woman. Had anything occurred to renew his affection? It was impossible, in their isolated condition, that he would hear from her. But perhaps the priest might have been a confidant of his past, and had recalled the old affection in rivalry of her? Or had she herself been unfortunate through any idle word to reopen the wound? Had there been any suggestion?—she checked herself suddenly at a thought that benumbed and chilled her!—perhaps that happy hour at the cross might have reminded him of some episode with another? That was the real significance of his rude speech. With this first taste of the poison of jealousy upon her virgin lips, she seized the cup and drank it eagerly. Ah, well—he should keep his blissful recollections of the past undisturbed by her. Perhaps he might even see—though SHE had no past—that her present life might be as disturbing to him! She recalled, with a foolish pleasure, his solitary faint sneer at the devotion of the Commander's Secretary. Why shouldn't she, hereafter, encourage that devotion as well as that sneer from this complacently beloved Mr. Hurlstone? Why should he be so assured of her past? The fair and gentle reader who may be shocked at this revelation of Eleanor Keene's character will remember that she has not been recorded as an angel in these pages—but as a very human, honest, inexperienced girl, for the first time struggling with the most diplomatic, Machiavellian, and hypocritical of all the passions.

In pursuance of this new resolution, she determined to accept an invitation from Mrs. Markham to accompany her and the Commander to a reception at the Alcalde's house—the happy Secretary being of the party. Mrs. Markham, who was under promise to the Comandante not to reveal his plan for the escape of herself and Miss Keene until the arrival of the expected transport, had paid little attention to the late vagaries of her friend, and had contented herself by once saying, with a marked emphasis, that the more free they kept themselves from any entanglements with other people, the more prepared they would be for A CHANGE.

"Perhaps it's just as well not to be too free, even with those Jesuits over at the Mission. Your brother, you know, might not like it."

"THOSE JESUITS!" repeated Miss Keene indignantly. "Father Esteban, to begin with, is a Franciscan, and Mr. Hurlstone is as orthodox as you or I."

"Don't be too sure of that, my dear," returned Mrs. Markham sententiously. "Heaven only knows what disguises they assume. Why, Hurlstone and the priest are already as thick as two peas; and you can't make me believe they didn't know of each other before we came here. He was the first one ashore, you remember, before the mutiny; and where did he turn up?—at the Mission, of course! And have you forgotten that sleepwalking affair—all Jesuitical! Why, poor dear Markham used to say we were surrounded by ramifications of that society—everywhere. The very waiter at your hotel table might belong to the Order."

The hour of the siesta was just past, and the corridor and gardens of the Alcalde's house were grouped with friends and acquaintances as the party from the Presidio entered. Mrs. Brimmer, who had apparently effected a temporary compromise with her late instincts of propriety, was still doing the honors of the Alcalde's house, and had once more assumed the Mexican dishabille, even to the slight exposure of her small feet, stockingless, in white satin slippers. The presence of the Comandante and his Secretary guaranteed the two ladies of their party a reception at least faultless in form and respect, whatever may have been the secret feelings of the hostess and her friends. The Alcalde received Mrs. Markham and Miss Keene with unruffled courtesy, and conducted them to the place of honor beside him.

As Eleanor Keene, slightly flushed and beautiful in her unwonted nervous excitement, took her seat, a flutter went around the corridor, and, with the single exception of Dona Isabel, an almost imperceptible drawing together of the other ladies, in offensive alliance. Miss Keene had never abandoned her own style of dress; and that afternoon her delicate and closely-fitting white muslin, gathered in at the waist with a broad blue belt of ribbon, seemed to accentuate somewhat unflatteringly the tropical neglige of Mrs. Brimmer and Miss Chubb. Brace, who was in attendance, with Crosby, on the two Ramirez girls, could not help being uneasily conscious of this, in addition to the awkwardness of meeting Miss Keene after the transfer of his affections elsewhere. Nor was his embarrassment relieved by Crosby's confidences to him, in a half audible whisper,—

"I say, old man, after all, the regular straight-out American style lays over all their foreign flops and fandoodles. I wonder what old Brimmer would say to his wife's full-dress nightgown—eh?"

But at this moment the long-drawn, slightly stridulous utterances of Mrs. Brimmer rose through the other greetings like a lazy east wind.

"I shall never forgive the Commander for making the Presidio so attractive to you, dear Miss Keene, that you cannot really find time to see your own countrymen. Though, of course, you're not to blame for not coming to see two frights as we must look—not having been educated to be able to do up our dresses in that faultless style—and perhaps not having the entire control over an establishment like you; yet, I suppose that, even if the Alcalde did give us carte blanche of the laundry HERE, we couldn't do it, unaided even by Mrs. Markham. Yes, dear; you must let me compliment you on your skill, and the way you make things last. As for me and Miss Chubb, we've only found our things fit to be given away to the poor of the Mission. But I suppose even that charity would look as shabby to you as our clothes, in comparison with the really good missionary work you and Mr. Hurlstone—or is it Mr. Brace?—I always confound your admirers, my dear—are doing now. At least, so says that good Father Esteban."

But with the exception of the Alcalde and Miss Chubb, Mrs. Brimmer's words fell on unheeding ears, and Miss Keene did not prejudice the triumph of her own superior attractions by seeming to notice Mrs. Brimmer's innuendo. She answered briefly, and entered into lively conversation with Crosby and the Secretary, holding the hand of Dona Isabel in her own, as if to assure her that she was guiltless of any design against her former admirer. This was quite unnecessary, as the gentle Isabel, after bidding Brace, with a rap on the knuckles, to "go and play," contented herself with curling up like a kitten beside Miss Keene, and left that gentleman to wander somewhat aimlessly in the patio.

Nevertheless, Miss Keene, whose eyes and ears were nervously alert, and who had indulged a faint hope of meeting Padre Esteban and hearing news of Hurlstone, glanced from time to time towards the entrance of the patio. A singular presentiment that some outcome of this present visit would determine her relations with Hurlstone had already possessed her. Consequently she was conscious, before it had attracted the attention of the others, of some vague stirring in the plaza beyond. Suddenly the clatter of hoofs was heard before the gateway. There was a moment's pause of dismounting, a gruff order given in Spanish, and the next moment three strangers entered the patio.

They were dressed in red shirts, their white trousers tucked in high boots, and wore slouched hats. They were so travel-stained, dusty, and unshaven, that their features were barely distinguishable. One, who appeared to be the spokesman of the party, cast a perfunctory glance around the corridor, and, in fluent Spanish, began with the mechanical air of a man repeating some formula,—

"We are the bearers of a despatch to the Comandante of Todos Santos from the Governor of Mazatlan. The officer and the escort who came with us are outside the gate. We have been told that the Comandante is in this house. The case is urgent, or we would not intrude"—

He was stopped by the voice of Mrs. Markham from the corridor. "Well, I don't understand Spanish much—I may be a fool, or crazy, or perhaps both—but if that isn't James Markham's VOICE, I'll bet a cooky!"

The three strangers turned quickly toward the corridor. The next moment the youngest of their party advanced eagerly towards Miss Keene, who had arisen with a half frightened joy, and with the cry of "Why, it's Nell!" ran towards her. The third man came slowly forward as Mrs. Brimmer slipped hastily from the hammock and stood erect.

"In the name of goodness, Barbara," said Mr. Brimmer, closing upon her, in a slow, portentous whisper, "where ARE your stockings?"

CHAPTER VI

A MORE IMPORTANT ARRIVAL

The Commander was the first to recover his presence of mind. Taking the despatch from the hands of the unlooked-for husband of the woman he loved, he opened it with an immovable face and habitual precision. Then, turning with a military salute to the strangers, he bade them join him in half an hour at the Presidio; and, bowing gravely to the assembled company, stepped from the corridor. But Mrs. Markham was before him, stopped him with a gesture, and turned to her husband.

"James Markham—where's your hand?"

Markham, embarrassed but subjugated, disengaged it timidly from his wife's waist.

"Give it to that gentleman—for a gentleman he is, from the crown of his head to the soles of his boots! There! Shake his hand! You don't get such a chance every day. You can thank him again, later."

As the two men's hands parted, after this perfunctory grasp, and the Commander passed on, she turned again to her husband.

"Now, James, I am ready to hear all about it. Perhaps you'll tell me where you HAVE been?"

There was a moment of embarrassing silence. The Doctor and Secretary had discreetly withdrawn; the Alcalde, after a brief introduction to Mr. Brimmer, and an incompre-hensible glance from the wife, had retired with a colorless face. Dona Isabel had lingered last to blow a kiss across her fan to Eleanor Keene that half mischievously included her brother. The Americans were alone.

Thus appealed to, Mr. Markham hastily began his story. But, as he progressed, a slight incoherency was noticeable: he occasionally contradicted himself, and was obliged to be sustained, supplemented, and, at times, corrected, by Keene and Brimmer. Substantially, it appeared that they had come from San Francisco to Mazatlan, and, through the influence of Mr. Brimmer on the Mexican authorities, their party, with an escort of dragoons, had been transported across the gulf and landed on the opposite shore, where they had made a forced march across the desert to Todos Santos. Literally interpreted, however, by the nervous Markham, it would seem that they had conceived this expedition long ago, and yet had difficulties because they only thought of it the day before the steamer sailed; that they had embarked for the isthmus of Nicaragua, and yet had stopped at Mazatlan; that their information was complete in San Francisco, and only picked up at Mazatlan; that "friends"—sometimes contradictorily known as "he" and "she"—had overpowering influence with the Mexican Government, and alone had helped them, and yet that they were utterly dependent upon the efforts of Senor Perkins, who had compromised matters with the Mexican Government and everybody.

"Do you mean to say, James Markham, that you've seen Perkins, and it was he who told you we were here?"

"No—not HIM exactly."

"Let me explain," said Mr. Brimmer hastily. "It appears," he corrected his haste with practical businesslike precision, "that the filibuster Perkins, after debarking you here, and taking the Excelsior to Quinquinambo, actually established the Quinquinambo Government, and got Mexico and the other confederacies to recognize its independence. Quinquinambo behaved very handsomely, and not only allowed the Mexican Government indemnity for breaking the neutrality of Todos Santos by the seizure, but even compromised with our own Government their claim to confiscate the Excelsior for treaty violation, and paid half the value of the vessel, besides giving information to Mexico and Washington of your whereabouts. We conse-quently represent a joint commission from both countries to settle the matter and arrange for your return."

"But what I want to know is this: Is it to Senor Perkins that we ought to be thankful for seeing you here at all?" asked Mrs. Markham impatiently.

"No, no—not that, exactly," stammered Markham. "Oh, come now, Susannah"—

"No," said Richard Keene earnestly; "by Jove! some thanks ought to go to Belle Montgomery"—He checked himself in sudden consternation.

There was a chilly silence. Even Miss Keene looked anxiously at her brother, as the voice of Mrs. Brimmer for the first time broke the silence.

"May we be permitted to know who is this person to whom we owe so great an obligation?"

"Certainly," said Brimmer, "She was—as I have already intimated—a friend; possibly, you know," he added, turning lightly to his companions, as if to corroborate an impression that had just struck him, "perhaps a—a—a sweetheart of the Senor Perkins."

"And how was she so interested in us, pray?" said Mrs. Markham.

"Well, you see, she had an idea that a former husband was on board of the Excelsior."

He stopped suddenly, remembering from the astonished faces of Keene and Markham that the secret was not known to them, while they, impressed with the belief that the story was a sudden invention of Brimmer's, with difficulty preserved their composure. But the women were quick to notice their confusion, and promptly disbelieved Brimmer's explanation.

"Well, as there's no Mister Montgomery here, she's probably mistaken," said Mrs. Markham, with decision, "though it strikes ME that she's very likely had the same delusion on board of some other ship. Come along, James; perhaps after you've had a bath and some clean clothes, you may come out a little more like the man I once knew. I don't know how Mrs. Brimmer feels, but I feel more as if I required to be introduced to you—than your friend's friend, Mrs. Montgomery. At any rate, try and look and behave a little more decent when you go over to the Presidio."

With these words she dragged him away. Mr. Brimmer, after a futile attempt to appear at his ease, promptly effected the usual marital diversion of carrying the war into the enemy's camp.

"For heaven's sake, Barbara," he said, with ostentatious indignation, "go and dress yourself properly. Had you neither money nor credit to purchase clothes? I declare I didn't know you at first; and when I did, I was shocked; before Mrs. Markham, too!"

"Mrs. Markham, I fear, has quite enough to occupy her now," said Mrs. Brimmer shortly, as she turned away, with hysterically moist eyes, leaving her husband to follow her.

Oblivious of this comedy, Richard Keene and Eleanor had already wandered back, hand in hand, to their days of childhood. But even in the joy that filled the young girl's heart in the presence of her only kinsman, there was a strange reservation. The meeting that she had looked forward to with eager longing had brought all she expected; more than that, it seemed to have been providentially anticipated at the moment of her greatest need, and yet it was incomplete. She was ashamed that after the first recognition, a wild desire to run to Hurlstone and tell HIM her happiness was her only thought. She was shocked that the bright joyous face of this handsome lovable boy could not shut out the melancholy austere features of Hurlstone, which seemed to rise reproachfully between them. When, for the third and fourth time, they had recounted their past history, exchanged their confidences and feelings, Dick, passing his arm around his sister's waist, looked down smilingly in her eyes.

"And so, after all, little Nell, everybody has been good to you, and you have been happy!"

"Everybody has been kind to me, Dick, far kinder than I deserved. Even if I had really been the great lady that little Dona Isabel thought I was, or the important person the Commander believed me to be, I couldn't have been treated more kindly. I have met with nothing but respect and attention. I have been very happy, Dick, very happy."

And with a little cry she threw herself on her brother's neck and burst into a childlike flood of inconsistent tears.

Meantime the news of the arrival of the relief-party had penetrated even the peaceful cloisters of the Mission, and Father Esteban had been summoned in haste to the Council. He returned with an eager face to Hurlstone, who had been anxiously awaiting him. When the Padre had imparted the full particulars of the event to his companion, he added gravely,—

"You see, my son, how Providence, which has protected you since you first claimed the Church's sanctuary, has again interfered to spare me the sacrifice of using the power of the Church in purely mundane passions. I weekly accept the rebuke of His better-ordained ways, and you, Diego, may comfort yourself that this girl is restored directly to her brother's care, without any deviousness of plan or human responsibility. You do not speak, my son!" continued the priest anxiously; "can it be possible that, in the face of this gracious approval of Providence to your resolution, you are regretting it?"

The young man replied, with a half reproachful gesture:

"Do you, then, think me still so weak? No, Father Esteban; I have steeled myself against my selfishness for her sake. I could have resigned her to the escape you had planned, believing her happier for it, and ignorant of the real condition of the man she had learnt to—to—pity. But," he added, turning suddenly and almost rudely upon the priest, "do you know the meaning of this irruption of the outer world to ME? Do you reflect that these men probably know my miserable story?—that, as one of the passengers of the Excelsior, they will be obliged to seek me and to restore me," he added, with a bitter laugh, "to MY home, MY kindred—to the world I loathe?"

"But you need not follow them. Remain here."

"Here!—with the door thrown open to any talebearer OR PERHAPS TO MY WIFE HERSELF? Never! Hear me, Father," he went on hurriedly: "these men have come from San Francisco—have been to Mazatlan. Can you believe that it is possible that they have never heard of this woman's search for me? No! The quest of hate is as strong as the quest of love, and more merciless to the hunted."

"But if that were so, foolish boy, she would have accompanied them."

"You are wrong! It would have been enough for her to have sent my exposure by them—to have driven me from this refuge."

"This is but futile fancy, Diego," said Father Esteban, with a simulated assurance he was far from feeling. "Nothing has yet been said—nothing may be said. Wait, my child."

"Wait!" he echoed bitterly. "Ay, wait until the poor girl shall hear—perhaps from her brother's lips—the story of my marriage as bandied about by others; wait for her to know that the man who would have made her love him was another's, and unworthy of her respect? No! it is I who must leave this place, and at once."

"YOU?" echoed the Padre. "How?"

"By the same means you would have used for her departure. I must take her place in that ship you are expecting. You will

　　　　　　　Bret Harte

give ME letters to your friends. Perhaps, when this is over, I may return—if I still live."

Padre Esteban became thoughtful.

"You will not refuse me?" said the young man, taking the Padre's hand. "It is for the best, believe me. I will remain secret here until then. You will invent some excuse—illness, or what you like—to keep them from penetrating here. Above all, to spare me from the misery of ever reading my secret in her face."

Father Esteban remained still absorbed in thought.

"You will take a letter from me to the Archbishop, and put yourself under his care?" he asked at last, after a long pause. "You will promise me that?"

"I do!"

"Then we shall see what can be done. They talk, those Americanos," continued the priest, "of making their way up the coast to Punta St. Jago, where the ship they have already sent for to take them away can approach the shore; and the Comandante has orders to furnish them escort and transport to that point. It is a foolish indiscretion of the Government, and I warrant without the sanction of the Church. Already there is curiosity, discontent, and wild talk among the people. Ah! thou sayest truly, my son," said the old man, gloomily; "the doors of Todos Santos are open. The Comandante will speed these heretics quickly on their way; but the doors by which they came and whence they go will never close again. But God's will be done! And if the open doors bring thee back, my son, I shall not question His will!"

It would seem, however, as if Hurlstone's fears had been groundless. For in the excitement of the succeeding days, and the mingling of the party from San Antonio with the new-comers, the recluse had been forgotten. So habitual, had been his isolation from the others, that, except for the words of praise and gratitude hesitatingly dropped by Miss Keene to her brother, his name was not mentioned, and it might have been possible for the relieving party to have left him behind—unnoticed. Mr. Brimmer, for domestic reasons, was quite willing to allow the episode of Miss Montgomery's connection with their expedition to drop for the present. Her name was only recalled once by Miss Keene. When Dick had professed a sudden and violent admiration for the coquettish Dona Isabel, Eleanor had looked up in her brother's face with a half troubled air.

"Who was this queer Montgomery woman, Dick?" she said.

Dick laughed—a frank, reassuring, heart-free laugh.

"Perfectly stunning, Nell. Such a figure in tights! You ought to have seen her dance—my!"

"Hush! I dare say she was horrid!"

"Not at all! She wasn't such a bad fellow, if you left out her poetry and gush, which I didn't go in for much,—though the other fellows"—he stopped, from a sudden sense of loyalty to Brimmer and Markham. "No; you see, Nell, she was regularly ridiculously struck after that man Perkins,—whom she'd never seen,—a kind of schoolgirl worship for a pirate. You know how you women go in for those fellows with a mystery about 'em."

"No, I don't!" said Miss Keene sharply, with a slight rise of color; "and I don't see what that's got to do with you and her."

"Everything! She was in correspondence with Perkins, and knows about the Excelsior affair, and wants to help him get out of it with clean hands, don't you see! That's why she made up to us. There, Nell; she ain't your style, of course; but you owe a heap to her for giving us points as to where you were. But that's all over now; she left us at Mazatlan, and went on to Nicaragua to meet Perkins somewhere there—for the fellow has always got some Central American revolution on hand, it appears. Until they garrote or shoot him some day, he'll go on in the liberating business forever."

"Then there wasn't any Mr. Montgomery, of course?" said Eleanor.

"Oh, Mr. Montgomery," said Dick, hesitating. "Well, you see, Nell, I think that, knowing how correct and all that sort of thing Brimmer is, she sort of invented the husband to make her interest look more proper."

"It's shameful!" said Miss Keene indignantly.

"Come, Nell; one would think you had a personal dislike to her. Let her go; she won't trouble you—nor, I reckon, ANYBODY, much longer."

"What do you mean, Dick?"

"I mean she has regularly exhausted and burnt herself out with her hysterics and excitements, and the drugs she's taken to subdue them—to say nothing of the Panama fever she got last spring. If she don't go regularly crazy at last she'll have another attack of fever, hanging round the isthmus waiting for Perkins."

Meanwhile, undisturbed by excitement or intrusion of the outer world, the days had passed quietly at the Mission. But one evening, at twilight, a swift-footed, lightly-clad Indian glided into the sacristy as if he had slipped from the outlying fog, and almost immediately as quietly glided away again and disappeared. The next moment Father Esteban's gaunt and agitated face appeared at Hurlstone's door.

"My son, God has been merciful, and cut short your probation. The signal of the ship has just been made. Her boat will be waiting on the beach two leagues from here an hour hence. Are you ready? and are you still resolved?"

"I am," said Hurlstone, rising. "I have been prepared since you first assented."

The old man's lips quivered slightly, and the great brown hand laid upon the table trembled for an instant; with a strong effort he recovered himself, and said hurriedly,—

"Concho's mule is saddled and ready for you at the foot of the garden. You will follow the beach a league beyond the Indians' cross. In the boat will await you the trusty messenger of the Church. You will say to him, 'Guadalajara,' and give him these letters. One is to the captain. You will require no other introduction." He laid the papers on the table, and, turning to Hurlstone, lifted his tremulous hands in the air. "And now, my son, may the grace of God"—

He faltered and stopped, his uplifted arms falling helplessly on Hurlstone's shoulders. For an instant the young man supported him in his arms, then placed him gently in the chair he had just quitted, and for the first time in their intimacy dropped upon his knee before him. The old man, with a faint smile, placed his hand upon his companion's head. A breathless pause followed; Father Esteban's lips moved silently. Suddenly the young man rose, pressed his lips hurriedly to the Father's hand, and passed out into the night.

The moon was already suffusing the dropping veil of fog above him with that nebulous, mysterious radiance he had noticed the first night he had approached the Mission. When he reached the cross he dismounted, and gathering a few of the sweet-scented blossoms that crept around its base, placed them in his breast. Then, remounting, he continued his way until he came to the spot designated by Concho as a fitting place to leave his tethered mule. This done, he proceeded on foot about a mile further along the hard, wet sand, his eyes fixed on the narrow strip of water and shore before him that was yet uninvaded by the fog on either side.

The misty, nebulous light, the strange silence, broken only by the occasional low hurried whisper of some spent wave that sent its film of spume across his path, or filled his footprints behind him, possessed him with vague presentiments and imaginings. At times he fancied he heard voices at his side; at times indistinct figures loomed through the mist before him. At last what seemed to be his own shadow faintly impinged upon the mist at one side impressed him so strongly that he stopped; the apparition stopped too. Continuing a few hundred paces further, he stopped again; but this time the ghostly figure passed on, and convinced him that it was no shadow, but some one actually following him. With an angry challenge he advanced towards it. It quickly retreated inland, and was lost. Irritated and suspicious he turned back towards the water, and was amazed to see before him, not twenty yards away, the object of his quest—a boat, with two men in it, kept in position by the occasional lazy dip of an oar. In the pursuit of his mysterious shadow he had evidently overlooked it. As his own figure emerged from the fog, the boat pulled towards him. The priest's password was upon his lips, when he perceived that the TWO men were common foreign sailors; the messenger of the Church was evidently not there. Could it have been he who had haunted him? He paused irresolutely. "Is there none other coming?" he asked. The two men looked at each other. One said, "Quien sabe!" and shrugged his shoulders. Hurlstone without further hesitation leaped aboard.

The same dull wall of vapor—at times thickening to an almost impenetrable barrier, and again half suffocating him in its soft embrace—which he had breasted on the night he swam ashore, carried back his thoughts to that time, now so remote and unreal. And when, after a few moments' silent rowing, the boat approached a black hulk that seemed to have started forward out of the gloom to meet them, his vague recollection began to take a more definite form. As he climbed up the companion-ladder and boarded the vessel, an inexplicable memory came over him. A petty officer on the gangway advanced silently and ushered him, half dazed and bewildered, into the cabin. He glanced hurriedly around: the door of a state-room opened, and disclosed the indomitable and affable Senor Perkins! A slight expression of surprise, however, crossed the features of the Liberator of Quinquinambo as he advanced with outstretched hand.

"This is really a surprise, my dear fellow! I had no idea that YOU were in this affair. But I am delighted to welcome you once more to the Excelsior!"

CHAPTER VII

THE RETURN OF THE EXCELSIOR

Amazed and disconcerted, Hurlstone, nevertheless, retained his presence of mind.

"There must be some mistake," he said coolly; "I am certainly not the person you seem to be expecting."

"Were you not sent here by Winslow?" demanded Perkins.

"No. The person you are looking for is probably one I saw on the shore. He no doubt became alarmed at my approach, and has allowed me quite unwittingly to take his place in the boat."

Perkins examined Hurlstone keenly for a moment, stepped to the door, gave a brief order, and returned.

"Then, if you did not intend the honor of this visit for me," he resumed, with a smile, "may I ask, my dear fellow, whom you expected to meet, and on what ship? There are not so many at Todos Santos, if my memory serves me right, as to create confusion."

"I must decline to answer that question," said Hurlstone curtly.

The Senor smiled, with an accession of his old gentleness.

"My dear young friend," he said, "have you forgotten that on a far more important occasion to YOU, I showed no desire to pry into your secret?" Hurlstone made a movement of deprecation. "Nor have I any such desire now. But for the sake of our coming to an understanding as friends, let me answer the question for you. You are here, my dear fellow, as a messenger from the Mission of Todos Santos to the Ecclesiastical Commission from Guadalajara, whose ship touches here every three years. It is now due. You have mistaken this vessel for theirs."

Hurlstone remained silent.

"It is no secret," continued Senor Perkins blandly; "nor shall I pretend to conceal MY purpose here, which is on the invitation of certain distressed patriots of Todos Santos, to assist them in their deliverance from the effete tyranny of the Church and its Government. I have been fortunate enough to anticipate the arrival of your vessel, as you were fortunate enough to anticipate the arrival of my messenger. I am doubly fortunate, as it gives me the pleasure of your company this evening, and necessitates no further trouble than the return of the boat for the other gentleman—which has already gone. Doubtless you may know him."

"I must warn you again, Senor Perkins," said Hurlstone sternly, "that I have no connection with any political party; nor have I any sympathy with your purpose against the constituted authorities."

"I am willing to believe that you have no political affinities at all, my dear Mr. Hurlstone," returned Perkins, with unruffled composure, "and, consequently, we will not argue as to what is the constituted authority of Todos Santos. Perhaps to-morrow it may be on board THIS SHIP, and I may still have the pleasure of making you at home here!"

"Until then," said Hurlstone dryly, "at least you will allow me to repair my error by returning to the shore."

"For the moment I hardly think it would be wise," replied Perkins gently. "Allowing that you escaped the vigilance of my friends on the shore, whose suspicions you have aroused, and who might do you some injury, you would feel it your duty to inform those who sent you of the presence of my ship, and thus precipitate a collision between my friends and yours, which would be promotive of ill-feeling, and perhaps bloodshed. You know my peaceful disposition, Mr. Hurlstone; you can hardly expect me to countenance an act of folly that would be in violation of it."

"In other words, having decoyed me here on board your ship, you intend to detain me," said Hurlstone insultingly.

"'Decoy,'" said Perkins, in gentle deprecation, "'decoy' is hardly the word I expected from a gentleman who has been so unfortunate as to take, unsolicited and of his own free will, another person's place in a boat. But," he continued, assuming an easy argumentative attitude, "let us look at it from your view-point. Let us imagine that YOUR ship had anticipated mine, and that MY messenger had unwittingly gone on board of HER. What do you think they would have done to him?"

"They would have hung him at the yard-arm, as he deserved," said Hurlstone unflinchingly.

"You are wrong," said Perkins gently. "They would have given him the alternative of betraying his trust, and confessing everything—which he would probably have accepted.

Pardon me!—this is no insinuation against you," he interrupted,—"but I regret to say that my experience with the effete Latin races of this continent has not inspired me with confidence in their loyalty to trust. Let me give you an instance," he continued, smiling: "the ship you are expecting is supposed to be an inviolable secret of the Church, but it is known to me—to my friends ashore—and even to you, my poor friend, a heretic! More than that, I am told that the Comandante, the Padre, and Alcalde are actually arranging to deport some of the American women by this vessel, which has been hitherto sacred to the emissaries of the Church alone. But you probably know this—it is doubtless part of your errand. I only mention it to convince you that I have certainly no need either to know your secrets, to hang you from the yard-arm if you refused to give them up, or to hold you as hostage for my messenger, who, as I have shown you, can take care of himself. I shall not ask you for that secret despatch you undoubtedly carry next your heart, because I don't want it. You are at liberty to keep it until you can deliver it, or drop it out of that port-hole into the sea—as you choose. But I hear the boat returning," continued Perkins, rising gently from his seat as the sound of oars came faintly alongside, "and no doubt with Winslow's messenger. I am sorry you won't let me bring you together. I dare say he knows all about you, and it really need not alter your opinions."

"One moment," said Hurlstone, stunned, yet incredulous of Perkins's revelations. "You said that both the Comandante and Alcalde had arranged to send away certain ladies—are you not mistaken?"

"I think not," said Perkins quietly, looking over a pile of papers on the table before him. "Yes, here it is," he continued, reading from a memorandum: "'Don Ramon Ramirez arranged with Pepe for the secret carrying off of Dona

Barbara Brimmer.' Why, that was six weeks ago, and here we have the Comandante suborning one Marcia, a dragoon, to abduct Mrs. Markham—by Jove, my old friend!—and Dona Leonor—our beauty, was she not? Yes, here it is: in black and white. Read it, if you like,—and pardon me for one moment, while I receive this unlucky messenger."

Left to himself, Hurlstone barely glanced at the memorandum, which seemed to be the rough minutes of some society. He believed Perkins; but was it possible that the Padre could be ignorant of the designs of his fellow-councilors? And if he were not—if he had long before been in complicity with them for the removal of Eleanor, might he not also have duped him, Hurlstone, and sent him on this mission as a mere blind; and—more infamously—perhaps even thus decoyed him on board the wrong ship? No—it was impossible! His honest blood quickly flew to his cheek at that momentary disloyal suspicion.

Nevertheless, the Senor's bland revelations filled him with vague uneasiness. SHE was safe with her brother now; but what if he and the other Americans were engaged in this ridiculous conspiracy, this pot-house rebellion that Father Esteban had spoken of, and which he had always treated with such contempt? It seemed strange that Perkins had said nothing of the arrival of the relieving party from the Gulf, and its probable effect on the malcontents. Did he know it? or was the news now being brought by this messenger whom he, Hurlstone, had supplanted? If so, when and how had Perkins received the intelligence that brought him to Todos Santos? The young man could scarcely repress a bitter smile as he remembered the accepted idea of Todos Santos' inviolability—that inacce-ssible port that had within six weeks secretly summoned Perkins to its assistance! And it was there he believed himself secure! What security had he at all? Might not this strange, unimpassioned, omniscient man already know HIS secret as he had known the others'

The interview of Perkins with the messenger in the next cabin was a long one, and apparently a stormy one on the part of the newcomer. Hurlstone could hear his excited foreign voice, shrill with the small vehemence of a shallow character; but there was no change in the slow, measured tones of the Senor. He listlessly began to turn over the papers on the table. Presently he paused. He had taken up a sheet of paper on which Senor Perkins had evidently been essaying some composition in verse. It seemed to have been of a lugubrious character. The titular line at the top of the page, "Dirge," had been crossed out for the substituted "In Memoriam." He read carelessly:

"O Muse unmet—but not unwept—
I seek thy sacred haunt in vain.
Too late, alas! the tryst is kept—
We may not meet again!

"I sought thee 'midst the orange bloom,
To find that thou hadst grasped the palm
Of martyr, and the silent tomb
Had hid thee in its calm.

"By fever racked, thou languishest
On Nicaragua's"—

Hurlstone threw the paper aside. Although he had not forgotten the Senor's reputation for sentimental extravagance, and on another occasion might have laughed at it, there was something so monstrous in this hysterical, morbid composition of the man who was even then contemplating bloodshed and crime, that he was disgusted. Like most sentimental egotists, Hurlstone was exceedingly intolerant of that quality in others, and he turned for relief to his own

Bret Harte

thoughts of Eleanor Keene and his own unfortunate passion. HE could not have written poetry at such a moment!

But the cabin-door opened, and Senor Perkins appeared. Whatever might have been the excited condition of his unknown visitor, the Senor's round, clean-shaven face was smiling and undisturbed by emotion. As his eye fell on the page of manuscript Hurlstone had just cast down, a slight shadow crossed his beneficent expanse of forehead, and deepened in his soft dark eyes; but the next moment it was chased away by his quick recurring smile. Even thus transient and superficial was his feeling, thought Hurlstone.

"I have some news for you," said Perkins affably, "which may alter your decision about returning. My friends ashore," he continued, "judging from the ingenuous speci-men which has just visited me, are more remarkable for their temporary zeal and spasmodic devotion than for prudent reserve or lasting discretion. They have submitted a list to me of those whom they consider dangerous to Mexican liberty, and whom they are desirous of hanging. I regret to say that the list is illogical, and the request inopportune. Our friend Mr. Banks is put down as an ally of the Government and an objectionable business rival of that eminent patriot and well-known drover, Senor Martinez, who just called upon me. Mr. Crosby's humor is considered subversive of a proper respect for all patriotism; but I cannot understand why they have added YOUR name as especially 'dangerous.'"

Hurlstone made a gesture of contempt.

"I suppose they pay me the respect of considering me a friend of the old priest. So be it! I hope they will let the responsibility fall on me alone."

"The Padre is already proscribed as one of the Council," said

Senor Perkins quietly.

"Do you mean to say," said Hurlstone impetuously, "that you will permit a hair of that innocent old man's head to be harmed by those wretches?"

"You are generous but hasty, my friend," said Senor Perkins, in gentle deprecation. "Allow me to put your question in another way. Ask me if I intend to perpetuate the Catholic Church in Todos Santos by adding another martyr to its roll, and I will tell you—No! I need not say that I am equally opposed to any proceedings against Banks, Crosby, and yourself, for diplomatic reasons, apart from the kindly memories of our old associations on this ship. I have therefore been obliged to return to the excellent Martinez his little list, with the remark that I should hold HIM personally responsible if any of you are molested. There is, however, no danger. Messrs. Banks and Crosby are with the other Americans, whom we have guaranteed to protect, at the Mission, in the care of your friend the Padre. You are surprised! Equally so was the Padre. Had you delayed your departure an hour you would have met them, and I should have been debarred the pleasure of your company.

"By to-morrow," continued Perkins, placing the tips of his fingers together reflectively, "the Government of Todos Santos will have changed hands, and without bloodshed. You look incredulous! My dear young friend, it has been a part of my professional pride to show the world that these revolutions can be accomplished as peacefully as our own changes of administration. But for a few infelicitous accidents, this would have been the case of the late liberation of Quinquinambo. The only risk run is to myself—the leader, and that is as it should be. But all this personal explanation is, doubtless, uninteresting to you, my young friend. I meant only to say that, if you prefer not to remain here, you can accompany me when I leave the ship at nine o'clock with a small reconnoitring party, and I will give you safe escort back to your friends at the Mission."

This amicable proposition produced a sudden revulsion of feeling in Hurlstone. To return to those people from whom he was fleeing, in what was scarcely yet a serious emergency, was not to be thought of! Yet, where could he go? How could he be near enough to assist HER without again openly casting his lot among them? And would they not consider his return an act of cowardice? He could not restrain a gesture of irritation as he rose impatiently to his feet.

"You are agitated, my dear fellow. It is not unworthy of your youth; but, believe me, it is unnecessary," said Perkins, in his most soothing manner. "Sit down. You have an hour yet to make your decision. If you prefer to remain, you will accompany the ship to Todos Santos and join me."

"I don't comprehend you," interrupted Hurlstone suspiciously.

"I forgot," said Perkins, with a bland smile, "that you are unaware of our plan of campaign. After communicating with the insurgents, I land here with a small force to assist them. I do this to anticipate any action and prevent the interference of the Mexican coaster, now due, which always touches here through ignorance of the channel leading to the Bay of Todos Santos and the Presidio. I then send the Excelsior, that does know the channel, to Todos Santos, to appear before the Presidio, take the enemy in flank, and cooperate with us. The arrival of the Excelsior there is the last move of this little game, if I may so call it: it is 'checkmate to the King,' the clerical Government of Todos Santos."

A little impressed, in spite of himself, with the calm

forethought and masterful security of the Senor, Hurlstone thanked him with a greater show of respect than he had hitherto evinced. The Senor looked gratified, but unfortunately placed that respect the next moment in peril.

"You were possibly glancing over these verses," he said, with a hesitating and almost awkward diffidence, indicating the manuscript Hurlstone had just thrown aside. "It is merely the first rough draft of a little tribute I had begun to a charming friend. I sometimes," he interpolated, with an apologetic smile, "trifle with the Muse. Perhaps I ought not to use the word 'trifle' in connection with a composition of a threnodial and dirge-like character," he continued deprecatingly. "Certainly not in the presence of a gentle-man as accomplished and educated as yourself, to whom recreation of this kind is undoubtedly familiar. My occupations have been, unfortunately, of a nature not favorable to the indulgence of verse. As a college man yourself, my dear sir, you will probably forgive the lucubrations of an old graduate of William and Mary's, who has forgotten his 'ars poetica.' The verses you have possibly glanced at are crude, I am aware, and perhaps show the difficulty of expressing at once the dictates of the heart and the brain. They refer to a dear friend now at peace. You have perhaps, in happier and more careless hours, heard me speak of Mrs. Euphemia M'Corkle, of Illinois?"

Hurlstone remembered indistinctly to have heard, even in his reserved exclusiveness on the Excelsior, the current badinage of the passengers concerning Senor Perkins' extravagant adulation of this unknown poetess. As a part of the staple monotonous humor of the voyage, it had only disgusted him. With a feeling that he was unconsciously sharing the burlesque relief of the passengers, he said, with a polite attempt at interest,

"Then the lady is—no more?"

"If that term can be applied to one whose work is immortal," corrected Senor Perkins gently. "All that was finite of this gifted woman was lately forwarded by Adams's Express Company from San Juan, to receive sepulture among her kindred at Keokuk, Iowa."

"Did she say she was from that place?" asked Hurlstone, with half automatic interest.

"The Consul says she gave that request to the priest."

"Then you were not with her when she died?" said Hurlstone absently.

"I was NEVER with her, neither then nor before," returned Senor Perkins gravely. Seeing Hurlstone's momentary surprise, he went on, "The late Mrs. M'Corkle and I never met—we were personally unknown to each other. You may have observed the epithet 'unmet' in the first line of the first stanza; you will then understand that the privation of actual contact with this magnetic soul would naturally impart more difficulty into elegiac expression."

"Then you never really saw the lady you admire?" said Hurlstone vacantly.

"Never. The story is a romantic one," said Perkins, with a smile that was half complacent and yet half embarrassed. "May I tell it to you? Thanks. Some three years ago I contributed some verses to the columns of a Western paper edited by a friend of mine. The subject chosen was my favorite one, 'The Liberation of Mankind,' in which I may possibly have expressed myself with some poetic fervor on a theme so dear to my heart. I may remark without vanity, that it received high encomiums—perhaps at some more opportune moment you may be induced to cast your eyes over a copy I still retain—but no praise touched me as deeply as a tribute in verse in another journal from a gifted unknown, who signed herself 'Euphemia.' The subject of the poem, which was dedicated to myself, was on the liberation of women—from—er—I may say certain domestic shackles; treated perhaps vaguely, but with grace and vigor. I replied a week later in a larger poem, recording more fully my theories and aspirations regarding a struggling Central American confederacy, addressed to 'Euphemia.' She rejoined with equal elaboration and detail, referring to a more definite form of tyranny in the relations of marriage, and alluding with some feeling to uncongenial experiences of her own. An instinct of natural delicacy, veiled under the hyperbole of 'want of space,' prevented my editorial friend from encouraging the repetition of this charming interchange of thought and feeling. But I procured the fair stranger's address; we began a corres-pondence, at once imaginative and sympathetic in expression, if not always poetical in form. I was called to South America by the Macedonian cry of 'Quinquinambo!' I still corresponded with her. When I returned to Quinquinambo I received letters from her, dated from San Francisco. I feel that my words could only fail, my dear Hurlstone, to convey to you the strength and support I derived from those impassioned breathings of aid and sympathy at that time. Enough for me to confess that it was mainly due to the deep womanly interest that SHE took in the fortunes of the passengers of the Excelsior that I gave the Mexican authorities early notice of their whereabouts. But, pardon me,"—he stopped hesitatingly, with a slight flush, as he noticed the utterly inattentive face and attitude of Hurlstone,—"I am boring you. I am forgetting that this is only important to myself," he added, with a sigh. "I only intended to ask your advice in regard to the disposition of certain manuscripts and effects of hers, which are unconnected with our acquaintance. I thought, perhaps, I might entrust them to your delicacy and consideration. They are here, if you choose to look them over; and here is also what I believe to be a daguerreotype of the lady herself, but in which I fail to recognize her soul and genius."

He laid a bundle of letters and a morocco case on the table with a carelessness that was intended to hide a slight shade of disappointment in his face—and rose.

"I beg your pardon," said Hurlstone, in confused and remorseful apology; "but I frankly confess that my thoughts WERE preoccupied. Pray forgive me. If you will leave these papers with me, I promise to devote myself to them another time."

"As you please," said the Senor, with a slight return of his old affability. "But don't bore yourself now. Let us go on deck."

He passed out of the cabin as Hurlstone glanced, half mechanically, at the package before him. Suddenly his cheek reddened; he stopped, looked hurriedly at the retreating form of Perkins, and picked up a manuscript from the packet. It was in his wife's handwriting. A sudden idea flashed across his mind, and seemed to illuminate the obscure monotony of the story he had just heard. He turned hurriedly to the morocco case, and opened it with trembling fingers. It was a daguerreotype, faded and silvered; but the features were those of his wife!

CHAPTER VIII

HOSTAGE

The revolution of Todos Santos had to all appearances been effected as peacefully as the gentle Liberator of Quinquinambo could have wished. Two pronunciamientos, rudely printed and posted in the Plaza, and saluted by the fickle garrison of one hundred men, who had, however, immediately reappointed their old commander as Generalissimo under the new regime, seemed to leave nothing to be desired. A surging mob of vacant and wondering peons, bearing a singular resemblance to the wild cattle and horses which intermingled with them in blind and unceasing movement across the Plaza and up the hilly street, and seemingly as incapable of self-government, were alternately dispersed and stampeded or allowed to gather again as occasion required. Some of these heterogeneous bands were afterwards found— the revo-lution accomplished—gazing stupidly on the sea, or ruminating in bovine wantonness on the glacis before the Presidio.

Eleanor Keene, who with her countrywomen had been hurried to the refuge of the Mission, was more disturbed and excited at the prospect of meeting Hurlstone again than by any terror of the insurrection. But Hurlstone was not there, and Father Esteban received her with a coldness she could not attribute entirely to her countrymen's supposed sympathy with the insurgents. When Richard Keene, who would not leave his sister until he had seen her safe under the Mission walls, ventured at her suggestion to ask after the American recluse, Father Esteban replied dryly that, being a Christian gentleman, Hurlstone was the only one who had the boldness to seek out the American filibuster Perkins, on his own ship, and remonstrate with him for his unholy crusade. For the old priest had already become aware of Hurlstone's blunder, and he hated Eleanor as the primary cause of the trouble. But for her, Diego would be still with him in this emergency.

"Never mind, Nell," said Dick, noticing the disappointed eyes of his sister as they parted, "you'll all be safe here until we return. Between you and me, Banks, Brimmer, and I think that Brace and Winslow have gone too far in this matter, and we're going to stop it, unless the whole thing is over now, as they say."

"Don't believe that," said Crosby. "It's like their infernal earthquakes; there's always a second shock, and a tidal wave to follow. I pity Brace, Winslow, and Perkins if they get caught in it."

There seemed to be some reason for his skepticism, for later the calm of the Mission Garden was broken upon by the monotonous tread of banded men on the shell-strewn walks, and the door of the refectory opened to the figure of Senor Perkins. A green silk sash across his breast, a gold-laced belt, supporting a light dress-sword and a pair of pistols, buckled around the jaunty waist of his ordinary black frock-coat, were his scant martial suggestions. But his hat, albeit exchanged for a soft felt one, still reposed on the back of his benevolent head, and seemed to accent more than ever the contrast between his peaceful shoulders and the military smartness of his lower figure. He bowed with easy politeness to the assembled fugitives; but before he could address them, Father Esteban had risen to his feet,—

"I thought that this house, at least, was free from the desecrating footsteps of lawlessness and impiety," said the priest sternly. "How dare YOU enter here?"

"Nothing but the desire to lend my assistance to the claims of beauty, innocence, helplessness, and—if you will allow me to add," with a low bow to the priest—"sanctity, caused this intrusion. For I regret to say that, through the ill-advised counsels of some of my fellow-patriots, the Indian tribes attached to this Mission are in revolt, and threaten even this sacred building."

"It is false!" said Father Esteban indignantly. "Even under the accursed manipulation of your emissaries, the miserable heathen would not dare to raise a parricidal hand against the Church that fostered him!"

Senor Perkins smiled gently, but sadly.

"Your belief, reverend sir, does you infinite credit. But, to save time, let me give way to a gentleman who, I believe, possesses your confidence. He will confirm my statement."

He drew aside, and allowed Hurlstone, who had been standing unperceived behind, to step forward. The Padre uttered an exclamation of pleasure. Miss Keene colored quickly. Hurlstone cast a long and lingering glance at her, which seemed to the embarrassed girl full of a new, strange meaning, and then advanced quickly with outstretched hands towards Father Esteban.

"He speaks truly," he said, hurriedly, "and in the interests of humanity alone. The Indians have been tampered with treacherously, against his knowledge and consent. He only seeks now to prevent the consequences of this folly by placing you and these ladies out of reach of harm aboard of the Excelsior."

"A very proper and excellent idea," broke in Mrs. Brimmer, with genteel precision. "You see these people evidently recognize the fact of Mr. Brimmer's previous ownership of the Excelsior, and the respect that is due to him. I, for one, shall accept the offer, and insist upon Miss Chubb accompanying me."

"I shall be charmed to extend the hospitality of the Excelsior to you on any pretext," said the Senor gallantly, "and, indeed, should insist upon personally accompanying you and my dear friends Mrs. Markham and Miss Keene; but, alas! I am required elsewhere. I leave," he continued, turning towards Hurlstone, who was already absorbed in a whispered consultation with Padre Esteban—"I leave a sufficient escort with you to protect your party to the boats which have brought us here. You will take them to the Excelsior, and join me with the ship off Todos Santos in the morning. Adieu, my friends! Good-night, and farewell!"

The priest made a vehement movement of protestation, but he was checked by Hurlstone, as, with a low bow, Senor Perkins passed out into the darkness. The next moment his voice was heard raised in command, and the measured tramp of his men gradually receded and was lost in the distance.

"Does he think," said the priest indignantly, "that I, Padre Esteban, would desert my sacred trust, and leave His Holy Temple a prey to sacrilegious trespass? Never, while I live, Diego! Call him back and tell him so!"

"Rather listen to me, Father Esteban," said the young man

earnestly. "I have a plan by which this may be avoided. From my knowledge of these Indians, I am convinced that they have been basely tricked and cajoled by some one. I believe that they are still amenable to reason and argument, and I am so certain that I am ready to go down among them and make the attempt. The old Chief and part of his band are still encamped on the shore; we could hear them as we passed in the boats. I will go and meet them. If I succeed in bringing them to reason I will return; if I find them intractable, I will at least divert their attention from the Mission long enough for you to embark these ladies with their escort, which you will do at the end of two hours if I do not return."

"In two hours?" broke in Mrs. Brimmer, in sharp protest. "I positively object. I certainly understood that Senor Perkins' invitation, which, under the circumstances, I shall consider equal to a command from Mr. Brimmer, was to be accepted at once and without delay; and I certainly shall not leave Miss Chubb exposed to imminent danger for two hours to meet the caprice of an entire stranger to Mr. Brimmer."

"I am willing to stay with Father Esteban, if he will let me," said Eleanor Keene quietly, "for I have faith in Mr. Hurlstone's influence and courage, and believe he will be successful."

The young man thanked her with another demonstrative look that brought the warm blood to her cheek.

"Well," said Mrs. Markham promptly; "I suppose if Nell stays I must see the thing through and stay with her—even if I haven't orders from Jimmy."

"There is no necessity that either Mr. or Mrs. Brimmer should be disobeyed in their wishes," said Hurlstone grimly. "Luckily there are two boats; Mrs. Brimmer and Miss Chubb can take one of them with half the escort, and proceed at once to the Excelsior. I will ride with them as far as the boat. And now," he continued, turning to the old priest, with sparkling eyes, "I have only to ask your blessing, and the good wishes of these ladies, to go forth on my mission of peace. If I am successful," he added, with a light laugh, "confess that a layman and a heretic may do some service for the Church." As the old man laid his half detaining, half benedictory hands upon his shoulders, the young man seized the opportunity to whisper in his ear, "Remember your promise to tell her ALL I have told you," and, with an other glance at Miss Keene, he marshalled Mrs. Brimmer and Miss Chubb before him, and hurried them to the boat.

Miss Keene looked after him with a vague felicity in the change that seemed to have come on him, a change that she could as little account for as her own happiness. Was it the excitement of danger that had overcome his reserve, and set free his compressed will and energy? She longed for her brother to see him thus—alert, strong, and chivalrous. In her girlish faith, she had no fear for his safety; he would conquer, he would succeed; he would come back to them victorious! Looking up from her happy abstraction, at the side of Mrs. Markham, who had calmly gone to sleep in an arm-chair, she saw Father Esteban's eyes fixed upon her. With a warning gesture of the hand towards Mrs. Markham, he rose, and, going to the door of the sacristy, beckoned to her. The young girl noiselessly crossed the room and followed him into the sanctuary.

Half an hour later, and while Mrs. Markham was still asleep, Father Esteban appeared at the door of the sacristy ostentatiously taking snuff, and using a large red hand-kerchief to wipe his more than usually humid eyes. Eleanor Keene, with her chin resting on her hand, remained sitting as he had left her, with her abstracted eyes fixed vacantly on the lamp before the statue of the Virgin and the half-lit gloom of the nave.

Padre Esteban had told her ALL! She now knew Hurlstone's history even as he had hesitatingly imparted it to the old priest in this very church—perhaps upon the very seat where she sat. She knew the peace that he had sought for and found within these walls, broken only by his passion for her! She knew his struggles against the hopelessness of this new-born love, even the desperate remedy that had been adopted against herself, and the later voluntary exile of her lover. She knew the providential culmination of his trouble in the news brought uncon-sciously by Perkins, which, but a few hours ago, he had verified by the letters, records, and even the certificate of death that had thus strangely been placed in his hands! She knew all this so clearly now, that, with the instinct of a sympathetic nature, she even fancied she had heard it before. She knew that all the obstacles to an exchange of their affection had been removed; that her lover only waited his opportunity to hear from her own lips the answer that was even now struggling at her heart. And yet she hesitated and drew back, half frightened in the presence of her great happiness. How she longed, and yet dreaded, to meet him! What if anything should have happened to him?—what if he should be the victim of some treachery?—what if he did not come?—what if?—"Good heavens! what was that?"

She was near the door of the sacristy, gazing into the dim and shadowy church. Either she was going mad, or else the grotesque Indian hangings of the walls were certainly moving towards her. She rose in speechless terror, as what she had taken for an uncouthly swathed and draped barbaric pillar suddenly glided to the window. Crouching against the wall, she crept breathlessly towards the entrance to the garden. Casting a hurried glance above her, she saw the open belfry that was illuminated by the misty radiance of the moon, darkly shadowed by hideously gibbering faces that peered at her through the broken tracery. With a cry of horror she threw open the garden-door; but the next moment was swallowed up in the tumultuous tide of wild and half naked Indians who surged against the walls of the church, and felt herself lifted from her feet, with inarticulate cries, and borne along the garden. Even in her mortal terror, she could recognize that the cries were not those of rage, but of vacant satisfaction; that although she was lifted on lithe shoulders, the grasp of her limbs was gentle, and the few dark faces she could see around her were glistening in childlike curiosity. Presently she felt herself placed upon the back of a mule, that seemed to be swayed hither and thither in the shifting mass, and the next moment the misty, tossing cortege moved forward with a new and more definite purpose. She called aloud for Father Esteban and Mrs. Markham; her voice appeared to flow back upon her from the luminous wall of fog that closed around her. Then the inarticulate, irregular outcries took upon themselves a measured rhythm, the movement of the mass formed itself upon the monotonous chant, the intervals grew shorter, the mule broke into a trot, and then the whole vast multitude fell into a weird, rhythmical, jogging quick step at her side.

Whatever was the intent of this invasion of the Mission and her own strange abduction, she was relieved by noticing that they were going in the same direction as that taken by Hurlstone an hour before. Either he was cognizant of their movements, and, being powerless to prevent their attack on the church, had stipulated they were to bring her to him in safety, or else he was calculating to intercept them on the way. The fog prevented her from forming any estimation of the numbers that surrounded her, or if the Padre and Mrs. Markham were possibly preceding her as captives in the vanguard. She felt the breath of the sea, and knew they were traveling along the shore; the monotonous chant and jogging motion gradually dulled her active terror to an apathetic resignation, in which occasionally her senses seemed to swoon and swim in the dreamy radiance through which they passed; at times it seemed a dream or nightmare with which she was hopelessly struggling; at times she was taking part in an unhallowed pageant, or some heathen sacrificial procession of which she was the destined victim.

She had no consciousness of how long the hideous journey lasted. Her benumbed senses were suddenly awakened by a shock; the chant had ceased, the moving mass in which she was imbedded rolled forward once more as if by its own elasticity, and then receded again with a jar that almost unseated her. Then the inarticulate murmur was overborne by a voice. It was HIS! She turned blindly towards it; but before she could utter the cry that rose to her lips, she was again lifted from the saddle, carried forward, and gently placed upon what seemed to be a moss-grown bank. Opening her half swimming eyes she recognized the Indian cross. The crowd seemed to recede before her. Her eyes closed again as a strong arm passed around her waist.

"Speak to me, Miss Keene—Eleanor—my darling!" said Hurlstone's voice. "O my God! they have killed her!"

With an effort she moved her head and tried to smile. Their eyes, and then their lips met; she fainted.

When she struggled to her senses again, she was lying in the stern-sheets of the Excelsior's boat, supported on Mrs. Markham's shoulder. For an instant the floating veil of fog around her, and the rhythmical movement of the boat, seemed a part of her mysterious ride, and she raised her head with a faint cry for Hurlstone.

"It's all right, my dear," said Mrs. Markham, soothingly; "he's ashore with the Padre, and everything else is all right too. But it's rather ridiculous to think that those idiotic Indians believed the only way they could show Mr. Hurlstone that they meant us no harm was to drag us all up to THEIR Mission, as they call that half heathen cross of theirs—for safety against—who do you think, dear?—the dreadful AMERICANS! And imagine all the while the Padre and I were just behind you, bringing up the rear of the procession—only they wouldn't let us join you because they wanted to show you special honor as"—she sank her voice to a whisper in Eleanor's ear—"as the future Mrs. Hurlstone! It appears they must have noticed something about you two, the last time you were there, my dear. And—to think—YOU never told me anything about it!"

When they reached the Excelsior, they found that Mrs. Brimmer, having already settled herself in the best cabin, was inclined to extend the hospitalities of the ship with the air of a hostess. But the arrival of Hurlstone at midnight with some delegated authority from Senor Perkins, and the unexpected getting under way of the ship, disturbed her complacency.

"We are going through the channel into the bay of Todos Santos," was the brief reply vouchsafed her by Hurlstone.

"But why can't we remain here and wait for Mr. Brimmer?" she asked indignantly.

"Because," responded Hurlstone grimly, "the Excelsior is expected off the Presidio to-morrow morning to aid the insurgents."

"You don't mean to say that Miss Chubb and myself are to be put in the attitude of arraying ourselves against the constituted authorities—and, perhaps, Mr. Brimmer himself?" asked Mrs. Brimmer, in genuine alarm.

"It looks so," said Hurlstone, a little maliciously; "but, no doubt, your husband and the Senor will arrange it amicably."

To Mrs. Markham and Miss Keene he explained more satisfactorily that the unexpected disaffection of the Indians had obliged Perkins to so far change his plans as to disembark his entire force from the Excelsior, and leave her with only the complement of men necessary to navigate her through the channel of Todos Santos, where she would peacefully await his orders, or receive his men in case of defeat.

Nevertheless, as the night was nearly spent, Mrs. Markham and Eleanor preferred to await the coming day on deck, and watch the progress of the Excelsior through the mysterious channel. In a few moments the barque began to feel the combined influence of the tide and the slight morning breeze, and, after rounding an invisible point, she presently rose and fell on the larger ocean swell. The pilot, whom Hurlstone recognized as the former third mate of the Excelsior, appeared to understand the passage perfectly; and even Hurlstone and the ladies, who had through eight months' experience become accustomed to the luminous obscurity of Todos Santos, could detect the faint looming of the headland at the entrance. The same soothing silence, even the same lulling of the unseen surf, which broke in gentle undulations over the bar, and seemed to lift the barque in rocking buoyancy over the slight obstruction, came back to them as on the day of their fateful advent. The low orders of the pilot, the cry of the leadsman in the chains, were but a part of the restful past.

Under the combined influence of the hour and the climate,

the conversation fell into monosyllables, and Mrs. Markham dozed. The lovers sat silently together, but the memory of a kiss was between them. It spanned the gulf of the past with an airy bridge, over which their secret thoughts and fancies passed and repassed with a delicious security; henceforth they could not flee from that memory, even if they wished; they read it in each other's lightest glance; they felt it in the passing touch of each other's hands; it lingered, with vague tenderness, on the most trivial interchange of thought. Yet they spoke a little of the future. Eleanor believed that her brother would not object to their union; he had spoken of entering into business at Todos Santos, and perhaps when peace and security were restored they might live together. Hurlstone did not tell her that a brief examination of his wife's papers had shown him that the property he had set aside for her maintenance, and from which she had regularly drawn an income, had increased in value, and left him a rich man. He only pressed her hand, and whispered that her wishes should be his. They had become tenderly silent again, as the Excelsior, now fairly in the bay, appeared to be slowly drifting, with listless sails and idle helm, in languid search of an anchorage. Suddenly they were startled by a cry from the lookout.

"Sail ho!"

There was an incredulous start on the deck. The mate sprang into the fore-rigging with an oath of protestation. But at the same moment the tall masts and spars of a vessel suddenly rose like a phantom out of the fog at their side. The half disciplined foreign crew uttered a cry of rage and trepidation, and huddled like sheep in the waist, with distracted gestures; even the two men at the wheel forsook their post to run in dazed terror to the taffrail. Before the mate could restore order to this chaos, the Excelsior had drifted, with a scarcely perceptible concussion, against the counter of the strange vessel. In an instant a dozen figures appeared on its bulwarks, and dropped unimpeded upon the Excelsior's deck. As the foremost one approached the mate, the latter shrank back in consternation.

"Captain Bunker!"

"Yes," said the figure, advancing with a mocking laugh; "Captain Bunker it is. Captain Bunker, formerly of this American barque Excelsior, and now of the Mexican ship La Trinidad. Captain Bunker ez larnt every foot of that passage in an open boat last August, and didn't forget it yesterday in a big ship! Captain Bunker ez has just landed a company of dragoons to relieve the Presidio. What d'ye say to that, Mr. M'Carthy—eh?"

"I say," answered M'Carthy, raising his voice with a desperate effort to recover his calmness, "I say that Perkins landed with double that number of men yesterday around that point, and that he'll be aboard here in half an hour to make you answer for this insult to his ship and his Government."

"His Government!" echoed Bunker, with a hoarser laugh; "hear him!—HIS Government! His Government died at four o'clock this morning, when his own ringleaders gave him up to the authorities. Ha! Why, this yer revolution is played out, old man; and Generalissimo Leonidas Perkins is locked up in the Presidio."

CHAPTER IX

LIBERATED

The revolution was, indeed, ended. The unexpected arrival of a relieving garrison in the bay of Todos Santos had completed what the dissensions in the insurgents' councils had begun; the discontents, led by Brace and Winslow, had united with the Government against Perkins and his aliens; but a compromise had been effected by the treacherous giving up of the Liberator himself in return for an amnesty granted to his followers. The part that Bunker had played in bringing about this moral catastrophe was, however, purely adventitious. When he had recovered his health, and subsequent events had corroborated the truth of his story, the Mexican Government, who had compromised with Quinquinambo, was obliged to recognize his claims by offering him command of the missionary ship, and permission to rediscover the channel, the secret of which had been lost for half a century to the Government. He had arrived at the crucial moment whcn Perkins' command were scattered along the seashore, and the dragoons had invested Todos Santos without opposition.

Such was the story substantially told to Hurlstone and confirmed on his debarkation with the ladies at Todos Santos, the Excelsior being now in the hands of the authorities. Hurlstone did not hesitate to express to Padre Esteban his disgust at the treachery which had made a scapegoat of Senor Perkins. But to his surprise the cautious priest only shrugged his shoulders as he took a complacent pinch of snuff.

"Have a care, Diego! You are of necessity grateful to this man for the news he has brought—nay, more, for possibly being the instrument elected by Providence to precipitate the denouement of that miserable woman's life—but let it not close your eyes to his infamous political career. I admit that he was opposed to the revolt of the heathen against us, but it was his emissaries and his doctrines that poisoned with heresy the fountains from which they drank. Enough! Be grateful! but do not expect ME to intercede for Baal and Ashtaroth!"

"Intercede!" echoed Hurlstone, alarmed at the sudden sacerdotal hardness that had overspread the old priest's face. "Surely the Council will not be severe with the man who was betrayed into their power by others equally guilty?"

Padre Esteban avoided Hurlstone's eyes as he answered with affected coolness,—"Quien sabe? There will be expulsados, no doubt. The Excelsior, which is confiscated, will be sent to Mexico with them."

"I must see Senor Perkins," said Hurlstone suddenly.

The priest hesitated.

"When?" he asked cautiously.

"At once."

"Good." He wrote a hurried line on a piece of paper, folded

Bret Harte

it, sealed it, and gave it to Hurlstone. "You will hand that to the Comandante. He will give you access to the prisoner."

In less than half an hour Hurlstone presented himself before the Commander. The events of the last twenty-four hours had evidently affected Don Miguel, for although he received Hurlstone courteously, there was a singular reflection of the priest's harshness in his face as he glanced over the missive. He took out his watch.

"I give you ten minutes with the prisoner, Don Diego. More, I cannot."

A little awed by the manner of the Commander, Hurlstone bowed and followed him across the courtyard. It was filled with soldiers, and near the gateway a double file of dragoons, with loaded carbines, were standing at ease. Two sentries were ranged on each side of an open door which gave upon the courtyard. The Commander paused before it, and with a gesture invited him to enter. It was a large square apartment, lighted only by the open door and a grated enclosure above it. Seated in his shirtsleeves, before a rude table, Senor Perkins was quietly writing. The shadow of Hurlstone's figure falling across his paper caused him to look up.

Whatever anxiety Hurlstone had begun to feel, it was quickly dissipated by the hearty, affable, and even happy greeting of the prisoner.

"Ah! what! my young friend Hurlstone! Again an unexpected pleasure," he said, extending his white hands. "And again you find me wooing the Muse, in, I fear, hesitating numbers." He pointed to the sheet of paper before him, which showed some attempts at versification. "But I confess to a singular fascination in the exercise of poetic composition, in instants of leisure like this—a fascination which, as a man of imagination yourself, you can appreciate."

"And I am sorry to find you here, Senor Perkins," began Hurlstone frankly; "but I believe it will not be for long."

"My opinion," said the Senor, with a glance of gentle contemplation at the distant Comandante, "as far as I may express it, coincides with your own."

"I have come," continued Hurlstone earnestly, "to offer you my services. I am ready," he raised his voice, with a view of being overheard, "to bear testimony that you had no complicity in the baser part of the late conspiracy,—the revolt of the savages, and that you did your best to counteract the evil, although in doing so you have sacrificed yourself. I shall claim the right to speak from my own knowledge of the Indians and from their admission to me that they were led away by the vague representations of Martinez, Brace, and Winslow."

"Pardon—pardon me," said Senor Perkins deprecatingly, "you are mistaken. My general instructions, no doubt, justified these young gentlemen in taking, I shall not say extreme, but injudicious measures." He glanced meaningly in the direction of the Commander, as if to warn Hurlstone from continuing, and said gently, "But let us talk of something else. I thank you for your gracious intentions, but you remember that we agreed only yesterday that you knew nothing of politics, and did not concern yourself with them. I do not know but you are wise. Politics and the science of self-government, although dealing with general principles, are apt to be defined by the individual limitations of the enthusiast. What is good for HIMSELF he too often deems is applicable to the general public, instead of wisely understanding that what is good for THEM must be good for

Bret Harte

himself. But," said the Senor lightly, "we are again transgressing. We were to choose another topic. Let it be yourself, Mr. Hurlstone. You are looking well, sir; indeed, I may say I never saw you looking so well! Let me congratulate you. Health is the right of youth. May you keep both!"

He shook Hurlstone's hand again with singular fervor.

There was a slight bustle and commotion at the door of the guard-room, and the Commander's attention was called in that direction. Hurlstone profited by the opportunity to say in a hurried whisper:

"Tell me what I can do for you;" and he hesitated to voice his renewed uneasiness—"tell me if—if—if your case is—urgent!"

Senor Perkins lifted his shoulders and smiled with grateful benevolence.

"You have already promised me to deliver those papers and manuscripts of my deceased friend, and to endeavor to find her relations. I do not think it is urgent, however."

"I do not mean that," said Hurlstone eagerly. "I"—but Perkins stopped him with a sign that the Commander was returning.

Don Miguel approached them with disturbed and anxious looks.

"I have yielded to the persuasions of two ladies, Dona Leonor and the Senora Markham, to ask you to see them for a moment," he said to Senor Perkins. "Shall it be so? I have told them the hour is nearly spent."

"You have told them—NOTHING MORE?" asked the Senor, in a whisper unheard by Hurlstone.

"No."

"Let them come, then."

The Commander made a gesture to the sentries at the guard-room, who drew back to allow Mrs. Markham and Eleanor to pass. A little child, one of Eleanor's old Presidio pupils, who, recognizing her, had followed her into the guard-room, now emerged with her, and momentarily disconcerted at the presence of the Commander, ran, with the unerring instinct of childhood, to the Senor for protection. The filibuster smiled, and lifting the child with a paternal gesture to his shoulder by one hand, he extended the other to the ladies.

"The Commander," said Mrs. Markham briskly, "says it's against the rules; that visiting time is up; and you've already got a friend with you, and all that sort of thing; but I told him that I was bound to see you, if only to say that if there's any meanness going on, Susannah and James Markham ain't in it! No! But we're going to see you put right and square in the matter; and if we can't do it here, we'll do it, if we have to follow you to Mexico!—that's all!"

"And I," said Eleanor, grasping the Senor's hand, and half blushing as she glanced at Hurlstone, "see that I have already a friend here who will help me to put in action all the sympathy I feel."

Senor Perkins drew himself up, and cast a faint look of pride towards the Commander.

"To HEAR such assurances from beautiful and eloquent lips like those before me," he said, with his old oratorical wave of the hand, but a passing shadow across his mild eyes, "is more than sufficient. In my experience of life I have been favored, at various emergencies, by the sympathy and outspoken counsel of your noble sex; the last time by Mrs. Euphemia M'Corkle, of Peoria, Illinois, a lady of whom you have heard me speak—alas! now lately deceased. A few lines at present lying on yonder table—a tribute to her genius—will be forwarded to you, dear Mrs. Markham. But let us change the theme. You are looking well—and you, too, Miss Keene. From the roses that bloom on your cheeks—nourished by the humid air of Todos Santos—I am gratified in thinking you have forgiven me your enforced detention here."

At a gesture from the Commander he ceased, stepped back, bowed gravely, and the ladies recognized that their brief audience had terminated. As they passed through the gateway, looking back they saw Perkins still standing with the child on his shoulder and smiling affably upon them. Then the two massive doors of the gateway swung to with a crash, the bolts were shot, and the courtyard was impenetrable.

* * * * *

A few moments later, the three friends had passed the outermost angle of the fortifications, and were descending towards the beach. By the time they had reached the sands they had fallen into a vague silence.

A noise like the cracking and fall of some slight scaffolding behind them arrested their attention. Hurlstone turned quickly. A light smoke, drifting from the courtyard, was mingling with the fog. A faint cry of "Dios y Libertad!" rose with it.

With a hurried excuse to his companions, Hurlstone ran rapidly back, and reached the gate as it slowly rolled upon its hinges to a file of men that issued from the courtyard. The first object that met his eyes was the hat of Senor Perkins lying on the ground near the wall, with a terrible suggestion in its helpless and pathetic vacuity. A few paces further lay its late owner, with twenty Mexican bullets in his breast, his benevolent forehead bared meekly to the sky, as if even then mutely appealing to the higher judgment. He was dead! The soul of the Liberator of Quinquinambo, and of various other peoples more or less distressed and more or less ungrateful, was itself liberated!

* * * * *

With the death of Senor Perkins ended the Crusade of the Excelsior. Under charge of Captain Bunker the vessel was sent to Mazatlan by the authorities, bearing the banished and proscribed Americans, Banks, Brace, Winslow, and Crosby; and, by permission of the Council, also their friends, Markham and Brimmer, and the ladies, Mrs. Brimmer, Chubb, and Markham. Hurlstone and Miss Keene alone were invited to remain, but, on later representations, the Council graciously included Richard Keene in the invitation, with the concession of the right to work the mines and control the ranches he and Hurlstone had purchased from their proscribed countrymen. The compla-cency of the Council of Todos Santos may be accounted for when it is understood that on the day the firm of Hurlstone & Keene was really begun under the title of Mr. and Mrs. Hurlstone, Richard had prevailed upon the Alcalde to allow him to add the piquant Dona Isabel also to the firm under the title of Mrs. Keene. Although the port of Todos Santos was henceforth open to all commerce, the firm of Hurlstone & Keene long retained the monopoly of trade, and was a recognized power of intelligent civilization and honest progress on the Pacific coast. And none contributed more to that result than the clever and beautiful hostess of Excelsior Lodge, the charming country home of James Hurlstone, Esq., senior partner of the firm. Under the truly catholic shelter of its veranda Padre Esteban and the heretic stranger mingled harmoniously, and the dissensions of local and central Government were forgotten.

"I said that you were a dama de grandeza, you remember," said the youthful Mrs. Keene to Mrs. Hurlstone, "and, you see, you are!"

ABOUT THE AUTHOR

 **Francis Bret Harte** (August 25, 1836–May 6, 1902) was an American author and poet, best remembered for his accounts of pioneering life in California.

Born in Albany, New York, Harte moved to California in 1853, later working there in a number of capacities, including miner, teacher, messenger, and journalist. He spent part of his life in the northern California coast town now known as Arcata, at the time it was just a mining camp on Humboldt Bay.

His first literary efforts, including poetry and prose, appeared in The Californian, an early literary journal edited by Charles Henry Webb. In 1868 he became editor of The Overland Monthly, another new literary magazine, but this one more in tune with the pioneering spirit of excitement in California. His story, "The Luck of Roaring Camp," appeared in the maga-zine's second edition, propelling Harte to nationwide fame.

As an established literary figure, he was appointed to the position of United States Consul in the town of Krefeld, Germany in 1878 and Glasgow in 1880. In 1885 he settled in London. During the thirty years he spent in Europe, he never abandoned writing, and maintained a prodigious output of stories that retained the freshness of his earlier work. He died in England in 1902.

Choose from Thousands of 1stWorldLibrary Classics By

A. M. Barnard
Ada Leverson
Adolphus William Ward
Aesop
Agatha Christie
Alexander Aaronsohn
Alexander Kielland
Alexandre Dumas
Alfred Gatty
Alfred Ollivant
Alice Duer Miller
Alice Turner Curtis
Alice Dunbar
Allen Chapman
Alleyne Ireland
Ambrose Bierce
Amelia E. Barr
Amory H. Bradford
Andrew Lang
Andrew McFarland Davis
Andy Adams
Angela Brazil
Anna Alice Chapin
Anna Sewell
Annie Besant
Annie Hamilton Donnell
Annie Payson Call
Annie Roe Carr
Annonaymous
Anton Chekhov
Archibald Lee Fletcher
Arnold Bennett
Arthur C. Benson
Arthur Conan Doyle
Arthur M. Winfield
Arthur Ransome
Arthur Schnitzler
Arthur Train
Atticus
B.H. Baden-Powell
B. M. Bower
B. C. Chatterjee
Baroness Emmuska Orczy
Baroness Orczy
Basil King
Bayard Taylor
Ben Macomber
Bertha Muzzy Bower
Bjornstjerne Bjornson

Booth Tarkington
Boyd Cable
Bram Stoker
C. Collodi
C. E. Orr
C. M. Ingleby
Carolyn Wells
Catherine Parr Traill
Charles A. Eastman
Charles Amory Beach
Charles Dickens
Charles Dudley Warner
Charles Farrar Browne
Charles Ives
Charles Kingsley
Charles Klein
Charles Hanson Towne
Charles Lathrop Pack
Charles Romyn Dake
Charles Whibley
Charles Willing Beale
Charlotte M. Braeme
Charlotte M. Yonge
Charlotte Perkins Stetson
Clair W. Hayes
Clarence Day Jr.
Clarence E. Mulford
Clemence Housman
Confucius
Coningsby Dawson
Cornelis DeWitt Wilcox
Cyril Burleigh
D. H. Lawrence
Daniel Defoe
David Garnett
Dinah Craik
Don Carlos Janes
Donald Keyhoe
Dorothy Kilner
Dougan Clark
Douglas Fairbanks
E. Nesbit
E. P. Roe
E. Phillips Oppenheim
E. S. Brooks
Earl Barnes
Edgar Rice Burroughs
Edith Van Dyne
Edith Wharton

Edward Everett Hale
Edward J. O'Biren
Edward S. Ellis
Edwin L. Arnold
Eleanor Atkins
Eleanor Hallowell Abbott
Eliot Gregory
Elizabeth Gaskell
Elizabeth McCracken
Elizabeth Von Arnim
Ellem Key
Emerson Hough
Emilie F. Carlen
Emily Bronte
Emily Dickinson
Enid Bagnold
Enilor Macartney Lane
Erasmus W. Jones
Ernie Howard Pie
Ethel May Dell
Ethel Turner
Ethel Watts Mumford
Eugene Sue
Eugenie Foa
Eugene Wood
Eustace Hale Ball
Evelyn Everett-green
Everard Cotes
F. H. Cheley
F. J. Cross
F. Marion Crawford
Fannie E. Newberry
Federick Austin Ogg
Ferdinand Ossendowski
Fergus Hume
Florence A. Kilpatrick
Fremont B. Deering
Francis Bacon
Francis Darwin
Frances Hodgson Burnett
Frances Parkinson Keyes
Frank Gee Patchin
Frank Harris
Frank Jewett Mather
Frank L. Packard
Frank V. Webster
Frederic Stewart Isham
Frederick Trevor Hill
Frederick Winslow Taylor

Friedrich Kerst
Friedrich Nietzsche
Fyodor Dostoyevsky
G.A. Henty
G.K. Chesterton
Gabrielle E. Jackson
Garrett P. Serviss
Gaston Leroux
George A. Warren
George Ade
Geroge Bernard Shaw
George Cary Eggleston
George Durston
George Ebers
George Eliot
George Gissing
George MacDonald
George Meredith
George Orwell
George Sylvester Viereck
George Tucker
George W. Cable
George Wharton James
Gertrude Atherton
Gordon Casserly
Grace E. King
Grace Gallatin
Grace Greenwood
Grant Allen
Guillermo A. Sherwell
Gulielma Zollinger
Gustav Flaubert
H. A. Cody
H. B. Irving
H.C. Bailey
H. G. Wells
H. H. Munro
H. Irving Hancock
H. R. Naylor
H. Rider Haggard
H. W. C. Davis
Haldeman Julius
Hall Caine
Hamilton Wright Mabie
Hans Christian Andersen
Harold Avery
Harold McGrath
Harriet Beecher Stowe
Harry Castlemon
Harry Coghill
Harry Houidini

Hayden Carruth
Helent Hunt Jackson
Helen Nicolay
Hendrik Conscience
Hendy David Thoreau
Henri Barbusse
Henrik Ibsen
Henry Adams
Henry Ford
Henry Frost
Henry James
Henry Jones Ford
Henry Seton Merriman
Henry W Longfellow
Herbert A. Giles
Herbert Carter
Herbert N. Casson
Herman Hesse
Hildegard G. Frey
Homer
Honore De Balzac
Horace B. Day
Horace Walpole
Horatio Alger Jr.
Howard Pyle
Howard R. Garis
Hugh Lofting
Hugh Walpole
Humphry Ward
Ian Maclaren
Inez Haynes Gillmore
Irving Bacheller
Isabel Cecilia Williams
Isabel Hornibrook
Israel Abrahams
Ivan Turgenev
J.G.Austin
J. Henri Fabre
J. M. Barrie
J. M. Walsh
J. Macdonald Oxley
J. R. Miller
J. S. Fletcher
J. S. Knowles
J. Storer Clouston
J. W. Duffield
Jack London
Jacob Abbott
James Allen
James Andrews
James Baldwin

James Branch Cabell
James DeMille
James Joyce
James Lane Allen
James Lane Allen
James Oliver Curwood
James Oppenheim
James Otis
James R. Driscoll
Jane Abbott
Jane Austen
Jane L. Stewart
Janet Aldridge
Jens Peter Jacobsen
Jerome K. Jerome
Jessie Graham Flower
John Buchan
John Burroughs
John Cournos
John F. Kennedy
John Gay
John Glasworthy
John Habberton
John Joy Bell
John Kendrick Bangs
John Milton
John Philip Sousa
John Taintor Foote
Jonas Lauritz Idemil Lie
Jonathan Swift
Joseph A. Altsheler
Joseph Carey
Joseph Conrad
Joseph E. Badger Jr
Joseph Hergesheimer
Joseph Jacobs
Jules Vernes
Julian Hawthrone
Julie A Lippmann
Justin Huntly McCarthy
Kakuzo Okakura
Karle Wilson Baker
Kate Chopin
Kenneth Grahame
Kenneth McGaffey
Kate Langley Bosher
Kate Langley Bosher
Katherine Cecil Thurston
Katherine Stokes
L. A. Abbot
L. T. Meade

L. Frank Baum
Latta Griswold
Laura Dent Crane
Laura Lee Hope
Laurence Housman
Lawrence Beasley
Leo Tolstoy
Leonid Andreyev
Lewis Carroll
Lewis Sperry Chafer
Lilian Bell
Lloyd Osbourne
Louis Hughes
Louis Joseph Vance
Louis Tracy
Louisa May Alcott
Lucy Fitch Perkins
Lucy Maud Montgomery
Luther Benson
Lydia Miller Middleton
Lyndon Orr
M. Corvus
M. H. Adams
Margaret E. Sangster
Margret Howth
Margaret Vandercook
Margaret W. Hungerford
Margret Penrose
Maria Edgeworth
Maria Thompson Daviess
Mariano Azuela
Marion Polk Angellotti
Mark Overton
Mark Twain
Mary Austin
Mary Catherine Crowley
Mary Cole
Mary Hastings Bradley
Mary Roberts Rinehart
Mary Rowlandson
M. Wollstonecraft Shelley
Maud Lindsay
Max Beerbohm
Myra Kelly
Nathaniel Hawthrone
Nicolo Machiavelli
O. F. Walton
Oscar Wilde

Owen Johnson
P.G. Wodehouse
Paul and Mabel Thorne
Paul G. Tomlinson
Paul Severing
Percy Brebner
Percy Keese Fitzhugh
Peter B. Kyne
Plato
Quincy Allen
R. Derby Holmes
R. L. Stevenson
R. S. Ball
Rabindranath Tagore
Rahul Alvares
Ralph Bonehill
Ralph Henry Barbour
Ralph Victor
Ralph Waldo Emmerson
Rene Descartes
Ray Cummings
Rex Beach
Rex E. Beach
Richard Harding Davis
Richard Jefferies
Richard Le Gallienne
Robert Barr
Robert Frost
Robert Gordon Anderson
Robert L. Drake
Robert Lansing
Robert Lynd
Robert Michael Ballantyne
Robert W. Chambers
Rosa Nouchette Carey
Rudyard Kipling
Saint Augustine
Samuel B. Allison
Samuel Hopkins Adams
Sarah Bernhardt
Sarah C. Hallowell
Selma Lagerlof
Sherwood Anderson
Sigmund Freud
Standish O'Grady
Stanley Weyman
Stella Benson
Stella M. Francis

Stephen Crane
Stewart Edward White
Stijn Streuvels
Swami Abhedananda
Swami Parmananda
T. S. Ackland
T. S. Arthur
The Princess Der Ling
Thomas A. Janvier
Thomas A Kempis
Thomas Anderton
Thomas Bailey Aldrich
Thomas Bulfinch
Thomas De Quincey
Thomas Dixon
Thomas H. Huxley
Thomas Hardy
Thomas More
Thornton W. Burgess
U. S. Grant
Upton Sinclair
Valentine Williams
Various Authors
Vaughan Kester
Victor Appleton
Victor G. Durham
Victoria Cross
Virginia Woolf
Wadsworth Camp
Walter Camp
Walter Scott
Washington Irving
Wilbur Lawton
Wilkie Collins
Willa Cather
Willard F. Baker
William Dean Howells
William le Queux
W. Makepeace Thackeray
William W. Walter
William Shakespeare
Winston Churchill
Yei Theodora Ozaki
Yogi Ramacharaka
Young E. Allison
Zane Grey